PRAISE FOR E.

"A rollercoaster of suspense, faith and love. I was hooked from the very first page! Laura and Lisa have penned an exceptional story that I read in one sitting. Once you pick it up, you won't be able to put it down."

DANI PETTREY, BESTSELLING AUTHOR OF THE
COASTAL GUARDIAN SERIES

"Laura has compassionately woven in difficult topics in *Expired Vows* including identity, grief, and the reality of brain injuries. This beautiful love story of faith and hope is made fuller by the depth of the people that Kelsey and Trace help. I highly recommend this thrilling romance - you will come away not only inspired but also deeply moved!"

CRISTABELLE BRADEN, RECORDING ARTIST AND
FOUNDER OF HOPE AFTER HEAD INJURY

"Laura Conaway has crafted an amazing romantic suspense novel filled with twists and turns, danger, surprises, and an incredible ending. This story will keep you not only turning the pages, but will also keep you guessing who is behind everything and why."

ALLYSON, GOODREADS

A NOTE FROM LISA

Dear Reader

We're at the end of the series! If you've been along the journey all the way, thank you! That comes from the bottom of my heart, and I'm sure all of us Last Chance Fire and Rescue authors as well. It's wonderful to be a writer, but we can't do this without readers who love great stories.

I've come to realize (not sure why it was such a revelation, haha) that my books always have strong themes of second chances, especially in the spiritual thread. And why not? Isn't that precisely what God did, sending His son Jesus to be our redemption? He washed away the past and offered us new life as part of His family. That is the best story – it's the one we get to live.

From the first time I heard the premise of *Expired Vows* I knew this was a story that had to be told. Two broken people, made whole in Jesus, finding peace and safety with each other. What a blessing. When it hit me that Kelsey was the maid of honor at Trace's wedding, I was hooked! Laura did a great job crafting a story where the path wasn't straight or easy, but it was the right one. Stalker stories are always so creepy, and this one wasn't short of tension! What a thrill ride.

Laura, you brought all that young adult energy and the wisdom of a deep relationship with Jesus to this project. It was wonderful to journey with you in crafting this book. I'm so excited for how your author career is already branching out, and hopeful for many more action-packed, heartfelt stories in the years to come.

Creating a community of readers is something every author wants to do. My readers are amazing people who are so friendly and supportive. So if you want to sign up for my newsletter and stay in the know, you can find the form on my website. Once you sign up, you get a free story and a link to the Discord reader server I have with a group of Christian Suspense authors whose names you'll know. Come join us!

And, as always, Happy Reading!

Lisa

*To the One who writes the best stories and
has filled my heart with praise.
Soli Deo Gloria.*

The Lord gave, and the Lord has taken away;
blessed be the name of the Lord.
Job 1:21b ESV

1

Trace Bently wasn't going to let anyone die on his watch—not today.

"You ready to go, partner?" Andi peeked her head around the driver's side door of the ambulance. Her voice echoed in the enclosed garage area of the Eastside firehouse.

"All set." Trace hit the side of the truck and jogged to the passenger side.

The tires squealed against the pavement as they made a sharp turn out of the station. Sunlight streamed through the windshield, and he pulled down the visor. Andi leaned forward and flicked the sirens on. Traffic steered to the shoulder, and they were given the right of way.

Trace spoke into the radio. "Ambulance 21 is on the way. Any updates on the situation?"

Static crackled through the line as he waited for a response. Hostage situations could get ugly fast, and he hoped a negotiator was already en route. Time was always of the essence. No telling what would tip the captor over the edge to do something stupid. He'd seen it too many times when he was a cop. Standing around, powerless to do anything.

Now that he was an EMT, he could focus on the victims rather than just who needed to be arrested. Saving lives was his job—and that's exactly what he was going to do.

He leaned forward and tapped his foot against the floorboard before sneaking a glance at Andi. A knowing look crossed her face as she raised her eyebrows. She was going as fast as possible. He knew that. But he didn't have to like how slow it felt in the meantime.

"We've got a male holding two kids at gunpoint," the commander on the other end of the line stated.

Trace winced. "Copy that."

"Kids?" Andi hissed.

Trace gritted his teeth. "I know."

"The wife escaped and is with an officer now but needs immediate medical attention. Gash to the forehead and cuts along her arm. Possible broken bone," the commander said.

"ETA seven minutes." Trace let go of the button.

Despite the clear skies and sunny morning, the flash of their blue and red lights illuminated the surrounding neighborhood and trailed down the street to encircle the corner property as they pulled in. Bystanders shifted their heads in an attempt to get a closer look at the commotion while officers blockaded the area.

Before Andi even rolled to a complete stop, Trace hopped out and scanned the area. As soon as she parked, he grabbed his bag, Andi not far behind.

Suburban neighborhood. The house had a front porch with a swing dotted with several decorative pillows. It could comfortably seat two. The front lawn was meticulous. Shrubs trimmed with precision, and the hanging plants vibrant with color.

Patches of brown grass were the only indication of trouble beyond the exterior of the property. Though that was simply from the cooler temperatures making way for winter weather. To the outside world, the family who lived here had a good life.

Lieutenant Basuto stood on the sidewalk. He waved them over. "Husband hit her on the head with the butt of his gun."

Trace looked over at the woman whose hand was propped against her head.

"On her way out, she tripped over an uneven sidewalk and slammed into the pavement with her arm." The lieutenant averted his gaze to the woman. "We already took her statement, so she's all yours."

Andi led the woman to sit on the curb.

Trace stayed with Basuto. "And the kids? Any injuries?"

"As far as we can tell—" He lowered his voice to a whisper. "—they're unharmed, though they're still inside with him. We're working to get them out."

"You'll need blueprints of the house layout to determine the best route in. I wonder if one of the side windows has open blinds. Maybe a drone would work to see in through the skylight." Trace took a few steps back and pointed in the direction of the roof.

Basuto's eyes scanned him up and down. "We've got it under control."

"Right." Trace nodded. "Keep it that way."

He'd slipped right back into cop mode. *Old habits.* Some things were ingrained, and he'd been a police officer for almost six years. But he would never go back. That season had taken too much of what he loved, and he'd never get it back.

Trace clenched his hand.

Now he had the power to save people on the front lines every day as a medic. This new job gave him purpose.

"If you're good to take over here, I have a patient to see to." He grinned, playing it off like a joke when nothing about this situation was funny. *Get your head straight.*

Lieutenant Basuto's eyebrows rose. "Sure thing, Bently."

Trace walked over to Andi, who had her stethoscope out and a blood pressure cuff around the woman's arm.

"Alice, this is my partner Trace. Trace, Alice." Andi released the valve, and air whooshed out before she packed up the cuff. "Glad you could finally join us." She shot Trace a look.

"Had a few things to tend to with Basuto." Trace waved his hand and crouched along the curb.

Alice had a cloth pressed against the side of her head, and she cradled her right arm against her chest. Tinges of white peeked through, but the majority of the cloth was saturated with hues of red.

The woman looked between the two of them and burst out in tears. "My kids. They're still in there with Gerald. He said he was going to take them." Her shoulders heaved with each sob.

"These officers are here to make sure that doesn't happen. They will do everything they can to keep the kids safe, Alice." He gave her a reassuring smile.

Inside, his stomach churned. He wanted to pray those kids made it out safely, like that would actually help. God had stripped him of those he loved. Why trust Him when the outcome here might not be any different?

Trace trusted that law enforcement here in Last Chance County had the training to resolve this peacefully. They'd find a way to take the guy down and reunite the kids with their mother.

Trace pulled back on his insecurities and focused. "Right now, we need to get that cut on your head taken care of." And make sure Alice didn't have a concussion.

Her sobs slowly eased up until only silent tears trickled down her face.

"BP is elevated, but everything else is good," Andi said.

"I'm going to move my finger, and I want you to follow it, okay, Alice?" Trace said.

She nodded and focused her gaze on his finger. He moved it side to side and up and down. Her eyes tracked, which was a good thing. But he didn't like how heavily her head wound was bleeding.

Trace pulled out gauze and bandages. "Alice, can you hand Andi the cloth so I can take a look at your head?" Trace donned a pair of gloves. The elastic snapped against his skin.

Blood trickled in a steady stream from the wound. The woman's hair was sticky and tangled, and it took a minute to clear the area to assess the cut. As he did, he glanced back at the cops, who stood around, waiting.

"Wishing you were over there with those tough guys?" Andi asked.

"When I can be here doing the real work? Nah." He chuckled.

Resolve stirred in him as he probed Alice's wound. *This* was where he was supposed to be.

"That's going to need sutures. Here." Andi handed him alcohol swabs. She cut some gauze and gave it to him.

The bandage would suffice for now, but they needed to get her to the hospital soon. Get a CT scan ordered to make sure there wasn't internal bleeding. The fact that she was coherent was a good sign. He didn't want that to change before the police resolved the situation and got her kids out of the house.

Trace observed the way she held her elbow. "Can you move your arm for me?"

"I-I'm not sure." Sweat beaded on her brow. "It hurts."

"That's okay." He held out his hands. "I'm just going to touch different areas and you tell me if you feel any pain."

Alice nodded. "I can't believe I tripped on my own front walk."

He worked his way from the shoulder down. When he applied pressure to the radial bone, she winced. "All right. I'm going to add a little more pressure. Bear with me." His fingers connected with her skin. She let out a hiss before biting her lip. "You've definitely got bruising at minimum, but only an X-ray will tell how bad the damage is."

A tear rolled from her eye. Trace placed her arm in a sling, and Andi put the supplies back in the bag.

A scream pierced the air.

"My babies!" Alice pushed herself off the curb with her good arm and managed a few steps before swaying. "What is he doing to them?"

"Whoa. We can't have you passing out now." Trace gingerly took hold of the woman's left arm as Andi held the other.

"He's hurting them!" She pushed against their grip.

"Hold up, okay?" Trace looked at Andi. "Can you look after her?" He turned to Alice. "I want you to sit, okay? I'll see what's going on."

"Trace." Andi's eyes held an edge of reluctance.

"I'll be right back, okay?"

He spotted Alex Basuto and figured the lieutenant would be able to fill him in a little on what just happened. Trace couldn't help it. Even though he wasn't a cop anymore, the instincts were still there. If someone was in danger, it was his responsibility to make sure others were safe—no matter what job he did.

Trace jogged across the street and weaved around several patrol cars. The scene commander yelled into his radio. Adrenaline hit him like electricity trying to find a circuit and catch a spark—the rush of running into a deadly situation, not knowing what would be on the other side of the door.

The child's scream still rang in his ears.

He just hoped no one else got hurt and the negotiator's skills proved infallible.

Trace approached Basuto. "Did they get the negotiator in there yet?"

It seemed like law enforcement was at a standstill. No one moved. Several heads were lowered in conversation—the scene commander, Chief Conroy Barnes, and a couple of other officers.

"The guy refuses to see one." The lieutenant frowned. "He said he'll only talk with his counselor."

That wasn't the cop way to solve a problem. "They could end up getting everyone hurt."

"Right now, it's the only option we have to work with if we want this resolved with those kids safe." Basuto's radio crackled to life and someone shared intel. "We're in a bind right now, Trace. None of us can do anything." Basuto spoke into the device. "What's her ETA?"

The radio crackled. "Five minutes out."

"Copy," Basuto said. "We'll continue to hold down."

The blinds in the house were shut. From this angle, Trace could see a tan fence enclosed the backyard. There was no way to monitor what was going on inside. The gunman had the upper hand, and he likely knew it.

A few minutes later, a blue Impala pulled up to the opposite corner of the house. Officers waved the crowd back, and a woman got out of the car. Trace couldn't make out who it was other than that she had long auburn hair.

A counselor empathized with someone's feelings. They weren't trained to de-escalate someone who clearly had other intentions in mind. She wouldn't know where to position herself in case any bullets went flying. There was no way he could sit back and do nothing.

The whole situation was crazy. "This woman could end up getting everyone killed."

His legs started moving before his mind caught up. He needed to talk some sense into this crew and brainstorm a plan B that didn't involve this counselor stepping in the crossfire.

"Dude, you can't go over there," Basuto called out.

Trace made it as far as the fire hydrant several yards from the front walkway before Basuto was in front of him, palm up, legs positioned in a defiant stance.

"They should really have a better plan in place. Or at least think through another option than this." Trace waved his hand in the direction of the team suiting up a woman who had no clue what she was doing.

He raised his heels and strained to see past the entourage of officers.

"You're not a cop anymore." Basuto crossed his arms. "And if you were, I'd be your superior. So back off."

The words sliced through the air and bound his good intentions in handcuffs. Being a cop hadn't helped him to save the one person who'd needed him. He'd vowed to never let that happen again, so he'd become an EMT. Yet here he was, stuck in a quandary.

He hated being useless.

Trace winced. "But..."

"Places everyone. We'll be ready to go in five." The chief's command came through loud and clear on the radio.

Basuto waved him off. "Go do your job, Trace. Let us take care of ours."

Trace shut his mouth. He looked over once more at the team assembling and let out a sigh. He made his way back to Andi who was still with their patient.

"Kelsey!" The name echoed through the air behind him.

Trace shifted to assess the commotion. That's when the counselor turned. She took something from an officer and slid her hand up to her ear to fit it in place. She gave a thumbs-up.

Kelsey.

She was the counselor? His heart beat faster against his chest at the realization that she was here at the scene. The roof of his mouth dried like flames had licked up the moisture. He'd moved here to escape his past, not come face-to-face with it again.

His mind spun with thoughts, but one question rang loudest. What was his dead wife's best friend doing in Last Chance County?

2

Out of all the ways she'd helped people over the years, walking into a hostage situation was quite possibly the stupidest idea she'd ever agreed to.

Lights flashed from every angle on the street, and pebbles crunched under her feet from the pavement. Kelsey took a few steps, unsure which direction to turn.

Like her clients, she understood sensory overload. If she was having a hard time focusing right now, she could imagine the agitation Gerald felt inside. Emergency personnel yelled commands, and even a few neighbors stood on their porches gawking. She focused her gaze on a group of officers to help her stay in the present moment and on her task at hand.

"Kelsey." An officer jogged over to her. "I'm Lieutenant Basuto." The man stuck out his hand before he lifted his sunglasses and met her eyes. "Thank you for coming on such short notice."

Basuto's cheery smile complemented his warm eyes. His disposition made up for his lack in height. He reminded her of her dad. Sorrow snuck its way into her heart at the memory of her loss, but she pushed it aside. Right now, she needed to help save a family from losing their father.

"I'm glad I could." She smiled. "Whenever one of my clients is in crisis, I want to make sure they receive the help they need."

"That's very admirable of you. We're here to make sure you and everyone else stays safe." He motioned to her earpiece. "Stay in contact."

"Right. Thank you." She smiled. His confidence and concern for people's safety gave her comfort. She was entrusting her life to the skills of these officers.

Basuto frowned. "But please understand the severity of this situation. This is not a typical counseling session." His tone was kind, but his words gave her pause before she spoke.

"I'm well aware of that, Lieutenant Basuto." A nervous laugh escaped. "I can assure you, though, it's not his fault. Gerald is a wonderful man. He's experienced brain trauma, which affects his impulse control."

"Which is exactly why this situation is high risk." Basuto signaled for another officer to come over. "We can talk while we suit you up."

"Excuse me?"

"Protective gear. To make sure you're safe." A female officer whose nameplate read *Tazwell*, a blonde not much older than Kelsey, handed her a black vest.

She took it and slid her arms through. "I see." After a few cleansing breaths—like she always told her clients—she let go of some of the tension.

The woman adjusted the Velcro straps on the sides.

"Why do you think Gerald's choices aren't his fault?" Basuto asked.

Kelsey fell back on what she knew. "He's not always self-aware, and his emotional responses are not reflective of his actual character. His brain is trying to compensate for stimulus overload."

He frowned. "Has he had any other excessive outbursts lately?"

"Nothing that I wasn't able to work through with him and his family. We've made great progress in therapy sessions."

Officer Tazwell tugged on the straps, then said, "Put this over the top of the vest to make sure it stays hidden." She handed Kelsey back her leather jacket.

"Thanks." The added warmth helped. The wind had picked up, and the cold gusts made her shiver. Or perhaps it was her nerves.

Basuto got her attention again. "Your goal is to distract Gerald and keep him away from the kids so our SWAT team can go in and safely remove them. You'll have direct communication with us the whole time."

"I'll need to talk with him first." She raised her brows. "So I can understand what started this whole situation." Otherwise it could end badly.

"This isn't a catch-up session. The longer it takes to extract the children, the higher the risk of injury."

"Lieutenant Basuto." She averted her eyes to the ground and counted to five. She could handle her job, and the safety of two children was at stake. "Gerald is a wonderful man when he's in a sound mind. When he's overwhelmed, it takes time to help him think through his decisions to realize the irrational side."

"Unfortunately, that's not going to work. Time is of the essence here."

Kelsey's jaw clenched. Time was the most imperative part of this whole operation. "You called me here to do my job because there wasn't another way. So let me do it."

Basuto furrowed his brow. "Comms check."

The words came through loud and clear in her earpiece.

"Places everyone. We're all set." He spoke into his radio, then nodded at Kelsey, who started walking toward the house.

She rapped on the front door and held her breath.

"Who is it?" Gerald asked in a gruff tone.

A whimper traveled through the air. She swiveled on her heel and scanned the front yard, but no one was there. To her left, the front window was open. "It's Kelsey Scott, Gerald. May I come in and talk to you?"

"The door's unlocked."

She twisted the knob and let herself in before closing the door behind her. The cops didn't need line of sight for one of their snipers to shoot Gerald before she even had a chance to talk to him. The click of the door echoed in the hallway.

"I'm inside." She hoped Basuto was still able to hear her on the other end.

"Copy that," he replied in her earpiece.

"Gerald, where are you and the kids?" She eased through the entryway.

"In the kitchen." She recognized Lily's voice and the thread of fear in it.

Kelsey rounded the corner on her right and stepped into the open kitchen. Natural light streamed through the windows to display the shattered plates strewn across the tile floor. Water and soap suds dripped from the sink, where dishes lay in a heap. A calm morning turned upside down.

The two kids, Brandon and Lily, only eleven and eight, stood in front of their dad by the island. Gerald had a gun, his hand fiery red from the tight grip he had on the weapon. It gave Kelsey minimal comfort to see the gun pointed at the floor when that stance could quickly change.

"Gerald, it's good to see you. And Brandon and Lily." She tried to smile as she placed herself on the opposite side of the island. That way she would be able to duck behind the cabinets if necessary.

"Thank you for coming." The muscles in Gerald's face relaxed a fraction.

"I'm happy to help." She looked down at the kids.

Tears streaked Lily's face, while Brandon's remained stoic. The trauma these kids were experiencing made her want to shake the man until he realized what he was doing. People only saw a shell of this man. He was a wonderful father and husband who needed to learn to cope with a new reality.

The clock on the wall ticked loudly, and emergency personnel could still be heard talking outside. Kelsey needed to bring the tensions down for Gerald. In a calm voice she said, "Walk me through what happened. Let's see if we can find a solution."

Basuto's voice came through her earpiece. "SWAT is ready to move. Just get Gerald away from the kids."

Heat permeated her cheeks. With all due respect to him, Lieutenant Basuto didn't understand the benefits of empathy. Or utilizing that connection to help people think clearly about their feelings and choices.

"I just—just wanted to take the kids hunting today." His voice grew in momentum, and his breath came in short gasps.

"Was this a trip you and Alice talked about?" Kelsey knew the wife was outside with some injuries. Now it was all about rescuing the kids.

"It was planned for a week. We had it planned for some time. I was going to catch a buck. With—with my boy."

"That sounds like it would be fun." She propped her hands on top of the counter so they were visible. "Then what happened?"

"Alice got nervous. Said we weren't ready for a big trip." He pushed himself away from the island and teetered to the side.

His feet crisscrossed each other, and Kelsey took a step closer in case he began to fall. The TBI's effect on Gerald's vestibular system caused him to lose balance easily. And the last thing he needed was another head injury.

The kids cowered in the corner away from their dad.

"I'm fine! I can't let this injury hold me back. I want to be okay." Gerald shook his hands, the gun still in his unsteady grip. The veins in his neck bulged. "I'm trying hard. Really hard." He pinched his eyes shut. Then opened them.

Kelsey took a step back while her heart thrummed in her ears. "It can be hard to accept what life throws at us."

Lily's eyes darted between her dad and Kelsey before she squeezed them closed. Brandon shuffled closer to her and wrapped his arm around her waist. The small gesture sent warmth coursing through Kelsey. The love these two siblings had for each other—even in the face of severe trauma—was incredible.

She was grateful they could lean on each other. Unlike her experience as an only child. When her dad had died from a stroke, she'd shifted focus and comforted her grieving mother. No one had ever cared about her feelings or what it had been like to suddenly lose her dad. Someone who had at one point encouraged and championed her. In a way, these kids were experiencing a similar void.

She threaded her fingers through her hair. "I know how much this trip meant to you, Gerald. And you've made great progress in our sessions."

Gerald might still be alive, but the dad Lily and Brandon once knew was trapped in this aggressive man's body. It was critical for her to help this family work through their challenges and experience some normalcy.

Kelsey held her ground. "Brandon, did you want to spend the day with your dad?"

"I did." The kid peered down at his shoes.

She could read between the lines. Brandon *had* wanted to go to the lake to hunt with his dad. But not anymore. Not with his daddy acting like this.

"Brandon." She waited for him to look at her. "It's wonderful you wanted to spend time with your daddy. I know that means a lot to both of you."

The little boy pursed his lips and blew out a slow breath.

She smiled at him, hoping to convey how proud she was of him for using the technique she'd taught him. He would consider the words he used and encourage his dad rather than risk triggering any frustrating emotions. If he'd vocalized just now how he didn't want to go anymore, who knew how Gerald would respond? The father's actions weren't in the child's control, but positive reinforcement could de-escalate situations in a lot of cases.

They were getting somewhere—hopefully—but she couldn't afford to let her guard down yet.

Kelsey shifted her weight from one side to the other to give her foot some relief. "I know how much your kids and wife love you, Gerald. Why don't we schedule a time to come into my office and we can talk about how to make this trip happen?"

"I don't know. It wasn't always like this." He rubbed his free hand down his face. "Why is this happening? Why?"

Basuto's voice came through her earpiece. "All positions, ready for go."

Kelsey's breath hitched. No, they couldn't barge in yet.

Gerald let out an exasperated sigh and moved toward the counter. "Alice ran out when I tried talking to her." He pointed at the sliding glass doors that exited to the patio, the gun still in his hand.

That was when she noticed the trail of blood across the floor. What had happened? *I need to find a way to get us out of this situation safely, Lord.* Kelsey sent up the silent prayer.

If he'd put down the weapon, they could defuse the situation. "Gerald, we can work this out. But you need to put the gun down."

The police would rush in any moment. She wanted to

scream. Gerald could start shooting if they entered. But if she reached for the kids, it would tip him off to what was happening outside.

Tears gathered in Kelsey's eyes. "I'm so sorry for the way this injury is affecting your family's life."

"I want to take these kids hunting. I want my life back. Don't let them stop me!" He grabbed his kids by the shoulders and pulled them closer to the patio door. Lily let out a sob.

"Gerald." Kelsey stepped away from her cover and walked a few steps toward them. "We can talk to the cops about going on the trip, see when it can happen." One of the SWAT guys walked past the glass door. Another officer stepped onto the patio. What were they doing? She hadn't given them the signal.

Gerald must have noticed her pause, because he swiveled around. "They're going to take my kids from me."

His head whipped back. The look in his eyes bored through Kelsey and sent shivers down her spine.

He shoved the kids aside. Their weight hit the floor with a thud, and screams tore through the air.

"You're supposed to help me!" Gerald roared.

She needed to get out now. Her mind screamed at her to run, but she couldn't leave the kids behind.

Gerald's six-foot frame barreled toward her even as he swayed side to side. Kelsey ran for the front door, but his iron grip jerked her back.

The SWAT team rushed in. Officers swarmed from all angles.

Gerald let out a grunt as he fell into the wall and loosened his grip on her arm. The abrupt motion sent her grasping for the doorknob. She opened it and tumbled down the front steps. Pain shot through her knee. She glanced behind her to see one officer handcuff Gerald while another held her weapon at the ready.

Someone called out to her. "Don't get any ideas about joining the force, rookie."

She'd recognize that voice anywhere. It couldn't be.

Kelsey lifted her gaze to the man standing on the grass to her right. She frowned. "Trace?"

3

T race's past collided with his present in a matter of seconds as he stood feet away from Kelsey. He shifted his attention between the front door and the grass where Kelsey sat, her leg splayed out in an uncomfortable position from her tumble. Still, all the memories threatened to showcase a lowlight reel in his mind. Everything that once was rushed back, along with the sharp reminder it was no longer the life he lived.

He rubbed his forehead to stop his mind from taking him back to an unwelcome place. He needed to focus on the situation at hand.

He latched on to her elbow and helped her stand. "Let's go, hero."

Despite the scowl on her face, Kelsey hadn't changed much since college. Her auburn hair swayed in the breeze, and a spatter of freckles still covered the bridge of her nose and cheeks. She'd filled out too, and not in a bad way, but rather more toned. Those piercing green eyes still bore through him, as if she could read all his thoughts.

"I didn't realize you worked in town." Her voice pulled him from his thoughts.

The sun glistened behind her, high in the sky, and Trace shielded his eyes. "For a couple years now."

"I see. Well, it's good to see you, but I should really go find the kids. Make sure they're okay." She started to walk down the sidewalk, a limp evident in her step.

"You're going to pay—pay for this, Kelsey!" Gerald's voice echoed through the air as a cop escorted him to a waiting patrol car. "You can't lie to me."

Trace balled his hands into fists. What was it with men who thought they could treat a woman however they pleased? For Gerald's sake, it was a good thing Trace wasn't the cop handling this case.

He caught up to Kelsey and took hold of her forearm. "Hey, not so fast." Redness permeated her cheeks as his fingers connected with her skin, but he ignored her response. "I'm still a first responder." He motioned to his shirt. "And you need to get checked out."

"I'll be fine. The kids come first." She turned her shoulder in an attempt to brush him off.

"Uh-uh." He shook his head, fully back in his role of EMT. "Your arm is bleeding, and by the look of that limp, your leg could use some attention too."

She followed his gaze to her elbow and winced. Blood trickled down to her hand. Clearly the pain hadn't set in yet.

"I'll go, but can we please find the kids first? I want to make sure they're okay. Gerald threw them pretty hard across the floor. And Alice." Her hand flew to her mouth, her eyes wide. "Oh no, is Alice okay? There was blood on the kitchen floor. I think he hit her."

"Alice is fine. My partner is taking care of her."

"Your partner?" Her brow furrowed, and he swore she

looked down at his left hand, but she blinked, and the expression disappeared.

"Andi. The other medic I ride with."

"Oh. Right."

He scanned the area, assessing the officers and other personnel coming and going. He tilted his head to speak into his radio. "I have the counselor with me. Forearm needs bandaging and possible injury to her right leg. Any status on the kids?"

"Copy that. An officer is escorting the kids to the truck now," Andi replied.

"This way." He motioned with his finger toward the sidewalk on the other side of the street. Kelsey started to walk, but she grimaced in the process. "Why don't you stay here, and I'll bring my bag over?"

"I could run a marathon right now. Of course I can walk." She stood taller, her shoulders back as she hobbled slowly in the direction of the ambo.

He let out a cough to cover his laugh. Still as independent and feisty as she had been in college. They weaved their way through the mass of people. The two kids broke away from the officer and raced toward Kelsey.

"Ms. Kelsey, what are they doing with Daddy?" Tears streaked the young girl's face. She wrapped her arms around Kelsey's torso for a second.

Kelsey moved her injured arm out of the way and positioned Lily on her other side. Brandon took his sister's hand in his.

Instead of crouching to eye level, Kelsey straightened her leg and leaned forward to speak to the girl. "We're going to help your dad get better so he can come home. But first, let's find your mom and get you two checked out to make sure you're okay." She rubbed the girl's back and nodded at the boy. The kindness in her expression glistened in her eyes.

Trace's heart ached at the gentle, motherlike exchange. The void it left threatened to overtake him, and his head swam. He cleared his throat. All three pairs of eyes turned and waited for him to speak while he tried to gather his resolve.

"Let's get you two taken care of so you can see your mom." They nodded in response. "Ms. Andi over there—" He pointed to where two ambulances were now parked beside each other. "She'll get you checked out in no time."

Andi waved at them as they approached, then turned her back to the kids. "The mom is stable, but I called in another ambo to take her to the hospital. I'm going to have them assess the kids en route as well so they can stay with their mom."

"Copy that. While you get them settled, I'll tend to Kelsey." Trace led her to the back of his ambulance and tapped his hand on the ledge. She raised her eyebrows. It was his duty to make sure everyone was safe on his watch, and he wouldn't have it any other way. "The kids are being treated. Now please, let me make sure you're okay."

She let out a sigh and sat down, her legs dangling off the bumper.

He pulled out his bag and took her vitals, then grabbed an alcohol swab. He held her arm in his hand, inspecting her elbow. By now, the blood had caked and dried around the exposed skin.

"I have to clean the wound out, so it's going to sting."

"I've endured worse."

Trace took pause at her comment, unsure how to respond. He ripped open the wrapper and wiped around the cut first before dabbing at the exposed skin. Her muscles tensed at the contact, but she didn't let out a sound.

"So, you're back in Last Chance County?" He hoped distraction would help.

"Only temporarily. For six more months."

"What for?"

"I helped secure a grant program for the therapy center that Dean Cartwright oversees. We're hoping to get a family and behavioral counseling section running and fully staffed. The goal is to treat the whole person and keep families intact as they learn to cope when someone close to them has experienced a medical trauma."

"Which explains why you were called to the scene today?" He discarded the alcohol pads in a small plastic biohazard box and grabbed some gauze.

"Exactly. I've been working with Gerald's family after his injury to help them learn to cope with his behavioral changes in order for them to live as normal of a life as possible as a family."

"The concept sounds like a great idea. Even if today it backfired. You or someone else could have been seriously hurt." All his cop instincts were going off. Surely she could see the danger these types of situations imposed. Mentally unstable people weren't always predictable, which was obvious today. And yet, she'd waded in despite the danger.

She crossed her arms and lifted her chin. "He's a great guy, Trace. You only witnessed one percent of who he is. Gerald has made great progress in our sessions, and he even got connected with a brain injury support group. Today he just got more flustered than usual."

"I'd say it was more than being flustered." He searched her eyes.

"Someone has to believe in him." Pain flashed in her eyes, but she seemed to shrug it off. "What brought you to Last Chance?" She changed the topic fast, and what was left unspoken from her question hung in the air like thick smoke.

He did not want to have this conversation right now. "Had a friend share about an opening here. He knew I'd just gotten certified. I'd already decided it was time to hang up the badge and take an EMT job. The cop life wasn't for me anymore." He pulled out some medical tape. "Can you put your finger right here to hold the bandage?"

He ripped off a piece of tape, hoping she caught on to his deflection and wouldn't pry.

"How have you been?"

There it was. The dreaded question. If anyone else had asked, he could have gotten away with a simple answer about how he was feeling that day. But she wanted the real answer. How was he *really* doing? He should have guessed she'd ask, considering her training was all about helping people process their emotions.

But he didn't need her help, because he wasn't one of her mentally unstable patients. He was *fine*. Time moved on whether he liked it or not, and he'd learned to adjust to life without Renee.

He lifted his gaze to meet hers, and once again the sea of freckles splattered along her cheek bones added a softness to her that drew him in. "I get to save people every day with this job. One call at a time."

"You know that's not what I asked, Trace," she whispered.

He ignored her response and put the tape back in the bag before zipping it up. "Your arm will be good as new in a few weeks. Just make sure to change out the bandage every day and keep it clean." He handed her a roll of gauze. "This should hold you over. Now, let's take a look at that leg. Where does it hurt?"

"I'm sure it's just bruised. I can ice it when I get home and keep it elevated." She placed her arms on the edge of the truck, ready to push off.

"I'd still feel better if I took a quick look."

"Really, I'll be fine. I still need to talk with Lieutenant Basuto and give him back my, uh, equipment." She pointed to the earpiece still snug in her ear.

He moved in front of her. Of course, she could deny the medical treatment, and he would have to accept it. It was her legal right as a patient. But he didn't want to feel responsible if a more serious injury had been overlooked. "At least let me make sure nothing is broken. Or bleeding."

To his relief, she sank back onto the edge of the truck.

"Where does it hurt?"

"My knee. It's definitely sore." She had it positioned straight instead of bent like her left one.

"How far in can you bend it?" The range of motion would tell him how serious the problem might be.

She moved it ever so slowly inward and made it to about eighty degrees.

"I'm just going to see if it's swollen." He moved his fingers along her patella and could feel the tenderness. Swollen for sure. He gathered the bottom of her pant leg and lifted it above her knee.

He inhaled at the sight before him. And chided himself just as quickly at his response. Her kneecap was red and puffy and a bruise had already formed. But it wasn't the state of her knee that had taken him by surprise.

Right below her knee, screwed in around the flesh, was a prosthetic leg.

Questions flooded his mind, but he didn't know what to say, and it didn't seem appropriate to ask. Especially considering he'd already shut down a response when she'd inquired about how he was doing.

"Am I good to go now?" Kelsey asked.

He noticed she bit her lip, something she'd always done whenever the nerves crept in. Embarrassment flooded his cheeks. "Like you said, ice it and elevate it for a few days. Don't do anything to aggravate the inflammation." He rolled her pant leg back down.

"Thanks." She gave him a weak smile and slid off the truck. "I'm going to go find Basuto. It was nice to see you, Trace."

"Likewise, Kelsey."

He watched her head in the direction of the patrol cars. She'd endured far worse than the injuries she'd sustained today. Just like him, she had her secrets. Painful reminders of what had been taken from her.

So what had happened that warranted such a devastating loss?

4

"Y ou're going to work yourself to death if you don't take time to relax." Natalie Atkinson popped her head into Kelsey's office, her hand resting on the doorframe.

Kelsey finished scribbling a few notes on a client's paperwork and lifted her gaze. "What if I find this work relaxing?" She leaned forward and propped her hands on her desk. Her temporary office space remained bare. Void of any personal touches. But Natalie's golden, flowy shirt with bright fall leaves on it made her wish her day-to-day space popped with color.

"Puh-lease." Natalie rolled her eyes. "I'm all for helping people, but you need to let your brain think of something else once in a while so you have the energy to meet the needs of people who walk through these doors."

"Thanks for the counseling session."

"Anytime. That's what I'm here for." Natalie paused. "Why don't you come with the rest of the staff to the Backdraft Bar and Grill for dinner? You have to be hungry. And it's a Friday night, for goodness' sake."

"I don't know." After what happened with Trace yesterday, she wasn't sure she could face more people. He might not know the details of how she lost her leg, but he'd witnessed her failure to talk down Gerald. Then, as an added cherry on top, she'd fallen right in front of him. The whole situation had been an embarrassing reintroduction to an old friend and someone she'd once had a crush on. Who knew what stories might circulate about her competency?

"I know you're technically only here for six more months, but it would be good to build team comradery. And put into practice the whole relaxing thing." She winked.

As if on cue, Kelsey's stomach rumbled. "All right. I'll join."

"Great! Let's carpool so you don't have the chance to back out."

Kelsey let out a laugh. She was incredibly grateful for Natalie and the friendship they'd formed so quickly when she'd started at the office. They kept each other sane at work and always found something entertaining to talk about. Even the fact they'd both been held hostage a few months ago hadn't put a damper on their friendship—nor had Natalie's blooming relationship with a certain fire chief.

"Let me just put these files away, then I'll be ready."

"Sounds good. I'll meet you downstairs."

After checking her levels and adjusting her insulin as needed, Kelsey opened her mini-fridge and grabbed an orange juice as a backup measure. That would stabilize her blood sugar until their orders came at the restaurant.

Fifteen minutes later, as she opened the door to Backdraft, music and chatter flooded her senses.

This grill was a step up from what she'd expected with the sleek style. Several booths occupied the outer walls, and long bench tables sat in the middle of the establishment next to two pool tables, where one party already battled it out.

"Wow this place is..."

"Amazing, right?" Natalie finished for her. "They even have a rooftop area, which is equally as spectacular."

Kelsey waved to Dean, his wife Ellie, and the rest of the team sitting at one of the tables. Directly behind them was the entire fire and rescue squad, including Trace.

"C'mon, let's go join everyone, and I'll introduce you."

Before Kelsey could interject, Natalie walked over.

"Look who I brought with me tonight." Natalie stretched out her hand in Kelsey's direction.

"Good to see you could join us. At least those clients aren't holding you up on a Friday night." Amara, another coworker, offered a tight smile. "If you ever need help, let me know."

"Thanks for letting me crash." Kelsey ignored her other comment. Amara hadn't been thrilled when Dean, her supervisor, had given Kelsey the grant position.

"You're part of the team." Amara shrugged and held up her menu.

Natalie took Kelsey's hand and pulled her over to the other table.

Nothing like being the center of attention. Kelsey was grateful for the dimmer lighting overhead, because heat crept into her cheeks as everyone turned her way.

"Welcome." A man with neatly combed dark-brown hair stood and extended his hand to her. He sported a tan bomber jacket that accentuated his brown eyes. His firm handshake, along with his stance, shouted confidence. "I'm Logan. Firefighter with the crew."

"Nice to meet you." She nodded.

Natalie introduced each person round-robin.

"And this is Trace."

She kept her response to a professional nod. "Good to see you again."

"You too, Kelsey. How's the leg today?" He took a sip of what she guessed was Coke.

"Still sore, but nothing time won't mend." Except it wouldn't heal the real problem.

"That's right. You two already met at the callout yesterday," Natalie said.

"Well, we actually knew each other from college." The words spilled from Kelsey's mouth before she could stop them. She bit down on her lip and hoped the noise in the restaurant had drowned out her response.

Trace raised an eyebrow, clearly amused.

Obviously, she'd been loud enough for them to hear. *Great.*

"You knew each other in college?" Logan chimed in.

"Yeah, we had a few classes together. I was best friends with his wife." Kelsey immediately realized that was the wrong thing to say.

Trace's jaw set and his shoulders squared back. He stirred the straw in his Coke, avoiding eye contact with everyone.

"You're married?" Andi asked.

A few heads turned toward him. Despite the rowdiness of those around them, time stood still. Silence enveloped the table as everyone waited for his response. Some of the guys looked ready to crack a joke, but they refrained. And for that, she was grateful.

Clearly none of his coworkers knew about his past life. The seconds ticked by, and Kelsey stood there, waiting for him to open up to someone.

Trace's body language communicated the need to run, like he might just hop off the bench and bolt for the door. His foot thumped against the floor, but no one else seemed to notice. He took in a breath. "Was married." His gaze met Kelsey's. His eyes clouded over, and he swallowed hard.

"Oh. I'm sorry." Andi folded her hands on the table.

"Dude—" Macon started.

Trace cut him off. "We're not talking about it, okay?"

Her suspicions were confirmed. He wasn't okay, but she also couldn't ask him about it. Not here. Would he talk to her?

Trace glanced over, and she got her answer. No, he absolutely would not talk to her.

She awkwardly sat down at the table and Natalie slid in next to her.

"Welcome to the Backdraft. Can I get you started with an appetizer?" The waitress appeared at the end of the table, her blonde hair pulled back in a low ponytail. A pen and pad in one hand, she had a towel draped over her other arm.

Kelsey did a double take. It took a moment to place the woman. "Maeve?"

"Kelsey Scott. Oh my. I can't believe you're here in the flesh." A smile lit up her face. "It's wonderful to see you."

Kelsey stood up to give her old friend a hug. "It's been a long time."

"You don't say. What are you doing in town?"

"I took a temporary position at the Ridgeman Center. And you?"

"That's wonderful. Moved back to Last Chance after college, and I pick up some shifts here to help out."

"We need to catch up sometime soon."

"Sounds good." Maeve turned her attention back to the table. "What can I get everyone?"

"I'll take the steak salad with a side of fries, and add extra avocado, please," Kelsey said.

While everyone listed their orders, Kelsey studied Trace. Her comment earlier had prodded at something, and sorrow trickled into her heart at the realization she'd dredged up painful memories for him.

"Do you want your usual, Trace?" Maeve wrote on her pad.

"Sure." He offered her a smile, but Kelsey could tell it was forced. He was clearly distracted by other thoughts. Her mind sifted through different coping techniques and other tactics she could use to help him.

Slow down. She couldn't get ahead of herself before she even offered assistance, let alone got him to accept her help.

After their meal, everyone grabbed their drinks and headed to the rooftop. Kelsey's sweater and boots had been a good choice with the September air so chilly. Several heater towers emitted their propane fuel, which added extra warmth. From this vantage point, the stars shone in the night sky, creating an ambiance that made the demands of work and the situation with Gerald disappear.

"Who wants to play a game of pool?" Macon shouted over the live band. Their jazzy music competed for attention through the speakers.

"Oh, you're on!" Natalie sauntered over to her boyfriend, her eyes laser focused on him.

It amused Kelsey to see the two of them banter like the best of friends. The story of how they had met was crazy. When Macon became the new fire chief, Natalie had been tasked with assessing the department's mental health. But a stalker had changed Macon and Natalie's professional relationship to a personal one.

At least Kelsey didn't have to worry about romance impacting her job. Better to be single and use her abilities to secure this grant. It gave her a way to help others cope with medical challenges in a healthy way as a family. Something her mom hadn't done.

"I'll join. It can't be that hard to pick up." Kelsey walked over to the pool table.

"Have you played before?" Trace picked up a cue.

"A time or two." She raised her brows in a challenge, happy they could go back to something light after she'd revealed his past to his coworkers.

"Let's see what you got." Trace hit the stick on the ground.

Macon removed the rack from the balls and nodded to Natalie. "Ladies first."

"If you insist." She smiled and took her aim. The balls ricocheted off one another and rolled in every direction on the table before one sank into the left corner hole.

"Looks like the stripes are ours, boys." Natalie grinned.

Macon stepped up to the short edge of the table. He focused in on the solid six ball closest to the cue ball. "I wouldn't get too ahead of yourself now." He shifted his gaze from Natalie to Trace. "We've got this in our back pocket." He pulled back the cue and let it connect with the ball. It rolled to the side of the table and stopped short of the hole.

"Uh-huh. Kelsey, show them how it's done." Natalie winked and Kelsey stifled a laugh.

She hadn't played pool in several years, but her dad had enjoyed the game, and it had given them something to bond over.

She closed one eye and fixed her gaze on two balls. If she hit it just right...

A crack exploded as the balls connected—right before they both sank into their respective holes.

"I thought you said you'd only played a time or two." Trace eyed her, then shifted his gaze to the table.

"That may have been a slight understatement."

Natalie burst out laughing.

They finished their game, and she and Natalie high-fived each other.

"I think the firehouse needs more training." Kelsey smirked.

Trace shook his head. "We were just warming up."

"Agreed. A rematch is warranted." Macon put his cue on the table.

"Can't stand losing?" Kelsey chuckled.

"That's not true." Macon frowned. "We just like friendly competition." He set up the balls once more.

"Maybe they need a mini counseling session on being good sports." Natalie nudged Kelsey.

"No way," Trace and Macon responded in unison.

"We'll give you two time to practice before another round." Natalie winked. "Next week, babe."

The crew began to trickle out and say their goodbyes. Kelsey wanted to catch Trace before he called it a night, but didn't want to make a scene in front of everyone else. After Natalie and Macon left, she spotted him standing in a corner, occupied with something on his phone.

"Hey."

He looked up, and the light from the screen illuminated his features against the darkness around them. The light stubble on his face accentuated his chiseled jaw, but she could see the faint lines on his forehead from all the burdens he carried. "Hey." Much had changed about the man she'd once admired in school.

"I want to apologize for earlier and the comment I made about Renee." She waited for a response, watching him. Sure enough, his forearm muscles tightened and a vein in his neck protruded. "I—"

"There's no need to apologize. You didn't know about my coworkers' lack of knowledge."

"Right." That was one way to put it. "Well, if you want to talk about it, I'd be happy to listen." She shifted her stance to put more weight on her left foot. The dull ache in her injured leg began to throb.

"I don't need counseling, Kelsey."

"That's not it." His wife still held his heart, and she wanted to see him move past the hurt and pain. He didn't deserve to live life carrying that burden. But she couldn't help him if he didn't want it. "I meant as a friend. Can we grab coffee tomorrow morning at eight?"

Trace let out a sigh. "Sorry. I didn't mean to sound so stern. I appreciate the thoughtfulness, but I don't think I need coffee."

She wanted to correct him but knew what he meant. In his line of work, the man ran on coffee. He just didn't need coffee with her.

"Well, if you change your mind, I'll be at Bridgewater Café at eight."

"Note taken. But I'm fine, and I don't need anything else you have to offer either." He averted his eyes and shuffled his feet.

The response burned more than the alcohol pad on her wound from the other day, considering she and Trace had once been good friends.

Despite the hostility, Kelsey still wanted to get to the root of Trace's pain and help ease the ache. She couldn't help it; the instinct was in her blood.

The burdens he carried weighed heavily on his shoulders. She knew, because they were the same as hers. Yet God could do something good despite the pain. She was a walking testimony of that.

For the sake of seeing him heal, she would find a way to get him to accept her help.

5

Trace hooked his arm to the right and connected hard before coming around from the other side to knock the weight back in the other direction. The satisfaction of the contact sent an adrenaline rush through his veins.

He glanced at his watch, which told him he'd been at the workout for the last forty minutes and was in his target heart-rate zone. The early morning light just now peeked through the window in the workout space he'd created in the spare room in his apartment. Most people found it convenient to go to the gym and use equipment. He much preferred adding to his own space where he could go undistracted and forget about his thoughts.

Including the ones that had tried to keep him up last night.

The ones everyone said time would heal.

Nightmares he'd been able to shove into the recesses of his heart, until his team had learned a sliver of the truth, which had brought with it the raw reminders. As if that weren't bad enough, Kelsey's face when she'd asked if he needed help haunted him.

Like she thought she had to save him.

Trace jabbed at the boxing bag again as sweat trickled down his forehead.

Five years since his world had crashed to a halt around him and stripped him of everything he held dear.

Five years since he'd failed the one person he'd vowed to protect.

A drop of perspiration fell into his eye and sent a burning sensation through it. He grabbed a towel from the rack behind him and hit the red X on his watch to end the workout.

He'd managed to hide his secrets behind fireproof doors when he moved to Last Chance in hopes of starting fresh. Now the past resurfaced to remind him of the mistakes he'd made and how he'd failed. Who knew what Andi and the firefighters at Eastside would say after last night? He couldn't bear the thought of their pity.

Trace took a swig from his water and headed to the bathroom.

If his coworkers felt sorry for him, they might question if he was capable of performing his duties. That doubt was far from the truth. He worked to save people and never lose someone else again.

A cold shower would solve the problem—maybe. He pulled his cargo pants and blue medic shirt from the closet and turned on the water.

It terrified him how easily Kelsey had read his thoughts last night. He'd seen the way her discerning eyes had surveyed him and taken note of his body language. Even in college she'd had the keen ability to know when someone wasn't being honest.

He let out a grunt.

From this vantage point, a few feet from the mirror, the circles under his eyes stood out. He just hoped no one mentioned anything on shift today. The Lord could at least allow him that, couldn't He? All Trace wanted was to be able to live the life he was left with. Minus all the blows God had dealt him being shoved back in his face.

He watched the water swirl down the drain, but all it reminded him of was the fact his entire life had gone that way. And what did that leave him with?

After he changed, Trace brewed a cup of coffee while he scrambled some eggs. His phone rang and vibrated on the counter. He put a bagel in the toaster and answered the call. "Bently."

"Trace, it's Andi." Concern laced her voice.

"What's up?" He'd have to face her questions soon enough. His partner would want to know why he'd never mentioned Renee, but it was still too fresh. Did they have to do it now?

"I know you're coming in for shift soon, but I wanted to give you a heads-up that Gerald got bail."

"What?" Trace paced between the kitchen sink and stove and eyed the burner. "How'd you find out?"

"He made a threat at the station about putting people in their place. I guess he wasn't too thrilled about us taking care of the kids. But they still arraigned him this morning, and he got bail pending the trial. He's on the streets."

"Thanks for the heads-up." The toaster popped and alerted him to a golden bagel ready for the taking.

Silence lengthened over the line, and Trace braced himself for what was coming.

"I'm sorry about your wife," she whispered.

Trace clenched his hand against his mouth. "You didn't have any control over it."

"Still, it can't be easy."

"Yeah. Well, it's in the past." He wished those words rang true.

"Just don't let it occupy too much space, okay?" Andi's voice held a gentle tone.

He knew what she didn't explicitly express. If it began to

impede his work, he'd be back in for a mental health evaluation like a few months ago when the whole Eastside department had been evaluated by Natalie Atkinson following Mickey's death.

"It won't." Trace grabbed the butter from the fridge.

"Good. I'll make sure the guys leave it alone too."

"Thanks." He hung up and compiled the fixings for a breakfast sandwich. At least Andi understood. Trace was grateful for the comradery he'd built with everyone in the department. At least they didn't think he was broken and needed fixing.

Unlike Kelsey.

Now one fire had been extinguished, but another one still posed a threat. Trace did not like the fact Gerald roamed about. His gut told him nothing good could come from this, never mind what Kelsey said about the guy. Trace needed to make sure she understood the severity of the situation and watched her back. Gerald's anger was proof enough the guy was capable of anything.

He dialed Kelsey's number, but it went to her voicemail.

"Kelsey, it's Trace. Gerald got bail. Please, watch your back and be mindful of your surroundings, okay?" Hopefully she got the message. The idea of Gerald making good on his threat to hurt her sickened him.

He inhaled a bite of his bagel sandwich and took a sip of dark roast coffee, just the way he liked it. It amazed him that people added cream or sugar. At that point, they enjoyed a glorified milkshake, not the delectable and energizing taste of pure caffeine.

A glance at the microwave told him it was 7:45. If Kelsey was still a woman who stood by her word, she'd be at the coffee shop. He could get there in time to warn her and make sure she was okay before he headed to the station.

With two more bites, he finished off his sandwich. He

grabbed his Tervis cup, keys, and a jacket and sprinted for his car.

A few quick turns and he rolled out onto the main road and accelerated. With one eye on the rearview, he checked his surroundings to make sure no patrol cars lurked—or Gerald. He wished he had cop lights, but he couldn't afford to be pulled over as a civilian either. By the time he explained the situation to an officer, he might miss Kelsey.

Five minutes later he pulled into the Bridgewater Café parking lot. The bell overhead rang as he stepped inside and scanned the establishment. The whir of the espresso machine resounded as the barista worked on an order. A handful of patrons stood by the counter waiting for their orders, most of them engrossed with their phones, while a few sat at tables.

Trace glanced at his wrist. Three minutes after eight. His heart sank when he finished his assessment.

No Kelsey.

He sat down at a table by the window that gave him a full view of the parking lot.

Ten minutes ticked by, and she still didn't show. He turned his phone ringer on in case she tried calling. Uneasiness formed in his stomach after twenty minutes went by. He checked his notifications once more and dragged his feet back to his car to make his way to the station.

Something else had probably come up, and she'd gotten sidetracked. He was overreacting and needed to relax. Although he hadn't seen Kelsey in years, if she suggested something, she showed up first. Maybe the girl he'd known in college had changed, and the woman who'd shown up back in town lived a different life.

Clearly, he'd missed the memo about Kelsey's amputated leg. When had that happened? She'd never mentioned anything in school about it.

He connected to his Bluetooth as he headed to the station. Time to open up his own investigation.

"Trace, hi." Maeve's sultry voice filled the car's interior. "What's the occasion, that I have the pleasure of talking to you?"

Trace winced. "I need to pick your brain on something." His tone remained neutral, and he hoped she didn't read into anything. He simply needed information. Nothing more.

"You got it. What's up?"

"Did you know Kelsey has a prosthetic leg?" He wasted no time trying to beat around the bush.

Silence lengthened on the other end.

"Maeve?"

"She never told you?"

"Apparently not. When did this happen?" They'd been good friends, and she hadn't cared to tell him something so important. He ground his back molars.

"I'm so sorry, Trace. I thought you knew. It truly was terrible of her to miss Renee's funeral."

"What do you mean?" Trace eased his foot on the brake, unsure what she'd say next.

"Her surgery happened a few days before, and she chose to stay home and recover that weekend."

Trace let Maeve's words sink in. There still seemed to be missing information, but at least he had some context to go off.

Trace parked in the back lot at the station. "Thanks for the info. I appreciate it."

"Anytime, Trace. I'm happy to help."

The car door slammed, and Trace winced as the sound reverberated.

"That bench press is still in the gym if you need it." The doors to the firehouse garage were rolled up, and Izan stuck his head around the corner.

"Thanks, but I'm good." Trace stepped inside.

"If you say so." Izan raised an eyebrow and went back to checking off items on his clipboard. They'd been partners for a while, but now—like Andi had—Izan was trying his hand at being a firefighter.

Trace headed to the bunker and dropped off his bag. Overnight shifts were always a gamble with how much sleep he'd actually get. But at least he'd come prepared to take a quick nap if the opportunity arose.

He made his way to the kitchen.

"Hey, man." Charlie Benning lifted his chin, already dressed in his off-duty clothes. "There's leftover donuts on the counter from yesterday. If you care about me at all, you'll eat one."

Trace chuckled. "Note taken." He grabbed a powdered donut. "How was your shift?" Eddie had called in sick, so Charlie had covered for him on Rescue.

"Can't complain." Charlie shrugged. "The chief sent out an email this morning with information about that hostage situation."

"Gotcha." Trace nodded.

"Well, I'm outta here. Shift's over and I need to go run some errands." Charlie slapped Trace's shoulder. "If it's any consolation, it takes two to make a relationship work."

Trace choked on his donut and coughed. He raced over to the trash can and deposited the remainder of the food.

Clearly Charlie had been caught up on the conversation from last night at Backdraft, but his assumptions were far from the truth.

"You're better off without her." Charlie winked, then disappeared around the corner.

Trace grabbed a napkin to wipe off the white powder that coated his fingers, then took a swig of coffee to wash down the ashen taste in his mouth.

How could his buddy act nonchalantly about the situation? He recoiled at the thought. Marriage was a beautiful gift, not something to take lightly. Maybe he needed to have a clarifying conversation to address the elephant in the room. Except it would have to wait until later.

Trace headed to Macon's office. He wanted the verbal scoop on Gerald and any other updates he needed to be aware of for today. He raised his fist to knock on the chief's door, but the alarm resounded through the building.

A dispatcher's voice came over the intercom. "Ambo 21, Rescue 5, and Truck 14 needed at North and Walnut Street. Hit and run. Person trapped."

Trace barreled to the engine bay while rescue squad and the engine firefighters popped out of rooms. Within seconds he was in the driver's seat of the ambulance, and Andi closed the passenger door.

He peeled out of the station, the trucks not far behind. Andi grabbed the radio to connect with dispatch. "Ambo 21 en route, over."

"Copy that. Single adult female in the vehicle, unconscious according to witness."

Adrenaline raced through Trace's veins, and he leaned over to turn on the lights and siren.

A few bystanders stood in the grass as they pulled up to the scene. Andi grabbed her stethoscope from the center console and the orange trauma bag from the back of the ambo and slung it over her shoulders.

Trace assessed the scene. The car lay at an angle in the dirt, the bumper pushed in and the driver's side dented inward. He could make out someone through the window, but there was no movement.

He turned to Andi. "I'll get the spine board while you check out the person's condition."

"Copy that." She nodded and headed down the embankment.

He unhooked the board from the truck and pulled it out.

"Trace," Andi called up.

He turned and swung the board under one arm and made his way to the edge of the hill.

She cupped her hands. "It's Kelsey!"

Trace's heart skipped a beat, and his stomach churned. With the stretcher in one hand, he zigzagged down the hill. Rocks littered the ground. His foot connected with a dislodged stone that sent him careening forward. The board slid down the hill. Trace jutted out his hands to stop himself from tumbling the rest of the way. Pebbles lodged in his palms and scratched at his wrists, but he kept going.

Trace pulled up next to Andi.

She glanced over. "You good?"

He slapped his hands together to brush off the dirt and bit back a wince. "You said it's Kelsey?"

"Behind you." Rescue squad's Lieutenant Crawford moved between them.

The truck firefighters started clearing the onlookers and blockaded the area to give them room to work.

"The door's bent and won't budge," Eddie yelled. "We need the jaws." Thankfully, Eddie was feeling better and back on Rescue today. Given the current situation, it was a good thing he'd only had a twenty-four-hour bug.

Logan walked over to the window and tapped on the glass. "Ma'am, if you can hear us, go ahead and nod." Kelsey nodded and gave a thumbs-up. "We're going to get you out shortly," Logan said.

Trace held his breath, waiting for the go-ahead to do his job. Rescue squad encircled the vehicle.

"Hey, it's that girl from last night," Logan said.

"We know." Trace moved closer to the scene. His fingers itched to do something. Anything. He flexed his hands. They couldn't leave Kelsey in there any longer. "Come on, guys."

Their lieutenant glanced back. "Back up, Trace. You can't do your job 'til we do ours." Bryce narrowed his eyes.

"Take it easy, bro." Andi propped her hands on her hips. "We've all had a lot happen in the last few days." She softened her features and studied Bryce until he relented and turned back to his duty.

"Just do it now. Time's a-ticking." Trace moved the stretcher so it would be close to the driver's door when they gave the go-ahead. He hated waiting around. Just give him a job and let him do it.

Logan straightened from the passenger side. "Does anyone else smell gas?"

Eddie stuck his head out from under the front bumper. "There's a leak!"

Bryce spun to Amelia, the truck lieutenant. "Get the hose down here now!"

Eddie yelled, "Lieutenant!"

Bryce shoved Trace away from the vehicle. "Everyone back!"

With one hand on the stretcher, Trace prepared to lunge forward the moment they extracted Kelsey.

They had seconds before the situation turned from bad to worse.

A fireball erupted from the hood of the car.

Kelsey screamed.

6

An unwelcome pounding rhythm reverberated through her skull. Kelsey wasn't sure if it was from the hit she'd taken to her head or the incessant sound of metal hitting metal as the firefighters worked to remove the car door.

Her heart beat an unsteady rhythm. She could have died. Or maybe she'd have a heart attack here and it would all be over. God had given her so many trials in life. She didn't blame Him. But if she were honest, it had become exhausting to find the strength to press forward.

Kelsey grabbed the steering wheel to ground herself only to jerk her hands back from the heat it emanated. The urge to vomit settled over her.

Gray smoke billowed in front of her, and she coughed. Sweat broke out on her brow as the temperature continued to rise in the enclosed space.

She used her arms to push herself up, but something prevented her from moving. The seatbelt must have locked up in the crash. She hit the red button, and the restraint bounced back into its holder. Kelsey yanked on the door handle, but it wouldn't budge.

Her head swam and dizziness invaded.

How was she going to get out?

Emergency personnel in black and reflective yellow coats and helmets surrounded her car. Dirt specks splattered the window, making visibility difficult. She let out a scream, but the noise was drowned out by the incessant pounding of the jackhammer.

She banged on the door window and gave it a shove. To her delight, a wave of fresh air swept over her face. Someone moved the door out of the way.

"It's all clear," a male voice called out.

Kelsey shoved a firefighter out of the way, ready to escape the claustrophobic space, not waiting for anyone's help. She'd had enough people fuss over her at Gerald's house. No one should be worried. She was alive and consciously coherent.

Her feet touched the solid ground. Kelsey wanted to shout for joy, but her surroundings seemed to tilt, and she took an extra step to the side.

"Whoa." Trace came up on her left, his arm sturdy and strong on her upper back. "We need to move you away from the blaze."

"I'm fine. Really. I don't need help." She shoved at his arm. Kelsey shifted so her back faced him.

"You need to take it easy." Trace placed his hand on her shoulder and guided her to an area away from the vehicle. "Sit."

"You know, I'm not a dog." She frowned.

"I didn't say you were one. It was simply an order."

"Right." Her fingers shook and she squeezed her eyes shut. This man worked all the time, ready to do whatever it took to stabilize the situation. But she could stabilize herself. She worked with trauma patients too.

She opened her eyes again and came face-to-face with a scowl. "Can you recall anything from the accident? The type of car? Who it might have been?"

Kelsey rubbed her temples. "I don't know. Why does this sound like an interrogation?" She wrapped her arms around her legs. "I should have paid more attention." She sucked in a breath and blew it out. Her foot tapped the grassy area.

If she'd focused on how fast the truck behind her had accelerated, this whole escapade could have been avoided. No one would've needed to respond to a distress call on her behalf. It was quite embarrassing.

Kelsey blew on the pad of her thumb to stimulate her vagus nerve in an attempt to calm down.

"You didn't know. It's okay." Trace took her trembling hand in his. He wrapped his fingers around her wrist and looked at his watch. "Can you bandage up the cut on her face?"

"Sure thing." Andi bent down to pull supplies from the bag. "Perhaps we should try to stop meeting each other like this." She chuckled.

"Agreed." Kelsey shifted on the ground to find a comfortable position on the hard surface and coughed.

"Here." Andi handed her an oxygen mask. The cold air filled her lungs and dissipated the smoke.

Trace squatted so he was at eye level. "Follow my finger."

She stared at him.

"Please."

Kelsey bit the inside of her cheek to keep from cracking a smile. She followed the direction of his finger until he lowered it.

"I'm going to check for signs of a concussion. Since you're not showing signs of a bleed, that's a good thing."

Kelsey nodded and lowered the mask.

"I want you to focus on my nose. When I move my finger, I want you to touch it, then touch your nose."

Kelsey did her best not to let her gaze wander to Trace's eyes, which proved harder than tapping his finger and her nose. With each touch, she told her heart to slow down. It didn't help that other people were at the scene. The last thing she needed was them picking up on her nervousness.

"Good job." Trace smiled. "I'm going to push down on your arms and legs, and I want you to resist it."

Without her jacket as a barrier, Trace's hand cooled her warm skin. Kelsey shifted her focus to the grass and worked to push back against the pressure Trace applied. There was a time in college when she would have melted in Trace's embrace, but life had turned out differently, and she wouldn't embarrass herself by falling for this man now.

"Your motor skills are good. Your eyes are tracking well too. Sometimes concussion symptoms are delayed, so keep an eye on how you feel. Any headaches, nausea, worsening dizziness, go to the hospital."

"Got it, thanks." Kelsey stretched out her legs in the grass.

"So, what happened, besides the obvious?" His frown deepened. On her other side, Andi worked on cleaning the side of her face. "You weren't at the coffee shop this morning."

She raised her eyebrows. That was not a declaration she'd expected to hear. "You went?"

"After I found out Gerald got bail, I tried calling you to give you a heads-up so you'd watch your back. When you didn't respond, I headed to the café."

"I see." So he'd gone out of concern for her safety. Not because he was willing to admit he needed help with whatever was going on behind those broad shoulders, that toned physique, and his rich, chocolatey eyes.

Oh, get it together, Kels. Now is not the time to notice how attractive he is.

"I had an emergency visit with one of my patients this morning and had to stop by the hospital. By the time I was finished, it was late, and I didn't expect..." She paused, not wanting to say what she'd thought.

But Trace finished for her. "You didn't expect me to show up."

"I decided to head to the office, but a gray pickup started tailing me. I figured it was an impatient driver running late for work, so I slowed down a bit. But when I rounded the corner, they hit me from behind. They made it appear like they were going to pass me, but then the truck sideswiped me. I lost control, and they sped off."

Trace's jaw clenched as she finished talking.

The sticky adhesive of a bandage greeted her cheek. "You're all good to go," Andi said. "It wasn't a deep cut."

"Thank you." Kelsey smiled and turned her attention back to Trace.

"Were you able to see who was driving the pickup? Or get a license plate number?"

"No, on both counts."

"If this was Gerald, I'm going to have something to say to him." Trace pushed himself off the ground.

He extended a hand to her, but she ignored the gesture and stood up.

A rush of blood whooshed its way through her head. Kelsey stood still until the feeling passed. "It was probably someone late to work who didn't want to be caught up in an accident. I doubt it was Gerald."

"Kelsey, he got bail. He's out on the street again." He picked up the orange medic bag.

Andi climbed the hill with the stretcher at her side.

Trace pulled out his phone from his back pocket. "I'm going to call in a favor and see if any information can be tracked down."

"No need. I'll take the investigation over from here." A uniformed officer, sergeant chevrons on both sleeves, walked up to them. "Aiden Donaldson, LCC Sergeant. We met at the hostage situation." He shook Kelsey's hand, his grip firm.

He had dark hair, almost black. His uniform and stance screamed business, but his expression was tender.

"I remember." Kelsey caught Trace's glance in her direction before he headed back up the hill to the waiting ambo.

Something made him fiercely protective of her. She'd love to crack Trace's outer shell somehow and get to the root.

"Why don't we start from the beginning." Donaldson pulled her attention back.

She recounted everything that had happened and watched him scribble notes on a pad.

"And now my car is a piece of junk." After the words left her mouth, Kelsey realized she hadn't noticed if they'd gotten the fire under control.

She did a one-eighty in the grass and stared at the hunk of metal. It wasn't pretty. The missing driver's door made it appear like a stunt car. The hood lay mangled and charred to a crisp. Glass and a few scraps of metal littered the area around the front tire.

"And you didn't get a look at the driver?"

"No, sir."

"Do you know of anyone who would want to hurt you, Ms. Scott?"

"I—" She paused and scratched her cheek. The bandage made her skin itchy. "I'm a clinical social worker who counsels patients who have suffered physical and mental setbacks. It can be challenging."

The sergeant frowned. "Would you be able to provide a list of names for us to look into?"

"That's strictly confidential." She crossed her arms. The motion made her muscles sore. "Unless you get a warrant, I can't hand over patient information."

A dull ache started to form at the side of her head, and she rubbed her temple. She needed to contact Dean and let him know where she was. She didn't know the time, but her boss would be concerned she hadn't shown up for work yet. And there were probably several missed calls from Natalie as well.

"Would you be able to see if my purse and phone are still in the car? I need to contact a few people."

Sergeant Donaldson radioed someone, and within a few minutes, a woman jogged over to them with her belongings.

He closed his pad. "That's all I need from you at the moment. Do you have someone who can give you a ride?"

"Thank you, I do."

"Excellent. We'll be in touch later."

She rummaged through her purse and pulled out her phone.

The screen lit up and, sure enough, there were several missed calls. She called Dean but left a voicemail explaining the situation.

Then she called Natalie. It barely rang once before she answered.

"Kelsey! Where are you? Are you okay?" The words rushed out of her friend's mouth.

"I'm fine. I had a slight fender bender this morning."

"And you think I'll believe that?" Natalie said. "I want details, please."

Kelsey sighed. If she sugarcoated the truth now, Nat would find out later, so it didn't matter. "I was in a car accident. Someone hit me from behind, and they ran me off the road."

"What?" Natalie's shriek pierced the line, and Kelsey moved the phone away from her ear. The high-pitched octave added to her growing headache.

She winced. "The medics checked me out, and the police are looking into it."

"You know Gerald got bail, right?" Natalie said.

"I heard."

"You don't think…" Her unspoken words said it all.

"I don't know. I don't want to believe it." She pinched the bridge of her nose.

"The patients we work with are troubled, Kels. That's why we're here, to help them. I would watch your back."

"That's exactly what Trace said."

"He's a wise man. Listen to that advice."

Kelsey sighed. "I'll be in the office once I get everything situated here." She would not inconvenience her friend and ask for a ride. Even if that meant she walked to work.

"I'll be there in fifteen minutes."

"What? No, I'm fine."

A door shut on the other end. "Nonsense. Your car needs to be repaired, right? And I know you won't ask for help."

Natalie hung up.

Kelsey scanned the area and shivered. At the top of the hill, the end of the guardrail was bent inward, and tire marks paved a path down to her vehicle.

Who had run her off the road?

If it wasn't an accident, that meant she'd angered someone. And if that were true, it meant her goal of helping people had backfired. Nerves coiled in her gut at the thought.

She might have made her first enemy.

7

The words on the computer screen taunted him, as if to drive home the point that today's call could have ended very differently. Trace finished filing the rest of the report in the common area at the station where the computers were housed. He sat back in the chair. His weight bent the mechanism so it reclined further.

He hadn't even been around Kelsey for more than seventy-two hours, and already memories of his wife haunted him. If they hadn't gotten the door off in time, Kelsey could have died in that car. And once more he'd had to wait to step in and help.

He laced his fingers behind his head and let out a breath.

"Bad call?" Logan asked. He'd just come on shift, covering for another lieutenant out sick this week.

Trace shot a glance over his shoulder. "Something like that."

Logan sidled into the breakroom, turned one of the other chairs around, and straddled it. He waited in silence for Trace to share what was on his mind.

"You ever want to talk some sense into someone so they take care of themselves and don't do something stupid?"

"Dude, if you have a problem with my daredevil stunts and jumping out of planes to fight wildfires, just say so," Logan said with a mischievous grin.

"Ha. Ha. Very funny. It just irks me. I don't want to see someone else get hurt, and she doesn't even realize she's in danger."

"I get it." Logan shrugged. "We have an inclination to protect and save people. It's the nature of our jobs, no matter the danger. We know what to do."

"Exactly." Trace leaned forward and propped his arms on his legs.

"But we also can't make someone do something they don't want to do. We can only encourage the right thing."

Trace didn't say anything, because Logan was right. Instead, he stared at the black computer screen, which had gone into power-saving mode.

"This wouldn't have anything to do with Kelsey, would it?" Logan tilted his head and gave him a knowing look. "We all know about the counselor and the hostage situation."

"I'm not buying the incident today as merely an accident. I don't want something worse to happen." Trace let out a sigh.

"She doesn't believe she's in danger?"

Trace said, "It's Kelsey. Whatever it is, she'll handle it herself." Except that *he* was the one who needed help.

"How close were the two of you in college?"

Of course Logan would press him about his feelings for Kelsey after the conversation at the Backdraft, but it wasn't like that. They had only ever been one thing. "Friends. A group of us hung out frequently." He stood up and grabbed the TV remote off the couch and turned up the volume on the news channel. The background noise added a nice distraction.

"I see."

Trace took two water bottles from the fridge and tossed one

to Logan. Even the brief mention of college brought back memories of his wife. Kelsey and Renee had been inseparable.

To his surprise, Logan didn't press further. "Kelsey seems to have a good head on her shoulders. She's self-sufficient and you can watch her back, right?" Logan popped off the plastic bottle cap.

And that was exactly what Trace feared. Kelsey was independent and strong-willed. Not a bad thing, but he'd seen it backfire with his wife. Now he lived with the regret of his wife's choices, his failure to help, and what it had cost them both.

"Yeah, I suppose you're right."

"Are you going to let anything happen to her?"

Trace frowned. "Of course not."

"There you go, then." Logan winked and gave Trace a firm slap on the back.

Trace headed to the locker room to change into running clothes. With the shift over, he needed to clear his mind.

Outside, the overcast sky only added to the fogginess of his thoughts. A slight breeze swept through the air and added to the cooler temperatures, although no rain appeared imminent in the forecast. Trace zipped up his jacket and climbed into his car.

Ten minutes later he pulled into the park and grabbed his ear buds from the center console cup holder. There was plenty of time to run before heading back to his apartment to cook dinner.

Alone.

A wave of tightness enveloped his chest and threatened to swallow him. Five years without Renee, and yet there were moments, like today, where it felt like the first.

He paused on the sidewalk to start a workout on his watch.

His feet hit the pavement, and he set off along the path lined with trees to his left. A soccer field lay in the center of the park to his right, and a few kids kicked a ball around as they tried to make a goal.

With each step of his foot, the rhythm set in, and soon everything else faded as he focused on his breathing and maintained a steady pace. He made it around the bend and started his ascent on the short, yet steep, incline that wrapped around the outer edge of the park.

His heart raced in unison with his thoughts.

He'd left Benson, Washington, to move on from his past, not come face-to-face with it again. He couldn't do his job and save people if they didn't recognize their need for help. Thankfully most folks he came into contact with on the job were ready to accept assistance.

Trace eased up as he started going downhill, the wind pushing him along.

Several park benches dotted the path. A few oak trees created a welcome cover with their leaves that stretched over the seating. One woman wore a sweatshirt and biker shorts and sat with a book in her hands. As he approached, the unmistakable mark of a prosthetic leg was exposed.

Kelsey.

He hoped she remained engrossed in her book and wouldn't notice him pass by, yet he also wanted to talk with her. To remind her she needed to take care of herself and watch her back. If he could prevent more heartache for them both, it was worth it. She should be at home resting, not out here exposed where anything could happen.

The book must not have been all that interesting, because at the sound of his feet approaching, she lifted her gaze. Weariness clouded her expression.

She realized it was him, and her face softened. "Clearing your head?" It wasn't accusatory; rather, a gentle smile crossed her lips.

"Yeah." He paused the workout on his watch and stepped off to the side in the grass.

"It's a nice day for it."

"You like dreary, overcast days?"

"When you put it like that it sounds depressing." She laughed. "You know, God didn't only make sunny days. There's something peaceful and quiet about cloudy days. While everyone else stays holed up inside, you get to enjoy nature, and no one bothers you."

She closed her book and set it down beside her.

"Good point." Although, the circumstances in his life made him wonder if God had only given him cloudy days. "But shouldn't you be resting at home? Considering you were just in a car accident."

Alertness flared in her eyes, and she sat a little straighter against the back of the bench. "Oh no. I hope I'm not forgetting." Kelsey's eyes widened, even as she tried to refrain from grinning. "Amnesia might have set in, and I wouldn't be any the wiser. But if I recall correctly, I was cleared by the medic on scene." She tilted her head to the side and scrunched her forehead. "He said something about me being okay unless I started to experience concussion-like symptoms."

He coughed to cover his laugh. She was adorable. "You know, I do remember those orders. Fair enough."

"Thank you." She turned and gave him a wink.

He didn't want to be rude, but he couldn't help staring at her leg—well, what had been her leg. Her quirkiness and enthusiasm for life remained intact. But something drastic had happened between college and now that had physically affected her body, and Trace wanted to know what. Maeve hadn't given him much context, but Kelsey had been close to him once. So whatever had happened, she'd seen a need to hide it.

If life had taught him anything, it was that pain snuck in with a sucker punch without warning, and it took joy with it.

"It's not as bothersome as it looks." She shoved her hands in her sweatshirt pocket and bent her head. "You get used to it."

"I'm sorry. I really didn't mean to, uh"—Trace stumbled over his words—"stare."

"It's a natural response." Kelsey's gaze met his.

The wind blew loose strands of hair that escaped her ponytail, and he had the strong urge to tuck them behind her ear. For some reason, he wanted to envelope her in a hug, comfort her. The unspoken hardship evident in her soft-spoken words. And Trace wanted her to share more. Her dismissal of the injury confirmed there was more to the story.

He took a step closer.

His proximity allowed him to count each freckle on her face. The splatter of brown dots shone in unison with the golden strands of her hair and made him forget about the overcast sky—like the dark clouds overhead and within his heart didn't hold the final say.

The wind picked up momentum and several leaves fluttered to the ground around them.

Kelsey shivered and wrapped her arms around her waist.

"You're cold." Trace took off his sweatshirt and handed it to her. Their fingers brushed, and the subtle interaction stoked the kindling of dangerous fuel on a fire weather watch day.

Trace sucked in a breath and took a step back to give them both space.

"I'm fine." She swallowed. "Really, it's not necessary." Her eyes searched his.

Trace nodded, unable to muster anything else.

Why did his heart pound like a jackhammer? He should not feel *anything* for Kelsey. She was simply a familiar face. A safe place in his world—one that allowed him to go back in time and remember the good moments when Renee had been there.

"Are you free to go grab that coffee?" Trace held his breath, unsure how she would respond. She'd already attempted twice, and he'd declined her offers.

Kelsey grabbed her backpack from the bench. "Hmm, I don't know."

Trace chided himself for asking. Of course she wouldn't want to. Not after how he'd responded to her.

She put her book inside, and slung it over her shoulder, not meeting his gaze. "As long as that's considered resting. I wouldn't want my doctor chastising me for not taking it easy, you know."

Trace burst out in laughter, and the breath he'd been holding let loose. "Okay, okay, you got me." He held up his hands.

She swatted at his bicep. "Of course we can go grab coffee."

"Great. I'll meet you there?"

"Actually, I walked here." She gave him a sheepish grin.

"Are you asking for help?"

"Never." She raised her eyebrows. "Simply informing you it may take a while for me to walk home and drive over."

No way would he leave her unprotected for that long, and that amount of exertion wouldn't benefit her need to relax. "I can give you a ride."

The entire walk back to his car, his spine tingled. Was it from close proximity to Kelsey, or because someone lurked in the shadows?

Kelsey climbed in the passenger seat, and Trace paused on his way to the driver's side.

He scanned the parking lot and followed the trail of foliage along the perimeter. Nothing appeared out of sorts, but Trace knew better than to simply trust his naked eye.

Someone could be hiding nearby and keeping tabs on Kelsey.

But who?

8

Kelsey squirmed in her seat at Bridgewater Café while Trace took a sip of his drink. Her chair rocked back and forth from the uneven legs. A line of people waited at the enclosed glass bakery section, ready to experience a sliver of delicacy that the owner, Meg Andrews, prided herself on.

It had been over six years since she and Trace sat down and talked. Sure, they'd kept in touch here and there, but careers, marriage, and distance changed how often they updated each other on life. And small talk seemed silly now, but it was a place to start.

"What?" He eyed her across the tiny round table and raised an eyebrow, clearly amused at her response.

"I'll never understand how people drink their coffee black."

"I'm convinced the caffeine jolt is stronger."

"If you say so."

He took a bite of the egg sandwich he'd ordered. Her stomach sat in a web of knots so she couldn't eat much even if she'd wanted to, but she bit into her slice of avocado toast topped with red pepper flakes and salt.

The heat from the pepper only enhanced the warmth still coursing down her arms from her and Trace's *moment* at the park. Her shiver then had everything to do with the way he'd studied her. Like she could be the one to help him grow and see the beauty in life again.

She found him attractive enough that she now sat across from him, wanting to spill all her secrets, which was crazy. Trace might be a friend, but it had been years since they'd hung out. And right now, they were supposed to work on his problems.

The whole goal of getting coffee had been for her to learn what was really going on behind that handsome face of his. Not to let him infiltrate her every thought. She should really practice what she preached to her clients. *Don't let emotions dictate your feelings.*

No, she couldn't find him attractive. Even with his admirable mentality of saving people. This was her best friend's husband, after all. He belonged to Renee, and Kelsey refused to betray her friend. This interaction was simply business—no feelings allowed. A meeting to get to the root of what hurts he held on to.

She'd seen the curiosity in his eyes. If it helped him share, she could tell him more about how she lost her leg.

"I see you're still health conscious." Trace winked then grabbed a napkin from the holder in the corner of the table and dabbed his mouth.

Sure, Trace meant well, but his words struck a pang in her. The difficulties she faced with her health went far deeper than she'd ever admitted to him before. "I wouldn't dream of it. I prefer simple drinks like green tea." She raised her to-go cup in the air. "More antioxidants and none of the junk of processed sugar." The steam rose through the hole in the lid, and she blew on it before taking a sip.

"Does that philosophy have anything to do with what happened?" Tenderness graced his expression.

Hot liquid burned her tongue, but she took another sip anyway. Better to rip the bandage straight off. Still, her pulse beat in her ears. "I realized how detrimental it was to my health."

"I remember you missed classes sometimes because of the diabetes."

Kelsey nodded. "My body had already been through a lot after the virus attacked my pancreas as a child. When my dad died, my mom couldn't function in normal life, let alone stock the pantry with healthy foods. I was told to learn how to cope with the symptoms and it would eventually go away. Except it got worse. So yes, I missed class to work through the symptoms myself."

Even saying the words out loud sounded silly to her ears. She knew a lot more now about her health than she had back then. If she'd had people supporting her then, the road she walked would have been much easier.

Warmth flooded her face, but it wasn't from the drink or the man across from her. How foolish of her to think Trace would understand. When he discovered the whole story, certainly he'd walk away. That was the risk with vulnerability. It left the person exposed.

Silence flitted between them even as the sound of the espresso machine and orders being called filled the air.

"You don't have to share more if you don't want to." Trace slid his hand across the table. Instead of taking her fingers in his, he stopped short. The millimeters of space spoke volumes.

She would finish. If she could show Trace she trusted him with pieces of her story, then he might open up about his so she could help him.

"I changed my diet because I didn't want to be controlled by an illness. But the damage had already been done. I didn't have a consistent team of doctors once I was in college, so it was hard for anyone to keep my medical history straight. There was so much to manage during that time." She pulled in a breath, remembering all the days she tirelessly tracked which types of sugar and carbs she consumed. Even when her roommates had come home with cheesecakes and savory desserts, she'd stayed the course. "Despite the lifesaving insulin and lifestyle changes, it got worse. I woke up one morning and realized I couldn't feel my leg. I told myself it would go away, like my mom said." She paused.

"But it didn't." Trace finished the thought for her.

No, it hadn't. The memory of that day haunted her.

Kelsey didn't know how to word the next part without it sounding grotesque. Trace was in the medical field. He'd probably seen much worse and could put the pieces of what she wasn't saying together.

"I'd been taking my diagnosis seriously, but once the numbness crept in, an open wound got infected. I lost color in my leg, and my doctor said it needed to be amputated." She gulped down more of her tea, the liquid cooler now.

"Wow. I didn't realize."

She flicked her hand in the air. The last thing she wanted was his pity. "My mom's voice echoed in my head, telling me it would go away." She paused.

"But it didn't." Trace finished the thought for her.

"I was embarrassed to say anything because I thought I was managing everything better. By the time I got an appointment with the doctor, it was too late." The memory of that day haunted her. "I'm just sorry it prevented me from coming to Renee's funeral."

Trace's brown eyes clouded over like the dark sky outside. "What do you mean?"

"When you called about the accident, I wanted to be there to support you and honor her life. But my surgery was scheduled on the same day as the service, and it wasn't an option to push my surgery back."

She waited for his response. Her leg bounced underneath the table. Part of her always wondered if he held a grudge over her absence that day.

"Maeve said your surgery happened earlier and you were recovering."

"I wish. I tried to change my surgery date, but they wouldn't let me."

"Hmmm." Trace stared at the space behind her.

Kelsey still read between the lines. "At the time you were mad, though."

"Maybe. Yeah, a little." He brushed his fingers through his hair. "In my mind I knew you cared. But I told myself otherwise. Because Maeve came, but it felt weird without you or—" He stopped short.

Tears misted in his eyes, but Kelsey didn't want to draw attention to it. "I should have at least sent a card. But it seemed like a cheap Band-Aid to such great pain."

Trace cleared his throat, shoved the last bite of food in his mouth, and crumpled the napkin. "I blame myself for her accident. Right before she left for her trip that day, we had a heated argument. I told her she shouldn't go. She said it was only for the weekend, and with my work schedule, I wouldn't even realize she was gone."

The words hung in the air, and his shoulders slumped as his hand clenched the mug.

She wanted to reach out and touch his hand. Run her fingers across his palm and assure him it would be okay.

There was no way she'd cross that line. Not when he still cared deeply about his wife. Emotions were already high, and Kelsey didn't want to add any confusion to the sacred moment.

Trace propped his hand underneath his nose. "How did you

learn to cope with the reality of losing something and still live your life?"

She let out a short laugh. "I didn't at first. I was bitter. Every time I looked at my leg, it was a reminder of the mistakes I'd made. No matter how hard I tried, I couldn't get it right."

"You can say that again," Trace said under his breath.

"Eventually I realized it could either be a stumbling block or the fuel to remind me to focus on valuing the important things in life."

"And just like that you're happy again?"

"It was a choice to either live with intentionality or let it eat me alive each day. I decided on the former."

The conflict of emotions in his eyes told her the wrestling wasn't easy for him either.

Kelsey leaned forward and everything else faded into the background. "No matter what consequences or hardships we endure, God has purpose behind it. He uses it for good—even when it doesn't make sense. I now have greater empathy for my clients and the trauma they've experienced because of what I've gone through."

"Well, clearly God and I aren't on the same team." A muscle in his neck flinched.

She leaned back against the chair. "Thank you for sharing with me."

"Don't get any ideas of marking this down as a counseling session, though. Simply friend to friend." Trace stood up fast and put his hands in his back pockets.

"I wouldn't dream of it." Kelsey eased out of her chair. She wasn't willing to raise a white flag yet, but she'd refrain from pressing further right now, or else he might not open up to her again.

They threw out their trash and Trace drove her home. When they got to her street, Trace pulled up to the curb and let the truck idle.

This wasn't a date, and yet sitting here in his truck after getting coffee made it feel like one. Kelsey fumbled for her keys and tried to buy time and figure out what to say. "Thanks for the ride."

He nodded. "Absolutely."

She reached for the door handle and hopped out.

"Kelsey."

She turned back around. "Yeah?"

"Keep an eye on your surroundings, would you?"

She gave him a nod and walked up to the porch. She could feel his stare on her back the entire way.

He doesn't care about you in that way, girl. Get a grip.

Making sure she got safely inside was sweet, but she needed to remind herself it was strictly because of what he'd said. He didn't think she was safe.

She opened the front door and took a step inside before she froze. The doorknob turned ice cold in her hand as she processed the scene in front of her. What in the world?

She swiveled around, straight into a hard torso, and let out a scream.

Trace grabbed her shoulders to keep her from falling.

She clamped her mouth shut and hoped the neighbors hadn't heard her pathetic cry.

"What's wrong?" Trace stepped around her and walked inside.

She flicked on the switch, and light filtered through the living room. Trace inhaled sharply.

The mess in front of her was crystal clear. Someone had ransacked her place.

In a millisecond, Trace had a gun pulled. "Stay here while I clear the house. I don't want anyone surprising us with their presence."

She sat down on her living room couch and waited, her hands clasped together. Photos and glass littered the floor.

Drawers hung open and papers lay strewn on the carpet. Even her coat rack had been knocked over. Her eyes scanned the room and fell on the mirror above her mantel.

The words displayed in red ink stole her breath. *Home-wrecker.*

"All clear." Trace rounded the corner. He holstered his gun and she stood up to meet him. "When did you leave your house today?"

"After lunch. That's when I headed to the park."

He didn't look at the fireplace. He hadn't seen that atrocious statement. Kelsey's fingers trembled.

"And you locked your doors?"

She nodded. "I don't know how someone got in."

Trace pulled out his phone and typed away. "Do you have a security system?"

"I've never needed one before."

"Well, you might want to reconsider."

"Thanks for stating the obvious," she snapped. Then sighed. "Sorry. I didn't mean to sound rude."

"I think I know how they got in." Trace pointed down the hall to the kitchen. "The back window is shattered. Someone must have climbed through."

Kelsey let out a groan.

"I'm going to call this in. Let the cops process everything, see if they can pick up prints."

"Okay, thanks." She wrapped her arms across her chest and walked to the kitchen. Sure enough, a gaping hole stood where the window had been. Glass littered the floor. The sparkles they radiated were anything but beautiful. A breeze rustled the papers on the counter.

"Come look at this." Trace's voice echoed down the hallway.

She walked back into the front room. *I already saw it.*

A scowl formed on Trace's face, and Kelsey's skin began to itch. A red patch formed as she scratched her forearm. What if word got back to Dean, and she couldn't finish the grant program because of the accusation?

He pointed to the mirror. "This guy is trouble. I knew it."

She wanted to argue with him but couldn't deny the inkling of doubt in her mind. Who would have done something like this? Could it really have been Gerald in a fit of rage?

Kelsey didn't want to believe it, but the words on her mirror told a different story. One where she played a part in their broken family.

Despite her best efforts, she was on someone's bad side. Enough they believed she had ruined their life.

And whoever did this wanted her to understand something. She had a target on her back, and they weren't afraid to hit the bull's-eye.

9

Trace stood in Kelsey's living room as Detective Savannah Wilcox and her team gathered evidence. Their gloved hands meticulously combed over each surface. They dusted for prints and bagged possible evidence. He just hoped they found something that would stick.

Kelsey had gone to her room to change into warmer clothes. He'd seen the way she shook, which meant either the shock had taken a toll or her blood sugar was low. He figured it was a mix of the two.

"If you need anything, I'll be in the kitchen," Trace said to the team of officers.

He headed to the back of the house. The clock on the wall told him it was almost eight in the evening. Considering all Kelsey had earlier was tea and toast, she must be starving.

He opened the fridge and assessed the available options. Several oranges sat in the fruit drawer, and he pulled one out.

He put the slices in a bowl. She had salad fixings and plenty of toppings, so he whipped up a strawberry spinach salad and tossed in almonds, onions, and berries with the greens. Unsure how much dressing she liked, he poured some in a small dish.

Someone shuffled their feet.

Trace turned around, tongs in hand.

Detective Wilcox stood by the kitchen table and cleared her throat. "Bro. I didn't even whip up something that fancy while pregnant with my kid." She raised an eyebrow.

Trace shrugged. So he could cook. The skill he'd learned as a kid came in handy from time to time. Especially at the station. Between him and Charlie, the team didn't go hungry. He'd never forget the first time he concocted lunch with delicately grilled shrimp on a bed of greens, drizzled with a soy ginger sauce. Everyone on the team had echoed their bewilderment.

"Hey." Kelsey walked in and froze in the middle of the room. She appeared lost in her own kitchen. She'd donned sweatpants, and fuzzy socks covered her feet. Even in the casual attire, she looked cute. She'd twisted her hair into a messy bun, and it still looked good.

He turned his head back to the food on the counter. He couldn't afford to think of her as pretty. It would dishonor Renee. The thought knocked the air from his lungs.

"I figured you must be hungry, so I made you a salad. I hope you don't mind."

"Not at all." She smiled at him, exhaustion in her eyes.

She pushed herself onto the edge of the island and let her feet dangle off the side. He grabbed the bowl of orange slices and handed it to her. "Eat these first. Make sure your blood sugar doesn't drop."

"Right, thanks."

While she ate the fruit, he popped a few strawberries in his mouth.

"I'm going to need to secure that window before I go to bed." She spoke between bites.

"You're not thinking of staying here tonight, are you?" There was no way she should be here by herself. They didn't know who might be lurking in the shadows.

She lifted her chin. "I'm not going to let whoever did this scare me out of my own house."

"You heard the threats Gerald made. There's no reason he won't come back and do something worse when you're home."

Kelsey hopped down from the counter and put her bowl in the sink before grabbing a fork for the salad. "Can't you let people make their own decisions? I'm a grown adult, Trace. I can take care of myself. And I don't like you talking about my clients like that. They aren't criminals." She sat down hard on the barstool.

"I know he hasn't been formally convicted yet. But these circumstances call for more protective measures."

"Do you really know that? Because you're insinuating something serious." She stabbed the salad and pierced a few greens before eating the mouthful.

Why did she have to be so defiant? He simply wanted to make sure no one hurt her worse than what she'd already suffered.

"I don't need a guard. And the last thing I want is to take you or anyone else away from your actual duties."

"This is my job." Renee would want him to protect Kelsey. And he'd do whatever he could to watch after those she'd cared about and honor her life while doing so.

She shook her head. "No, it's not. You tend to people who're injured. I'm not hurt."

He opened his mouth, ready to argue.

"Everything okay in here?" Savannah walked back in.

Trace ignored her frown. "Did you find anything worthwhile?"

"The lab will determine that. Whoever this was covered their tracks well. I'm not holding my breath for fingerprints, but we might get a hit on the substance used for the writing on the mirror that might prove useful."

"Thank you for all your help." Kelsey slid off the stool.

"Of course. All our work here is done, and we'll be in touch."

"So that means I can stay here tonight?" Anticipation laced her words.

Trace took a step toward Savannah. "I really don't think..." He gave her a look, pleading with her to say no. Maybe if Kelsey heard it from a woman, she'd understand the stakes.

Savannah pinched her lips. Her gaze lingered for a moment before she averted her eyes to the broken window behind Kelsey.

"If you cover the window well and lock the doors, I don't think whoever was here will be coming back tonight."

Kelsey let out a sigh of relief.

Savannah's expression turned stoic. "I highly recommend installing a security camera and being cautious with your safety until we know who did this."

"Fair enough," Kelsey said.

Trace didn't like the answer, but he wasn't going to say so. He wouldn't be getting any sleep tonight. Macon had scheduled him for an early morning shift, but it wouldn't deter him if it meant making sure no one came back to do anything stupid.

Of course, she didn't need to know his intention was to sleep in his truck. "Do you have any wood?"

"There should be some in the storage closet. Take a left at the end of the hall and it's the door on your right."

Kelsey picked up her plate to finish her food, and the officers bade them farewell.

Trace opened the closet, surprised to find several planks of wood and a small box of tools in the corner, which he grabbed. "You have a secret craftsmanship skill?"

A sheepish look crossed her face, and pink tinted her cheeks. This woman was full of surprises.

"I have a fascination with DIY projects and had plans to build an entryway table."

He opened the toolbox and found every tool imaginable that would fit in the portable container. Guilt tightened across his chest at the lack of confidence he'd displayed in her. This girl could hold her own.

"I'm sorry." Trace took out a hammer and nails and set them on the table.

"For what?" Kelsey rinsed her plate in the sink.

"I seriously underestimated your abilities." Part of him wanted to know he was useful for something. That he could do good in some way.

"Ah."

"You want to do the honors?" He extended the hammer to her.

She must have sensed his inner turmoil, because instead of taking it from him, she folded his hand back toward his chest. "No, you can have at it."

Within thirty minutes, he had the planks secured over the gaping hole. If anyone tried to tamper with it, they would be audible.

"That should do it." He closed the toolbox. "Are you sure you don't need anything else?"

"Thank you, but I'm fine. Really."

He let himself linger next to her a little longer. An urge to hug her built inside him. The thought sent a shiver down his back.

Her arms hung by her side, and she shuffled her feet. A flash of some emotion he couldn't pinpoint skittered across her face, then disappeared. What he wouldn't give to protect her from harm's way. If he could save Renee's best friend from a tragic fate, then maybe, just maybe, he could forgive himself for how he'd failed his wife.

Trace slid his feet back until they connected with the wall. He needed to leave in order to think clearly. He bent down to gather his belongings at the same time she reached for his bag, and their arms brushed.

The temperature rose in the enclosed hallway. If he wasn't careful, Trace would overheat under Kelsey's watchful gaze and disintegrate into a puddle of emotions.

He cleared his throat and took the bag from her grasp. "Take it easy." Unwilling to expose his heart further in front of her, Trace walked outside without a second glance.

When the lock clicked behind him, he let his shoulders relax as he walked down her front steps. His car engine roared to life when he twisted the key, and he turned to see the front blinds to Kelsey's windows snap shut.

With the truck in reverse, he rolled down past two homes, put it in park, and turned off his lights. He reached into the glove box, and his hand gripped a wrapper. Good thing he stocked extra energy bars in here, because they would come in handy tonight.

He reclined his seat back just enough to be comfortable but not risk dozing off and settled in for the stakeout.

A BUZZING NOISE MET HIS EARS, AND TRACE JERKED IN HIS SEAT. He fumbled to find his phone and turned off the alarm.

Five thirty in the morning. He groaned and stretched his hands above his head but couldn't go far before they hit the ceiling.

It had been silent all night. The only activity he caught had been racoons in search of treasure in the garbage.

No one called with any news, which he deemed a good sign.

Trace stretched his legs as best he could in the cramped space before he slid his seat forward. He had to be at work in the next half hour and didn't want to risk staying out here any longer in case Kelsey left early for the office.

There was no point in causing conflict before he'd even had a sip of joe.

With one more drive past her quiet house, he headed to the station.

Trace entered the lounge area, and Charlie let out a low whistle. "Woo wee." He sat on the couch, his feet propped up, nursing an early morning cup of coffee.

"That bad, huh?" Trace walked over and slapped the guy on the shoulder. He hadn't checked in a mirror, but the bags under his eyes would be a dead giveaway.

"Whoa, watch the gold now. Every drop is precious." Charlie lifted the cup higher to steady the sloshing liquid.

"Quiet night at home?"

Charlie took a sip. "Same old, same old. Living the bachelor life. Sometimes the quiet nights get old."

"Is that why you joined the squad?" Trace winked. "Get your thrill of adventure?"

"Exactly." Charlie snapped his fingers. "Life has to be exciting somehow. And it sure hasn't disappointed yet."

"You got that right." Trace headed to the cubbies and grabbed his clothes to change into. No sooner did he exit the locker room than the alarm blared.

"Ambo 21, Truck 14. Accident off the bypass on Chestnut Street. Overturned vehicle, driver trapped."

Trace raced to the garage and hopped in the driver's seat of the ambulance.

"Good morning to you." Andi reached for the radio in the ambo.

"Let's do our best to keep it that way." Trace hit the gas harder and merged onto the highway, siren blaring.

Several minutes later, they pulled off the exit ramp and weaved their way through backed-up traffic of people who wanted to get to work on their early morning commute.

But the scene in front of them told Trace no one would be getting to the office anytime soon. It was about to be a long shift.

A silver sedan lay overturned across the median, and a blue Honda sat close by off the side of the road, the back part of the car crushed. A man, Trace pegged him in his early sixties with his white hair and a suit and tie, stood next to the blue Honda and waved his hands frantically.

"I got the gurney." Andi hopped out of the ambo.

Trace jogged over to the man.

"There's a woman in the car over there. I..." The man's words rushed out in a jumbled sentence. "There was a mother duck and her ducklings in the street, and I didn't see them right away with the sun so low in the sky. The next thing I know my car was slammed from behind and the other vehicle flew over me." The man rubbed his hands down his cheeks. "Please make sure the woman is okay."

"Sir, we will do everything we can. Why don't you have a seat over here and take a few breaths." Trace escorted the guy to the side of the road and had him sit down in the grass with enough distance from the street that he wouldn't be in harm's way.

"I need a blanket over here, stat," Trace said into the radio.

"Copy." Andi headed in their direction and gave him the blanket, which he wrapped around the man.

Truck 14, Amelia and the guys, was already by the overturned car, assessing the situation. Trace frowned. "We need to get the woman out, pronto."

"You don't have to tell me twice," Andi said as they walked over to the wreck.

Trace stepped up to the passenger side door and rapped on

the window, mindful not to hit where the spider web of cracks disseminated. "Ma'am, can you hear me?"

The firefighters worked to get the driver's door open, but the woman gave no response.

Her eyes remained closed, and blood covered her face and neck.

He scanned the rest of the area for any other damage he could make out. That was when he noticed her oversized belly.

Oh, dear God. Please, no.

Trace staggered back away from the car, his breath coming in short pants. He turned to face Andi.

"We need to get her out, now." His voice squeaked.

He ran over to Amelia, who hovered near the car, working the jaws of life to get the door open. "We're trying."

They needed to get the neck brace. Trace turned to Andi. Except no words formed. Everything started to grow dim as his head spun. He was going to pass out.

"Get it together, Trace." Andi shook him.

The abrupt jerking should have brought him back to reality, but he wasn't at the scene of this accident anymore.

Instead, all he could picture was his wife.

10

K elsey stared at the office calendar that hung on the wall next to her desk. The conversation from last night with Trace played in her head.

The second floor had been quiet so far, considering it was mid-morning. Most of the counselors were either teaching group sessions or making house calls.

It might be Trace's duty to look out for people and care for them when they were sick, but she couldn't let him view her the same way. Eventually he'd realize how inconvenient it was to look after her and he'd walk away. When he recognized the grief he needed to deal with in his own life, she'd become an afterthought.

Exactly why she wouldn't let herself walk down that road.

She'd take self-defense classes if needed. Anything to avoid going back to the place where people made it clear they didn't have time to dote on her needs. Which was why she was going to talk to Detective Wilcox.

Her fingers flew across the keyboard as she typed in her next appointment for the day. Once the screen verified it had autosaved, she closed her computer and gathered her belongings. The one perk to her position was not needing to stay holed up in her office all day. Whether she did group therapy sessions or one-on-ones, she could complete them in-house or in an environment conducive to the patient's needs.

Today, she planned to visit Thatcher in the hospital. He was recovering from a recent surgery to try and shrink a tumor on the frontal lobe. It affected his demeanor and caused random outbursts and changes in his disposition.

But first, she needed to swing by the police department.

After checking her glucose levels, which read normal at the moment, she grabbed an orange juice from her mini-fridge for the road—just in case.

As she made her way outside, she passed Wren at the receptionist's desk. "I'll be back in this afternoon. Just forward any calls to my voicemail." Kelsey smiled.

"You got it." Wren waved, then went back to typing.

On the drive, Kelsey thought through techniques to go over with Thatcher today. He'd said his wife would be in as well, so Kelsey would be able to encourage them to fight as a team. The older couple had custody of their granddaughter, Lucy, which added an extra complication to the family dynamic. Kelsey could only imagine the extra patience it required for Chrissy, Thatcher's wife, even though they were both retired.

Kelsey found a parking spot at the station and walked through the automatic doors.

She headed for the receptionist, whose nameplate read *Crystal Rivers* and sat next to a bouquet of fake flowers. "Is Detective Wilcox in? I'd like to speak with her." She gave the woman her name.

"One moment." She picked up the phone. "What's your name?" Her cherry-colored nail polish stood in contrast to the dark phone color.

"Kelsey Scott."

A few minutes later, Wilcox made her way over and shook her hand. "Kelsey, it's good to see you."

"Thanks for seeing me on short notice, Detective."

"Please, call me Savannah." She smiled.

Kelsey followed her back to a conference room.

"Can I get you anything to drink? Coffee, tea?"

"Tea would be great." Kelsey pulled a peppermint bag from the stash on the counter, and Savannah handed her a steaming cup. "Thanks."

"What can I assist you with?" Savannah pulled out a chair and sat down. "Did someone attempt another break-in?"

"No, they didn't. Thankfully." She blew on her cup. "I just wanted to know if you had any leads."

"Not yet. We're still waiting for the DNA results. I have the process expedited, given the hit-and-run incident, but it still takes time."

"I see." Hopefully they'd have information soon. In the meantime, she'd do what she needed to resume a normal life. "I'm getting a security camera installed later today."

"That's a wise idea." Savannah pulled out a pen and paper. "Do you have any ideas of who might've done it?"

"Like I said, I try not to make enemies. My job is to help people. Make their lives better." Kelsey still couldn't believe someone had invaded her personal life and destroyed parts of her home, a sacred place. "I have a few disgruntled clients. But Trace seems to have his eye on Gerald," she mumbled.

"He's just concerned for your safety." Savannah folded her hands on the table.

"Clearly, since he staked out my house last night."

"Ah." Savannah grinned. "Sounds like something my husband would do."

Kelsey had heard stories of Savannah's husband, private investigator Tate Hudson.

"Did you sleep better last night knowing you had eyes on the place?" Savannah's features softened.

"I did," Kelsey admitted.

"Being independent is good. So is letting someone in to have your back when the need arises."

"You think so?" Kelsey furrowed her brow.

"I know so. That's what I love about this department. You never go into a situation alone. Someone is always watching out for you."

Alone.

Kelsey understood what that felt like. When her dad died from a stroke, her mom spiraled out of control with grief, unable to take care of herself. So Kelsey stepped in. Her dad had been the rock of the family. The sounding board when things got tough. Even though her mom was still alive, she'd lost both her parents that day.

A buzzing noise pulled Kelsey from her thoughts. An incoming call from Chrissy.

"I need to go, but when you have any leads, let me know." Kelsey stood up and pushed in her chair.

"Certainly." Savannah walked her out.

Kelsey listened to the voicemail from her client's wife.

I'm running a bit behind this morning, the woman huffed. *The babysitter who watches Lucy came late. But I'm on my way to the hospital now. Hopefully you don't mind pushing our appointment back a tad.*

Kelsey returned the woman's call and assured her she could take her time. "You're doing a great job, and I'll see you soon."

She slid the sun visor down as she drove, to prevent a headache.

Fifteen minutes later, Kelsey pulled into the visitor lot at the hospital and headed for the entrance. Commotion rose on her left, and a team of doctors and nurses rushed to the aid of an ambulance and wheeled a stretcher out the back. Trace hopped out of the vehicle and spoke to a man in a white lab coat as they went inside.

She had some time to spare before heading to Thatcher's room. And if she waited to talk with Trace, depending on the direction their conversation went, she could technically clock it as hours for counseling.

Five minutes passed before Trace and Andi walked out. Kelsey made her way over to the ambulance bay. "Rough morning?"

"Yeah." Trace leaned against the side of the building, his face pale and muscles taut. The overhanging canopy and the fence along the perimeter added a level of privacy from onlookers.

Cars whizzed past on the street parallel to the hospital and a horn blared.

"I'm sorry to hear that."

Kelsey turned to Andi, who gave her a *something's not right, you need to talk with him* stare before she said, "I'm going to grab more supplies to replenish our stock. I'll be right back."

"Why don't we go sit? There's a bench over there." She pointed in the direction of the visitor entrance. The color of Trace's skin concerned her.

"Sure." The one-word response seemed to be all he could muster.

They sat down, and Kelsey crossed the arms of her cardigan sweater against the cooler temperatures. "You want to talk about what happened?"

Trace shifted and wiggled out of his jacket. "Here. This should help."

She blinked at him. "Thanks." She took the jacket and wove her arms through. The smell of his cologne wafted to her nostrils, a woodsy pine scent that warmed her up.

"A call came in for a car accident. Entrapment." Trace

stretched his arm along the back of the bench. "It was her in the car."

"Who was?" Kelsey ran through a list of people she and Trace might be acquainted with in town.

"The woman we helped."

"You knew her?"

"No." He shook his head. "Not personally. But she—" He swallowed, studied the ground. "All I could see was Renee." Trace gripped the ring around his neck.

She understood his reaction now, all too well.

Kelsey had picked up the phone call from Trace five years ago, unaware of how her world would change.

"She's gone," he said with hysteria.

"We're going to the beach for the weekend. She didn't tell you?" Kelsey lugged her suitcase to the front door, her phone propped against her ear.

"No. Kels—" His breath hitched.

Kelsey froze.

"She was in a car accident. She's gone."

Trace's sobs that day echoed in her ears.

Pain sliced through her lip and the taste of blood met her tongue. Kelsey leaned back against the bench. "What did you do?" She prodded deeper. Even now, she wanted to help Trace, yet her own tears pricked the edge of her eyes.

"All I could see—" Trace fisted his hand over his mouth. An attempt to keep the tears at bay so she wouldn't see this grown man cry. She really hated the stigma around that mentality. Everyone needed an emotional release at times.

"I froze." He cleared his throat. "Everything in me went blank, and I put Andi at risk because I couldn't do my stinkin' job. I was helpless because all I could see was the past."

She put her hand on his leg. "I'm so sorry. It's hard when those moments sneak up on us." Kelsey wanted to trail her finger down his jawline. To erase the deep lines that tragedy had added. But she held back. "There are still times I go to call her. And then I remember." Kelsey hiccupped. "I never got to say goodbye." She leaned forward.

Tears rolled down her face. She licked one away, the taste of salt potent. She brushed more away with the back of her hand, but they refused to relent. "I'm sorry, this isn't very..." Kelsey shifted to look at Trace, who wrung his hands together in his lap.

The memories of Renee knocked at her subconscious.

"Come here." Trace wrapped his arms around her shoulders and drew her to himself. She tucked her head into the crook of his neck and let the tears fall. Each one served as a reminder of her and Renee's moments of laughter, hours of video calls, and every shared memory in between.

Several minutes passed before the tears subsided. She was supposed to be counseling Trace through his grief, not leaning on him for support with her own emotions. It was a good thing he wasn't an actual client. Professionalism remained key during sessions, and here she sat, snot and all, with an unraveled resolve.

Kelsey slid out of Trace's hold and wiped her hands on her pants. "Well, that overtook me. Sorry."

"Don't apologize." Trace shook his head. "You and Renee were two peas in a pod." He cleared his throat.

Kelsey laughed, but it came out sounding like a whimper.

Trace wiped a stray tear from her cheek, then stood.

She followed suit.

"There's something else you should know," Trace whispered.

"What's that?"

A shadow appeared in her peripheral vision, and Kelsey turned to see Maeve making her way over.

"Hello, you two." Maeve wore a black ball cap with the Backdraft logo on it and held a pizza box.

Kelsey smiled. "Making an early lunch delivery?"

"Those patients know what they want when they want it." Maeve chuckled.

"I don't blame them. That hospital food is not the most ideal." Trace grimaced.

"You got that right." Maeve glanced between them, but her gaze settled on Trace. "We should grab a meal together sometime soon, okay?"

When he didn't respond, Kelsey said, "You got it. I still have the same number, so feel free to text me with a time."

"Sounds good. See you guys later." Maeve waved and walked inside.

Kelsey shifted her attention back to Trace who fidgeted with the pen clipped to the side of his shirt pocket.

Interesting.

Several thoughts crossed her mind. "Didn't you and Maeve date in college?" The question tumbled from her lips before she realized she'd spoken it out loud.

Trace met her gaze with wide eyes. "What made you think of that?"

"The interaction just now. And you completely deflected my question."

He shoved his hands in his pockets. "We did for a brief time. But that's old history."

"I see." Kelsey tilted her head. "Are you guys hanging out again?"

"It's nothing." Trace dipped his chin.

Andi emerged from the building and opened the back doors to the ambo. "We're all good with supplies," she called out.

Trace made his way back over to the truck and Kelsey followed suit. With his back to her, Kelsey caught Andi's eye and mouthed the words, *We're making progress.*

Andi nodded and mouthed back, *Thank you.*

"Let's get back to the station, shall we?" Trace climbed into the truck.

Kelsey waved, then made her way back to the front entrance.

The conversation with Trace rolled through her mind, but especially his response to Maeve's presence. If he was interested in her, it could be a good indication that his heart was beginning to find healing.

The sliding doors opened, and a breeze of cool air whipped her hair. Kelsey tucked her arms further into her sleeves and realized she was still wearing Trace's jacket. Part of her wanted to keep it, as if it could somehow provide similar comfort to his embrace. But that was wishful thinking.

Kelsey walked into the lobby where Maeve stood by the window. Kelsey offered up a wave. Except the only greeting in return was a curt nod that sent a sinking feeling in her chest. If Maeve and Trace were indeed spending time together, it left no room for Kelsey in his life.

But Kelsey wanted Trace to find healing. If that meant she needed to step out of the way for him to rekindle something with their friend, so be it.

11

The sun's descent had left a cloudy, dark sky in its place.

Trace grabbed his ball cap and whistle from the glovebox and headed to the local elementary school's gym entrance. He needed to burn some energy, or the moment he closed his eyes tonight, the flashbacks and night terrors would greet him.

The ones where he chased after Renee and couldn't reach her.

Except the woman today hadn't experienced the same fate. The team had saved her life so her husband wouldn't get the call no one ever wanted to receive.

With a swift pull of the door, he stepped inside, and the sound of squeaky sneakers against the floor greeted him. The bounce of the ball and shouts of joy echoed through the hallway.

Trace slung the whistle over his head and resituated his hat backward. Macon waved to him from the first row of bleachers where several of the young boys huddled.

He jogged over to them, staying on the outer edge of the

court to avoid getting caught in the middle of the boys' warmups.

"Glad you could make it tonight." Macon lifted his fist.

Trace tapped it with his own. "I'm excited to see how they do." Perhaps the kids' energy would lift his own spirit after the heaviness of the day.

"Did you hear anything about that woman from earlier?"

Trace shook his head and watched the boys run drills. "Cleaned out the ambo for the next shift. We didn't have another callout, so there wasn't a chance to go to the hospital and check on her." He gritted his teeth. It was difficult to hand a patient over and not know the outcome of the situation. He might have done his job to rescue the person, but sometimes complications arose later, and he couldn't do anything about it then. "If it was anyone else, I might be okay with not knowing the outcome, but it hit too close to home."

"I gathered as much." Macon swung his whistle in a rhythmic circle on his finger. "It doesn't have anything to do with your wife, does it?"

Trace dragged his hand down his face.

"Charlie said it wasn't divorce." Macon lowered his voice.

"She died in a car accident." Trace's voice caught in his throat, and he coughed.

Macon stopped fiddling with his whistle and rested his hand on Trace's shoulder. "Dude, I'm sorry. I can't even imagine."

"Everything rushed back in that moment, you know? One second I was doing my job, and the next I see a woman hurt the same way my wife was."

"Life can be ugly and painful." Macon cleared his throat.

"You got that right."

"You can't blame yourself, man. It's chivalrous to want to save people, but only God can do that. We should do our part to help, but ultimately, we're not in control."

Macon's words rubbed against his fears like sandpaper.

Trace had witnessed the devastation Renee's death caused for others, including Kelsey. The way he'd held her today while tears wracked her haunted his mind. She was normally so strong, so put together. He couldn't take away her sorrow, and anger welled up in him at the realization. If God was good, why hadn't He stopped the pain from happening in the first place?

"Renee wouldn't want me to stop working hard. So I'm going to put these hands to use." One life saved at a time. Starting with Kelsey's safety.

"And right now, they can be used to corral the team." Macon clapped. "Anytime you want to chat, I'm here."

Trace nodded.

When Macon had asked Trace to consider being an assistant coach for the elementary boys basketball team for the fall season, it hadn't taken him long to agree. Houston, Macon's brother, had finally gotten Macon back into sports. Now that baseball was in the offseason, Macon had found another sport to invest in.

For Trace, it was a great way to pour into these kids while building team comradery and having fun. Now he just had to get his head in the game.

Macon blew his whistle, and the boys came together. "What's our goal for the game tonight?" He bent his head low toward the group.

Trace grinned and waited for their responses.

"Play with your teammates!" one of the boys shouted.

"That's right, Adam. How do we do that?" Macon looked around.

Boys started calling out their answers. "Pass the ball to the offense."

"Cheer each other on."

"Be ready to switch with someone on the bench."

"Exactly." Macon pumped his fist in the air. "All right, let's bring it in."

The boys stuck their hands in the middle of the circle.

Macon gave a thumbs-up. His cue. Trace turned to face each boy. "What's our team?"

"Cougars," the boys said.

"What's our team?"

"Cougars!" Prepubescent voices filled the space. The boys threw scrawny arms in the air, wide grins on their faces.

It might be game time, but Trace was grateful for the bigger principle at play here. These boys were learning their character was more valuable than their performance. Something his parents had never learned to do right. They'd taught him to always take the easy way out.

He'd fought hard to not follow in their footsteps when he married Renee. Rather, he'd fought for authenticity and perseverance—while his parents had shown him how to quit when things got hard instead of playing on the same team.

At least these boys had a head start on the right trajectory. What they didn't know was that sometimes you did everything right but the worst still happened, and there was nothing you could do about it.

The ref blew his whistle, and the boys lined up in their respective spots on the court. The shrill sound of the buzzer came through the intercom, and the clock began to tick.

Trace scanned the bleachers and made a mental note of which parents had come tonight to support their kid. Sure enough, when his eyes fixed on the center area, Natalie clapped and cheered, Kelsey beside her.

A warm sensation moved down his arms and, at the same time, brought more memories of earlier that day to the forefront of his mind. He'd almost cried in front of Kelsey. She could have signed off on his need for counseling and thought him incompetent because of how he'd handled the crisis—something he'd been trained to take in stride.

Except she'd shed the tears for him.

He'd sat there, frozen, unsure how to comfort her because he couldn't even find a way to comfort himself. So she really shouldn't waste her efforts on him. Not when his life lay in shambles.

"Anything going on between the two of you?" Macon's words pulled him from his thoughts.

He met his friend's gaze. Macon lifted his eyes to the bleachers. Trace's heartbeat picked up speed. "Why would there be?"

"Maybe because she's an attractive, single woman who loves Jesus and has made it her goal to help people in life. You're already friends. What's not to love?" Macon gave him that *you're not fooling me* look and crossed his arms.

"You think she's attractive? Need I remind you about your girlfriend sitting right next to her?" Trace wanted to whip his hand in the air but didn't want to make it obvious to the women by pointing in their direction.

"Whoa." Macon held up a hand. "Natalie is my one and only. That girl makes my heart stop. I was just stating the obvious to my single friend about *her* single friend."

"Yeah, yeah. I'm just giving you a hard time." Trace forced a chuckle.

"But really. I would get out of the friend zone if I were you." Macon raised his brow before walking down the court line to cheer on the team.

Trace glanced again at Kelsey, who laughed at something Natalie said, a look of pure joy on her face. Nothing seemed to faze her. Not even with a criminal possibly out to get her. That's where he wished she'd take things more seriously. But right now, he couldn't focus on those unknowns. He owed it to the kids to be here—with his attention and his presence as a coach.

He took a seat on the bench.

One of the opposing team's players blocked Jake, who was doing his best to find an opening to pass the ball. The kid pivoted several times, but his short stature made it hard. The other kid loomed over him.

Jake was starting to panic, his eyes darting every which way. Finally, he took a step forward with his right foot. The kid propelled his hands high in the air with as much force as possible to send the ball to Danny, who stood diagonally from him.

Everything shifted to slow motion as the ball went airborne. The other child threw his hands in the air. Instead of catching the ball, the kid's hands smacked the rubber. The ball flew back in Jake's face and pelted him head on. The sudden impact sent Jake stumbling backward with a cry. He landed with a thud on his right side.

Trace jumped to his feet and grabbed for his whistle to stop the game—even if the ref called it first. A glance at the clock told him ninety seconds remained in the first half. Enough time everyone could take an extended break.

He put the metal to his mouth and blew hard. The force made his head spin. Except no sound came out. Trace glanced down as he made his way onto the court and realized he'd pulled his ring chain instead. Renee's diamond glistened under the overhead lights. He quickly shoved it under his sweatshirt and tugged on the actual whistle.

Another ear-splitting call sounded, and the ref announced a time out.

"Move out of the way, folks," Trace bellowed. "Let's give him some space, all right?" He stepped through the crowd of boys and knelt down next to Jake. Blood spewed from the boy's nose.

"Oh my goodness, Jacob!" A woman's high-pitched voice echoed off the gymnasium walls from the bleacher.

"Boys, go get a drink and take a breather on the bench." He gave them all a stern look.

They got the message, afraid to displease their coach, and meandered back to the sidelines.

"Here's a bag if you need it." A young man, probably one of the dads, stepped up and handed him a medic duffel.

"Thanks." Trace unzipped it, in search of gloves and a cloth.

The mom rushed over. "Jacob, my baby. Oh, sweetie. Are you okay?" She crouched next to Jake's head as Trace continued rummaging in the borrowed bag. "Aren't you going to do something for my son? Why are you just sitting there!"

"I'm going to do everything I can." Trace pulled out what he needed and ignored the woman's comment. "One of you call 911, please."

"At least we'll be doing something helpful," the woman huffed.

He'd discovered that in moments of stress, people responded in different ways to cope. If the roles had been reversed and his son was injured, he might respond similarly.

"I'm calling them now." Jake's dad had his phone against his ear.

Tears leaked from the boy's eyes, and sorrow welled in Trace's heart. It was never fun to be sidelined in a game, especially with the intensity of physical pain.

"It hurts, Mommy," the boy whimpered. He tried to push himself to a propped-up position but succumbed to the floor. His sheet-white face hinted at his distress.

Jake's response sent pinpricks across Trace's skin as if someone were prodding him with needles. Trace looked down at his chest. The engagement ring dangled on the outside of his shirt once again. He wanted to tuck it underneath his collar but didn't want to draw attention to it.

"What hurts, Jake?" Trace snapped on the gloves.

"My...my a-arm and head and nose," he stammered.

Considering the impact on the hard wood floor, Trace wasn't surprised. "I'm going to help you sit up, and I'd like you to hold this cloth over your nose and pinch tight, okay?"

After a quick demonstration, Trace placed his arms under his back. On the count of three, he lifted Jake to a seated position.

Jake followed Trace's orders and whimpered.

"It's going to be okay, baby." His mom rubbed his back in a circular motion.

Trace took the boy's good arm and put his fingers over his wrist. His pulse beat steadily.

"Jake, I want you to follow my finger, okay?" The boy's left eye was sluggish and couldn't track Trace's movement. "Now I want you to stare at my nose, reach out and touch my finger, then tap your nose." Jake reached for Trace's finger then poked his cheek instead of his nose.

Trace turned to face the boy's parents. "He's showing signs of a concussion, and they can treat him better at the ER."

"Oh no." The father's eyes widened.

"It's certainly treatable if he gets the right therapy," Trace assured him.

"The blood too!" the mother wailed.

"Can I see the towel, bud?"

Jake handed it to him, the fabric covered in red. More dripped from his nostrils.

When he moved his hand away, Trace could see the black and blue marks on the bridge of his nose and under his eyes. "I think his nose is broken, so it will need to be x-rayed."

"Thank you for being here to help." The father nodded.

"My pleasure."

EMTs showed up, and Macon went outside with them as they escorted Jake off the court to go to the hospital. Trace grabbed several wipes and cleaned the blood-stained floor.

A ref approached him. "The remainder of the game is cancelled. The teams will reschedule for another day."

"Sounds good."

"Need any help?"

Trace turned to the female voice. Kelsey held open a plastic bag and crouched next to him.

"Thanks." He tossed the bundle of wipes in and stood up, tugging off the gloves as well.

Her eyes fixated on his chest, and for a second, Trace thought he had blood on his shirt. Then she whispered, "Her diamond was beautiful."

Instead of responding, he tucked the ring back under his shirt.

"I know there was something else you didn't get to share earlier at the hospital, considering the mess of my emotions and the timing of everything." Sympathy clouded her eyes. "Trace, I don't want you to live in the grief of it forever. Let me help, please."

"I don't need help. Really. If anything, I just need a friend." He took the plastic bag from her and tied it up. "Thanks."

He went to dispose of the trash and gather his belongings.

Because he'd rather rescue other people on the daily than work through the emotions of mending a broken heart.

12

A fter her interaction with Trace last night—and over the past few days—Kelsey needed time with her friend and mentor to process things.

Kelsey hit the ball to Jamie with a forehand swing. It soared over the net and landed right inside the back corner of the service box.

A cheer erupted from the father-daughter pair who played on the tennis court next to them. The locker room door closed as someone walked back over to their seat to cheer the duo and pulled out a sandwich from a Backdraft to-go bag.

I just need a friend.

Trace's words rattled in her brain. Couldn't he see that's why she'd offered to help? Because he was her friend.

His rejection had slapped her across the face.

All the brokenness Kelsey carried weighed on her like a sack of bricks.

She wanted a reprieve from the heaviness of loss. From losing her parents, to losing her friend and her leg—it seemed to never end.

Kelsey needed the Lord to carry the weight for her. But she didn't know how to shake free.

She might carry a streak of independence, but it came at a cost. She'd been pushed aside too many times. Her baggage was too much for anyone to carry, so she'd learned to bear it alone.

Somehow Jamie had snuck her way into Kelsey's life and hadn't left yet.

Jamie lunged with her racket for the ball but missed. "Nice one." Jamie grabbed another ball and bounced it a few times in her hand.

"That's just a warm-up." Kelsey laughed.

"Love, fifteen." Jamie lifted her racket high in the air. Her brunette hair swung in a ponytail. She leaned forward to favor her left leg and served the ball. The woman had quickly become like the sister Kelsey never had, even though they were the same age.

Back in high school, when she'd witnessed Kelsey's collapse during a pep rally, Jamie had stuck with her through the humiliation. From then on, Kelsey had found she could trust Jamie—just like she and Renee had formed an inseparable bond in college.

Kelsey's feet crisscrossed as she prepared for where Jamie would send the ball next. "I just don't get it," she said in between shots.

"I haven't practiced my backhand in a while," Jamie said.

"That's not what I'm talking about." Kelsey breathed hard as she ran to the net and smacked the ball. "Trace."

Jamie bounced the ball once but paused before her serve. "How many years has it been?"

"Five." Her mind wandered back to Renee's diamond around Trace's neck. She remembered the day her friend had shared the exciting news. They'd both squealed in excitement as Renee showed off the ring. Knowing Trace held Renee close like that proved what Kelsey believed—that her friend had been worthy of that kind of devotion.

Still, she couldn't help believing he needed to move on. Someday. He couldn't live in the past. It would only end in despair. If Trace closed himself off to the point he refused to open up to people, he'd sink deeper into an imprisonment that had no escape. He wanted to rescue others, but he didn't recognize his need to be rescued first.

"What's it like seeing him again?"

Kelsey focused on the ball while she talked. "You really want to know?"

"I asked, didn't I?"

She let out a sigh. "Weird at first after so many years. But then the memories and feelings flooded back." Especially the pain she still carried from the lack of closure from missing the funeral. "I keep reminding myself why it will never work."

"What's that?" Jamie missed the ball, and it bounced against the wall. "I need a water break."

"Sounds good."

They walked over to the benches. The indoor courts should have provided a nice reprieve from the chilly temperature outside. Instead, her inner turmoil added to the sweat on her brow.

"Renee was the better fit for him. Besides, I have way too many health problems, and he's clearly not over his wife." Kelsey stuck out a finger with each reason. If she wanted, she could add more to the list.

"Everyone deals with grief at a different pace."

"I just want him to find hope in life again." Kelsey propped her foot on the bench to stretch and chugged some water.

"He might need some coaxing. A little encouragement." Jamie smiled. "Like someone else I know."

Kelsey understood the reality of loss. She'd never gotten to say goodbye to her friend.

"I remember back when I met a timid, hurt girl who let fear dictate how she responded to situations." Jamie wiped sweat from her forehead. "And now look at what God has done."

"You're right. Even with all the loss and grief, God showed me it had purpose. And I could use my experience to comfort others." Kelsey blinked. Sometimes she couldn't believe all God had done. Truly a testament of His grace at work.

"Have you offered to help him?"

"He's denied every attempt. Claims he's fine. And I never want him to think I have ulterior motives. I just...hope to see him enjoy life again." She sighed. The lines etched across his brow last night when he'd pushed her away wedged their way between them. "But he doesn't see it that way."

"You're doing the right thing. Who knows what life will bring? Maybe one day he'll heal from his grief and have room in his heart to love again." Jamie winked. "Perhaps someone he's already close to."

Kelsey couldn't hide anything from Jamie, but the truth remained: she needed to focus on work and securing this grant so hurting people could receive empathy and be pointed toward a better future. If she failed to get the family counseling program running smoothly, she'd have one more tally mark for a broken family.

Right next to her own.

She doubted Trace would ever think of her as more than a friend—despite the whispers of her heart.

"On that note, shall we?" Kelsey picked up her racket and motioned to the court.

"Time for me to bring my A-game." Jamie swung her arms, then jogged over to the other side of the net.

"We'll see if it's good enough." Kelsey shot her friend a playful smirk.

"Now, tell me about what else is going on." Jamie swung her

racket hard, and Kelsey barely returned the serve. "Any ideas who ransacked your home?"

"None. I'm clueless and confused. I could have been robbed." Kelsey stated it matter-of-factly, but the words hung heavy in the air. "No one seems to have lightened up about Gerald either."

"They're concerned for your safety." Jamie whacked the ball back to Kelsey.

"Both Dean and Natalie pulled me aside for a 'chat' at work." Kelsey raised her fingers with air quotes.

"As your coworkers, they have valid concerns."

They'd expressed uneasiness about a possible repeat incident like when Leon had shown up and trapped Natalie in her office with a gun.

"I want normalcy. Not an entourage of personal security." Kelsey dove for the ball and it smacked the center of the racket.

"Someone who has your back and is willing to protect you is a good thing. It shows they care." Jamie hit the ball, but it soared out of bounds.

"Detective Wilcox mentioned something similar."

"Ahhh." Jamie's eyes sparkled. "Do they have a suspect?"

"They haven't arrested anyone. I get the feeling the police have no idea who broke into my house." Kelsey sighed. "If I could just talk to them…"

"I get it. You want to believe the best of everyone. If you ever need guidance on the situation, I'm here." Jamie never took a situation lightly and meant her offer. That kind of genuineness was rare.

Kelsey couldn't let anything jeopardize the strides she'd made with the new family counseling unit. *If* Gerald was the culprit behind the havoc to her life, what would that show the committee about her competence to pull off the family counseling that sought to treat the whole person?

If she missed the mark with one client, they'd never

consider implementing the initiative at the Ridgeman Center permanently.

"I need to get people to believe Gerald. Somehow." Kelsey returned Jamie's serve, and her friend missed the shot. "One win for each!" Kelsey pumped her fist. Her heart beat fast from the exertion, and she blinked in an attempt to clear her blurry vision.

She jogged over to the bench to sip more water. Her fingers trembled and the tips shone bright red. She needed to check her blood sugar, but her kit was in her bag.

"Want to play one more for a tiebreaker?" Jamie asked.

"I need a quick break. I'll be right back." Kelsey grabbed her bag but left the rest of her belongings on the bench.

The father and daughter still played on the other court. With spectators around, she couldn't risk making a scene.

Kelsey locked herself in a stall and pulled out the lancet. She squeezed her finger hard as blood bubbled onto the test strip.

The monitor beeped.

She needed a quick sugar. Kelsey opened a mango-orange juice. The tangy flavor seeped into her taste buds.

After several minutes, she headed back to the court and finished off her water bottle. "All right. I'm ready. Let's take it a little slower though." She couldn't disappoint her friend.

"Sounds good."

Instead of alleviating the symptoms, Kelsey's arm grew heavy as she served the ball. Each motion took extra force to perform, and she concentrated harder on the ball.

Floaters formed across her vision as the ball soared back and forth. The next hit barely made it over the net.

"About time for one of us to win." Kelsey propped her racket against her leg, breathing hard. "Good game." A cold sweat had begun to break out along her forehead, and Kelsey wiped the perspiration with her sleeve.

"Nothing like a victory dance." Jamie leapt in the air. "Thanks for playing."

"Anytime." It took all her energy to get the word out.

Kelsey made her way over to their belongings. Before she reached the bench, her eyes lost focus and the world shifted on its axis.

Kelsey dropped to the ground. Lightheadedness rushed over her, and she tucked her legs in toward her chest. Not good. She should have called it quits earlier. White dots danced in her vision.

"Kelsey, what is it?"

"I'm—" Kelsey huffed. What was she going to say? Her eyes roamed the field to reorientate herself. No one else played on the court. "Pass out."

"You're going to be okay." Jamie rubbed her back. "I'll call an ambulance."

"No." Kelsey gulped down air. "I'm fine. I'll never learn. I'm so naïve." Tears clouded her vision as she pushed herself up to sit. Just like the doctor had confirmed when she'd come out of surgery.

The nurses had her leg propped up on two pillows for comfort and to encourage blood flow from her thigh. The white blanket over the lower half of her body hid the evidence of what no longer existed. As if she needed a reminder of what she'd lost, the doctor entered and examined the nub.

"Everything went smoothly, and you should be on the road to recovery." He raised his gaze above the frame of his glasses. "That is, if you follow patient protocol. We wouldn't want a repeat on the left leg now."

She swallowed. "No, sir." Kelsey's heart ached, despite the lack of feeling she had elsewhere from all the pain meds. She had followed orders and taken her prescription insulin every day.

She turned her head to the side. Tears streamed down her cheek. She wouldn't give this man the satisfaction of witnessing her distress.

To her right, family surrounded the woman in the bed in the other part of the room.

And she had no one.

"Good." The doctor nodded and jotted something on his paper. "We need people to actually know how to take care of themselves," he mumbled under his breath.

Kelsey fisted the sheet as heat worked its way up the base of her neck.

A cool hand touched her arm. Jamie crouched beside her. "I should have suggested we stop while we were ahead. We were playing for almost two hours."

"No. My health always interferes with things. I'm tired of it controlling me."

She closed her eyes. What had she been about to say? Kelsey couldn't remember. She rubbed her hand along her leg but stopped when she touched the prosthetic at the hem of her track pants. A constant reminder of the trials in her life, and yet here she was repeating the past and letting things get bad.

"Here. Drink this." Jamie wrapped Kelsey's fingers around a bottle.

Kelsey opened her eyes and took a sip of the energy drink. The citrusy orange taste coated her tongue. Who did she think she was that someone else would bear her burdens with her?

My yoke is easy. My burden is light.

The Holy Spirit spoke the words of truth, but the reality of it seemed impossible to Kelsey.

She shouldn't have put herself in a position where she needed someone's help. Not until she learned to cope on her own. It wasn't fair to be a burden when—unlike her clients—Kelsey couldn't even make the right choices toward her own healing.

Thirty minutes later, Kelsey lifted her head off the wall. "I need to go." She stood up. Then pinched her eyes shut to ward off the rush of blood from her head.

"Let's make sure your sugars are fine first." Jamie placed the kit in Kelsey's hand.

"I've got it." Kelsey snatched the zippered pouch and checked her levels again. She hadn't meant to snap at Jamie, but her friend had better things to do than be inconvenienced by her problems.

The monitor dinged. Slightly elevated.

"You really don't have to wait around," Kelsey said. She just needed to relax and let the adrenaline of the morning wear off.

"Nonsense. You can't get rid of me that fast." Jamie sat on the floor and crisscrossed her legs.

She was a complete buffoon, making a scene so another person had to rush to her aid. No one would want to endure that on her behalf.

Not long term, anyway.

Her mom hadn't. So eventually Kelsey had stopped sharing about how she didn't feel well. She'd cried wolf one too many times, according to her mom, whose grief over her husband's death had forced Kelsey to push aside her own well-being to help her mom. Even those efforts hadn't been acknowledged or reciprocated.

After another hour, and a safe glucose level, she walked outside, not even glancing back once at the gym. Another monument that stood as a sign of her personal failures.

Her mind told her what her heart didn't want to accept.

No one could love her through this. It was too much to ask of anyone.

13

T race pushed the gurney through the emergency room hallway. The metal wheels squeaked against the shiny linoleum floor. "What's the status of the patient?" The doctor grabbed a pair of gloves from a dispenser on the wall and walked alongside them.

The woman's chest rose and fell as she took short, shallow breaths. Her face held no color and her eyelids fluttered. It was a good thing her roommate called when she had, or the outcome might have been different.

Trace focused on the doctor as they turned into a room. "Andrea Black, twenty years old. Out partying into the wee hours of the morning. BP 145 over 96. In and out of consciousness. Her roommate attested to her vomiting multiple times when they got back before she fell asleep. She didn't know how many drinks Andrea had, but reported it was a lot."

"Anything else?"

Trace shook his head. *Never move a patient or start assessing the situation without first relaying all the necessary information to the next round of medical personnel.* It was the easiest way to avoid confusion or unanswered questions.

Andi went around him and went to the opposite side of the gurney. "On three."

Trace counted, and the two of them, along with two nurses, slid the young woman onto the hospital bed.

"We've got it, thanks." The doctor never looked up from the patient.

Andi went to the nurse's station to fill out the paperwork while Trace maneuvered the gurney out of the way.

He leaned against the counter and groaned. The sound rose above the beeps and dings through the intercoms, and a few nurses turned his way.

Andi raised an eyebrow.

"I'm starving." His eyes widened. "It's been a while since I've had a real meal." The first call this morning came early enough that he hadn't eaten breakfast at that point. Then lunch hour had disappeared, and now his stomach was protesting.

"I hear you." Andi paused from writing. "Can you grab me a snack from the supply room? I'll meet you back at the truck."

"Copy that." Trace tapped the counter, then swiveled on his heel and pushed the gurney back toward the bay.

He entered the break room and grabbed two apple juices and a yogurt from the fridge, along with two granola bars and a muffin from the counter.

He shoved them in his pockets and made his way outside.

Andi secured the gurney in the back of the truck and shut the doors.

"Think fast!" Trace tossed a granola bar and juice to her, and Andi caught them one handed. He snorted. "Show off."

"Gotta keep things interesting somehow." She smirked.

Once they were back in the truck, Trace peeled back the wrapper of the granola bar and chomped down on half of it.

Andi chuckled. "I know never to withhold food from you."

"Exactly. It's not a pretty sight."

"You did good this morning, partner." Andi nodded, then put the truck in Reverse.

"As did you," Trace said between bites of the muffin.

"You ever wonder what it would be like to go back to your old job?"

"I used to. That's how I could serve people."

"How so?" Andi cocked her head.

"Police officers were my heroes at one time. When home life got messy with my parents fighting, they showed up and controlled the situation. They even gave me a cop star pin and a police teddy bear. To an elementary kid that was a big deal." Trace chuckled.

"Do you miss that life though?" Andi looked his way as she turned a street corner.

"Not anymore." Trace shook his head. Scenes from his former life as a cop blipped through his mind. The calls and traffic stops. And the standing around, idle, directing people while others took care of the injured. "This is where I'm making a difference now."

"Because of the accident?"

"Because of the accident," he whispered. Trace propped his arm on the windowsill and stared at the cars on the road. "I had a mission then, and I have a mission now. Being an EMT gives me a way to make sure someone else has a second chance at life. And every day we get a call"—he pointed to the radio on the center console—"is another chance to fulfill that goal. To save a life."

Trace leaned his head against the seat and sighed. His job fueled him. It gave him meaning, and he got to be a hero. So why couldn't he shake the emptiness that still hovered inside?

"You've got what it takes for the job. Just don't let the scoreboard keep you from giving yourself a second chance." Andi smiled. "God's not tallying your performance, waiting for you to hit the mark."

After all God had taken from him, how could Trace not try to earn some favor with the Lord? Maybe then God would spare him more pain. "Says the one who now has life all figured out." Trace playfully smirked.

"Without the Lord's saving grace, I'm just as jacked up of a sinner." Andi turned a corner, and mud squished under the tires, the ground still saturated from the overnight deluge of rain they'd gotten. "Now I get to serve Him with my work."

"Would you go back to fighting fires?"

"It was fun, but I'm better at this job. It comes more naturally."

"Glad to hear I won't be losing a partner."

"Same here." Andi nodded.

They got back to the station and parked the ambulance in the driveway.

Trace hopped out and surveyed the side of the truck. "This needs a serious cleaning." Mud clung to the white edges and tire rims.

"Good thing the forecast is calling for a dry spell the next few days. So you're on cleaning duty." Andi gave a salute.

"Hey now. You're just going to walk inside and hit the lounge?" Trace gave her a mock expression of hurt.

"After a long morning, you bet. I cleaned the truck last week."

"Okay, okay." Trace held up his hands and Andi sauntered inside.

Trace filled the bucket with water and rolled it out of the garage.

When he went back inside to gather the soap and sponges from the closet, he walked past Andi, Charlie, and Logan huddled in the common area.

Footsteps sounded behind him as Trace made his way back to the driveway. "You coming to help me clean this bad boy?" Trace turned around to see Charlie.

"Gotta do something to pass the time."

Trace grabbed a sponge and tossed it to Charlie. "Someone hasn't been busy enough, then." Trace poured soap into the bucket. "You want to take my next call?"

"I'll run into a burning building any day. Ask me to prick someone with a needle, no thanks." Charlie held up his arms, water dripping from the sponge.

"Ha." Trace grabbed the hose and sprayed down the ambo. "You ever wish you could check in on those we rescue and make sure they're doing okay?"

Charlie's lips thinned. "If we get too attached, it makes the next call harder. Better to separate emotion and get the job done."

"They're people too." Trace wouldn't deny the wound Charlie's words pricked at. "Man, do you know what it's like to lose someone? To never have the chance to hear their voice again? Or their laughter?"

Charlie folded his arms. "Sometimes emotions hurt too much."

Before Trace could say anything, the door opened. "Either of you want a sub for dinner?" Bryce popped his head outside and braced an arm on the frame. "I'm placing an order now."

"I'll pass." Trace's eating schedule today was all messed up, so he'd find something in the fridge to heat up later.

"You bet." Charlie rattled off his order and tossed his sponge in the bucket before making his way back to the building.

"Thanks for your help scrubbing down the truck." Trace chuckled.

"Food's calling my name, man." Charlie rubbed his stomach and disappeared inside.

Trace grabbed the soap and poured more into the bucket of water. The sun poked through the gray sky, as if he should do the same thing and face the pain to find a glimmer of hope.

He didn't know how long he'd been outside cleaning the truck. Charlie's comments had taken up residence in his mind and slowed down his work. The Backdraft Bar and Grill delivery car pulled around the corner, and Trace stood from his crouched position.

Maeve stepped out, balancing a holder of drinks and a bag while she waved to him with her other hand and kicked the car door shut with her hip. *Bryce's sub order.* She must've seen the ambo bay door rolled up and come this way on purpose.

Trace lifted his hand in a quick acknowledgement of her presence before turning back to his duties. Just because they'd known each other in college didn't mean they had to connect now, especially after that disastrous date.

Trace didn't get close to women now. All it did was interfere in his ability to do his job—the one thing that offered a chance to make up for his failures.

A minute later, she came back out from making her delivery to the kitchen. "Don't you think it's a little cold and rainy to be doing that today?" Maeve asked as she walked up to him.

"It's got to get done sometime." He shrugged and set the sponge in the now murky bucket. His hands dripped with foaming suds.

He didn't dry his hands off, figuring she wouldn't want to get wet and would stay a couple of steps back. She paid him far too much attention at Backdraft. The last thing he needed was Maeve making a habit of visiting him at the firehouse, thinking he might give dating her another try. Rather than give her mixed signals, he had to give her none.

"You have a point." She motioned over her shoulder to the doors. "Did you order dinner?"

"I did not."

"Ah, too bad." She pouted, and Trace could have pegged her reaction as flirtatious. He'd made that mistake once a few weeks after he moved here, when she'd called him after she got stranded on the road with a flat tire. Her blue eyes had looked so helpless, and he'd jumped at the chance to rescue her.

Maeve took a step closer to him so that the only thing dividing them was the bucket of water. "If you ever have a long shift and you're too exhausted to cook, I might be able to arrange something. If you give me a call."

He wouldn't rise to the bait this time. Maeve was definitely hitting on him. "I—"

"Great! Soup would be perfect. Something to warm you up." She winked and took a step forward, hand extended to touch his arm. In the process, she hit the bucket.

It clanked and toppled over. Water spilled over his feet and seeped through his shoes and socks. Trace winced.

She grabbed hold of his forearm and stared into his eyes. "Whoops. I'm so sorry."

More tires crunched over the gravel, and Trace shifted his gaze to the newcomer.

Kelsey's rental car rolled to a stop on the firehouse driveway. She blinked and stared at him as if contemplating what to do.

Maeve removed her hand from his arm. Trace took a step back to create space between them and waved to Kelsey. Within that brief moment, the engine roared back to life, and Kelsey drove out of the parking lot.

"I think you should head back to the restaurant." The words came out harsher than he wanted, but she got the point and began to back away.

Then he spotted the tiny smirk on her face.

She blew him a kiss. "That offer still stands."

Trace picked up the bucket and rubbed his hands on his pants. *Great.*

Why had it seemed as though Kelsey was mad at him? She hadn't caught him doing anything wrong. And what had she come to say?

It shouldn't bother him, though. She probably wanted to

sneak in another counseling session and get him to move on from the past.

He wasn't interested. Not if it meant opening a door to another relationship. After all, he'd turned Maeve down. And yet something about Kelsey's kindness drew him to her. If it was a contest between the two, he'd have run after her car.

No, he viewed his role with Kelsey as protector. He needed to watch her back.

His feelings were for her safety and well-being. Nothing else. His heart still belonged to Renee. Always would. Even Kelsey could pin it from a mile away.

Still, his mind replayed Kelsey's wide-eyed gaze as she drove away, and a tinge of sadness crept in.

14

Trace had lied to her. She'd seen it in his eyes—that connection. *With Maeve.*

Maybe it had always been Maeve.

She'd do what she'd promised herself. She'd give the space he needed if that meant he would heal. But his dishonesty was a slap in the face. Especially since he'd said he wanted a friendship. Friends didn't lie to each other.

Kelsey threw his jacket from the passenger seat to the backseat and hit the brakes at the approaching stop sign. He'd probably forgotten she even had his jacket. And she hadn't expected to see him at the basketball game, so she hadn't returned it yet. No traffic rounded the corner, which gave Kelsey a moment to sit there and gather her senses. All the thoughts she'd stewed on the night before still resided in her mind.

The smell of wings and buffalo ranch dressing wafted through the interior as its own unique car freshener. She'd come here wanting to pay him back for making her dinner after the break-in. Trace was a good man who'd suffered a devastating loss. His compassion for people made him a fantastic EMT. She'd seen it at the basketball game.

Then she'd gone and pressured him more that he needed help. *You know better.* He had to reach out on his own. She couldn't bully him into seeking healing. Everyone handled grief differently, and only he could decide when the right time was.

So why did her muscles tense?

He might never reach out for help. Not with the way Maeve had put her arm on Trace. The interaction shouldn't bother her. She pulled out her phone and sent a message to Jamie.

> KELSEY
>
> You were right. I like him.

Three dots danced on the screen to show Jamie typing back.

> JAMIE
>
> Why's that?

> KELSEY
>
> He's compassionate, gentle, and a go-getter. He's not afraid to call the shots and get something done.

> JAMIE
>
> What are you going to do about it?

Kelsey's fingers hovered over the screen.

> KELSEY
>
> Nothing. He's got to make his own decisions and I can't force anything.

Kelsey placed her phone next to the food containers and sighed.

She'd failed to be Trace's friend first and counselor second. All she wanted was to make up for her mistake. But if she gave him the meal, Trace would think she was trying to take Renee's place. Or worse yet, that she was jealous of his and Maeve's rekindling romance.

Kelsey slid her hand down her face and groaned. She'd read it all wrong. Despite his insistence there was nothing between him and Maeve, maybe he wanted there to be.

Kelsey turned up the heat a few degrees so the warmth blew through the air vents and sucked out the last of the chill. She might be feeling better physically after her tennis incident, but the inkling of hope in her heart that Trace might've been interested in her was as severed as the nerves in her leg.

She should have known better. He cared about her protection and safety. She'd fallen into the trap of thinking more could transpire. And it stung knowing Maeve had stepped into the picture.

She prided herself on her intuition for knowing what someone felt before they verbalized it. One of the skills Dean first saw in her when he'd agreed to have her join the staff for the grant program. How had she read the situation so wrong?

A car approached in her rearview mirror. With a flick of the signal, she checked both ways and turned.

Feelings should never guide emotions. She reminded her patients of that all the time—and wound up forgetting it herself. Hearts were too fragile. In a foolish move, she'd nearly given hers away.

Trace didn't care about her enough to move past his pain and be her friend too.

The stark reminder of that rejection took her back to when her mom had disregarded her needs. Even yelled at her and said she'd made a mess of her life. Brought her health fiascos on herself. All because Kelsey had fainted in front of five hundred students during her high school's pep rally. When the school nurse called to have her mom pick Kelsey up, it was too much to take her focus off being a widow for a moment and be attentive to her daughter. And her mom had made sure Kelsey knew it.

The ringing of her phone pulled her from her thoughts, and she connected the call to Bluetooth. "Hey, Natalie, what's up?"

"Are you headed back to the office soon? Want to grab dinner?"

"I have one more house call to make, but it should be brief." She shifted her attention from the road to the digital clock. "Give me an hour and I should be back."

"Sounds good. Do you want me to order anything for you?"

Normally, Kelsey packed extra food to ensure her blood sugar levels remained steady through the day. It was easier to monitor ingredients and nutrition facts if she bought and prepped it herself. But with all the other demands life brought at the moment, a trip to the grocery store stayed unchecked on her to-do list.

"Could you get me a gluten free chicken alfredo?"

"Ohhh. That sounds good. Maybe I'll get the same—except with all the gluten, of course." Natalie laughed.

Kelsey smiled. The conversation shift soothed the edges of hurt. "Sounds good. I'll see you soon."

Kelsey used the voice commands to send a message to Thatcher and let him know she was en route to his house. He'd been discharged from the hospital, which was great news. Now he and his wife could settle in back at home, and she hoped the recovery process and therapy sessions would prove just as successful.

Stepping onto the porch, Kelsey rapped firmly on the door. While she waited for someone to answer, she surveyed the area.

Their house sat right in the heart of town. Traffic bustled around as people finished their workday. Kelsey imagined for a moment what it would be like to live in Last Chance permanently. To have roots in an area where people greeted her by name while on a walk. And where, when she got home, her own family stood ready to welcome her.

The door opened behind her, and Chrissy stood with one hand on the door, her eyes accentuated by a thin strip of eyeliner. Redness and puffiness still peeked through the makeup as if she'd been crying.

Lucy stood next to her grandma, one arm wrapped around her leg.

"Good evening, Chrissy. How are you doing?"

"It's good to see you, dear. Come in, please." She stepped away from the door and ushered Kelsey in with a sweep of her hand. "Why don't you go watch a show on your tablet, okay?" Chrissy stooped down to speak to the young girl, who nodded and dashed off in response.

Kelsey took off her shoes in the foyer and placed them on the mat by the door. "Have you and Thatcher been able to get settled in?"

"Well, we're home, which is a good thing. No more hospital food." Chrissy's attempt at a smile fell short.

"Where is he?" Kelsey took note of the dimmed lights, an effective technique in helping someone avoid light sensitivity.

"Out on the patio, listening to the radio." She took a deep breath.

She didn't have to say anything further. That was one of the outlets she'd established with Thatcher if he ever needed to decompress. He loved listening to the soccer games, which took him back to his younger days when he played the sport himself.

"I'm sorry." Kelsey extended her arms to give the woman a hug.

"Don't be. I'm grateful he's still alive and that I get to love him, even when it's hard."

"Even with the outbursts?" Kelsey's mouth widened at the woman's response. Only the Holy Spirit could elicit that change. It was her goal as a counselor to have that attitude too, but it always amazed her how love could transcend even the worst of circumstances and still have a fighting chance.

"Even with. It's growing me too, you know." Chrissy made her way through the hallway into the kitchen, and Kelsey followed. "To look past my needs and serve him. To mourn the times the man I married is hidden behind a terrible disease. But to also cherish the moments where all is right."

Kelsey pondered the sweetness of those words. "That's beautiful. You two are wonderful for each other."

"That's all the Lord, hun." She pushed open the door, and they stepped out onto the screened-in porch. "We all need as much grace as we can get. For ourselves, and for each other."

Kelsey bit her lip. Grace proved hard to extend at times. Given her family had hurt her and didn't recognize how deep it cut. Or with Trace, when she wanted to shake him and make him see how things could change for the better. But she needed to remain patient.

Thatcher sported a bandage, although this one only covered the top portion of his bald head. His eyes flitted between her and Chrissy before he crossed his arms and pulled down his sunglasses.

"I want to be alone." He pushed himself up and planted his feet on the ground.

Trace's words rang in her ear. *You need to watch your back.*

She refused to accept that and give in to the fear. In all her time helping others, Gerald had been the one exception among a wonderful batch of patients she enjoyed working with. It didn't mean all her patients would turn out the same, or that Gerald himself couldn't be treated.

"I won't stay long," Kelsey said. "It's good to see you back home. And look at you. Standing up straight." She grinned.

He let out a grunt.

His ability to stand still in one place without falling over was huge progress. It showed the physical therapy was working.

Chrissy grabbed a folding chair propped against the wall and sat beside her husband.

Twenty minutes later, Chrissy held the front door open for her. "Thanks for sticking with him today."

"Of course. He's making progress." Kelsey grabbed the keys from her purse. "Just remember that. Between wrestling with the fact he has a brain tumor and the onset of mood changes, it's a learning curve for him."

"Thank you. For always being so willing to help." Chrissy gave her a hug.

"If you need anything, you have my number. Otherwise, I have another session scheduled with him at the Ridgeman Center in two weeks."

Chrissy nodded.

Kelsey climbed into her car and noticed she had a missed text from Natalie.

You coming back soon? I'm getting hungry and ready to devour both our meals.

Natalie had followed up the words with a hungry emoji.

Kelsey texted back.

On my way. Save at least a bite of it for me.

Kelsey's stomach growled. Not wanting a repeat of the tennis incident, she grabbed an apple juice from her purse, took a swig, then pulled onto the street.

Once she found a parking spot, Kelsey dropped off her files in her office before heading down the hall to Natalie's.

She knocked on the door, and it opened a few inches on its own. "Nat?" When she didn't reply, Kelsey pushed the door open farther and stepped into the office. "You ready to eat?"

Natalie's desk remained immaculate. She envied her friend for her ability to keep the space free of paperwork. Only a handful of papers piled on a tiered filer and two disposable cartons of food sat in the middle of the desk. One was open with a fork in it.

Kelsey let out a laugh.

Maybe Natalie had gone to the break room to grab a drink.

A thud reverberated against the desk. Then another one.

A hand emerged from the corner, and Kelsey stepped over to where Natalie writhed on the floor.

Her body convulsed. Her leg hit the desk drawer.

"Natalie!" Kelsey bent down and grabbed for her hand.

Her arm swung out, and Kelsey shifted to avoid getting whacked.

"Someone help!" Kelsey whipped out her phone and dialed 911.

She needed to find a way to move the desk, otherwise Natalie might sustain severe injuries. Kelsey stood up, but the abrupt change of posture sent a wave of dizziness over her. Passing out was not an option when her friend needed help.

"911. Where's your emergency?" The dispatcher's calm voice worked on Kelsey like a breathing exercise.

She wedged the device between her shoulder and ear. "I need an ambulance at the Ridgeman Center now. My friend is having a seizure."

Kelsey closed her eyes and the lightheadedness passed. She grabbed the edge of the desk and hefted it a millimeter in the air but quickly dropped it again. Her fingers cramped. It weighed too much, especially with full drawers.

She lowered the phone. "Someone help!"

"Medics are en route. Do your best to secure the area. Move any objects out of the way that could pose a hazard," the dispatcher said.

"I'm trying." Kelsey gritted her teeth and tried to move the desk again.

She put her phone on speaker in case the dispatcher said something else, and set it on the desk before going back over to Natalie.

"Nat, can you hear me? Wake up, please." Kelsey had never

dealt with someone having a seizure before. Seeing her friend in this state made her stomach flip.

She turned her head toward the hallway again. "I need help!"

"What's going on?" Dean stepped into the entryway.

"Natalie's having a seizure."

Dean hopped over the desk and crouched next to Natalie. He took her arms and turned her on her side.

"Can I have your jacket?" He extended his hand.

Kelsey wiggled her arms free and gave it to him. He folded it and stuck it under Natalie's head.

"Do you know how long she's been having the seizure?" Dean glanced at his watch.

She shook her head and tears clouded her vision. "When I came in about two minutes ago, I found her convulsing on the floor." She gasped. "I need to call Macon."

As a former Navy SEAL medic, Dean had been the town's unofficial EMT for a while, but that was a couple of years ago now. He would help until the rest of the crew arrived, and those seconds could be priceless.

But would it be enough to save her life?

15

"Do we know who it is?" Trace asked Andi from the driver's side of the ambulance.

"Not that I'm aware of." Andi flicked on the lights.

Trace grimaced and floored the gas. What if Kelsey had gone into a diabetic seizure? He was becoming terrible at protecting her. For all he knew, Kelsey could have stopped by yesterday to share something she'd discovered about the attempts on her life and decided it could wait because Maeve had interrupted.

He rubbed the nape of his neck.

Except it couldn't wait. And he shouldn't have let Kelsey's safety take the back burner.

A hand clamped down on his forearm. "Take a deep breath. You need to have your head on straight regardless of who's involved. Got it?" Andi pursed her lips and waited for him to respond.

"You're right." If he wanted to do his job well, he needed to remain focused. "Stabilize the patient and give them the best care possible." But if something had happened to Kelsey, Trace would never forgive himself.

"Exactly." Satisfied with his answer, she leaned back in the seat. "I don't want it to be Kelsey either," she whispered. "But if she needs our help, I want you to do what you do best to help her. I don't want to see you go through another episode like at the car wreck."

Trace ground his molars. So much for not reminding him of the slip in his normal demeanor. He shuddered. "Note taken. I just can't imagine anything happening to her."

"You've seen a lot, Trace. It wouldn't hurt to talk with someone about it all." Andi gave him a half smile.

He turned left onto the road that led up to the therapy center. They could discuss her thoughts on counseling later. Right now, they had work to do.

"Let's go, people!" Macon clapped his hands as Trace hopped out of the truck.

Terror had filled Macon's face as well when the call came in. Because if Natalie was hurt, he wanted to be the first one there.

Even if this call hadn't required the firefighters, Macon would have hopped in the ambulance. Protocol ensured the medics had a team of firefighters with them to clear the area in case the individual coming out of the seizure became confrontational.

Trace slung the medic bag onto the gurney and took the front end as Andi and he wheeled it inside.

"Excuse us," Trace said as they approached Wren at the receptionist desk.

"They're on the second floor. Follow me." She waved them through.

When they got to the room, Kelsey stood against the wall, and his shoulders relaxed. He let out a long breath. She turned, and a sheen of wetness covered her cheeks.

Are you okay? He mouthed the words and she nodded, even

though her arms wrapped around her chest told a different story.

He turned his attention to the scene. Dean crouched next to Natalie, who lay on the floor, her legs twitching. Her eyelids fluttered open for a few seconds before closing again. Her hair frizzed in a few places, her face pale.

"How long has the seizure been going, Dean?" Trace stepped over while Andi pulled out an IV. They needed to get meds in Natalie's system stat to stop the seizure completely. At least Natalie no longer flailed about.

"I can't say for sure, since I didn't get here until Kelsey called for help, but at least six minutes."

"I'm going to start an IV with medicine so you feel better, Nat." Andi ripped open an alcohol swab and cleaned Natalie's inner arm.

Trace couldn't help the smile that formed. Andi made a great partner who knew protocol. Six minutes was significant for a seizure.

Trace pulled out a glucose meter and took Natalie's other hand. With a prick, drops of blood collected on the test strip. The monitor beeped, and he read the number. *Normal.*

"Not induced by blood glucose levels." Trace assessed Natalie's other vitals. Her blood pressure and heart rate came back elevated, but at least her breathing pattern was normal.

"A line is running with diazepam," Andi said.

"Copy that."

A few minutes later, Natalie's leg stopped twitching, which was a good sign.

Natalie opened her eyes and moaned. "Ma..." she began, then her gaze landed on Macon, who stood by her desk.

He took a step forward, but Trace held out his arm. "Wait."

Blood trickled from Natalie's mouth onto her chin. "Did she hit her mouth on anything during the convulsions?" Trace turned to Dean.

"Not while I was with her," Dean said.

"She might have before I found her," Kelsey piped up.

Macon knelt down next to Natalie and propped her head in his lap. His hand stroked her hair, fixing her bangs and flyaways.

Andi wiped away the blood on Natalie's chin. A few seconds later, Natalie's sobs filled the room. Her hand fisted Macon's jacket, and her knuckles turned white from the tight grasp.

They needed some details and had to get her to the hospital.

"Hey, Nat," Andi said. "Can you tell me what happened?" Andi crouched next to Natalie.

Dean nodded at Natalie to go ahead.

She licked her lips. "I ordered the food and came back to the office to wait for Kelsey because we were going to eat together." She paused, then pulled in a labored breath before continuing. "I got the notification the food was ready early, so I picked it up. It smelled amazing and, well, I was hungry."

"Do you have any food allergies?" Trace interjected.

"None," Natalie confirmed. "I ate a helping of the alfredo to hold me over. Next thing I know, I'm filling out paperwork and nausea sweeps over me. I thought I might puke. I went to go get water, but I don't remember anything afterward."

Trace stood and picked up the food container. About half of it had been eaten.

"The food tasted a little funky," Natalie wheezed.

Trace sniffed the food, but all he got were hints of cheese and spices on the chicken. "What do you mean?"

"I figured they might have given both of us gluten free noodles, even though only one container had the GF mark."

"Can you stick out your tongue for me?" Andi asked. "I want to make sure there's no swelling."

Natalie obliged.

Trace shifted to get a better view. From his vantage point, her tongue was tinted blue.

Andi turned back to him as if reading his thoughts and confirmed his suspicion.

There could be several causes. From food dye to a lack of oxygen and blood flow. No way would they take any chances. She needed to get to the hospital, stat.

Natalie closed her eyes and ducked her chin. Perspiration formed on her forehead, and Trace looked for any other signs that her body would start reacting again.

"You okay, Nat?" Macon wiped her brow.

She shook her head. "I think I'm going to be sick."

Andi grabbed a biohazard bag and handed it to Macon. He barely opened it before Natalie heaved whatever remained of her lunch.

Several of the guys averted their eyes, whether out of privacy for Natalie or because they were grossed out. If Trace ever had a family, he'd be prepared for those moments with kids, because nothing fazed him. "Puking is good."

Macon frowned.

"She needs to get what's in the food out of her system."

He met Kelsey's gaze and realized she'd been watching him. Thoughts swirled through his mind and took him by surprise. Could he ever love someone again, long enough to build a family? Even if he could, the risk of losing them wasn't worth it. His heart held on to Renee.

Loving someone else meant he betrayed her and risked living this nightmare of a life without her all over again. Trace had made a vow to love her, and it seemed wrong to move on, even if he wasn't scared out of his mind at the possibility.

His thoughts waged war against each other. Telling him yes, no, screaming at him to focus on the task at hand. No, he couldn't love someone again, because it meant the risk of not being able to fully protect them. It could have been Kelsey having a seizure today.

Natalie could have food poisoning, although it wouldn't explain the seizure.

The food tasted funky. Her words reverberated in his mind.

"Bag that food, would ya?" Trace directed his statement to Izan.

"Make space, man." Izan squeezed past Zack in the tight office space and sealed both food containers before putting them in the bag.

The food could have been an attack. A sabotage against Kelsey, and somehow, Natalie had been the unfortunate recipient.

It might be nothing, but Trace had a hunch. He'd drop it off at the police station and see if Sergeant Donaldson would send it to the lab. Macon and Frees could both throw their weight behind the request if necessary.

"Let's get her loaded and en route," Andi said. The firefighters moved the gurney, and Andi and Trace lifted Natalie onto the stretcher.

"Let's go." Trace grabbed the IV bag, and Macon walked next to Natalie.

They loaded her in the back of the truck and zipped out of the parking lot.

If the incident had been an attack directed at Kelsey, someone had almost succeeded at murder.

16

Kelsey stood in front of the bathroom mirror down the hall from Wren's desk on the first floor and dabbed at the black circles under her eyes. She ran warm water over a paper towel, although it still glided across her skin like sandpaper.

Wren tried to ask if she could do anything to help, but Kelsey couldn't form the words and bypassed the woman without speaking.

Someone had tried to hurt Kelsey, and Natalie had ended up paying the price. More than a coworker, she had become a friend. And now she fought for her life.

Izan had bagged the food. Which meant Trace suspected foul play. If that was the case, *she* should be the one headed to the hospital. And because she'd gotten back to the office late, Natalie had suffered. But who would want to go to such extreme measures to hurt her? It made no sense.

A cry escaped her lips and echoed in the bathroom. The noise mocked her.

Natalie could have died today because of her.

What if people blamed her? Kelsey fidgeted with her earring, twisting the stud.

Natalie had become close to members of the fire department the last several months. She'd helped them work through their disagreements and bond. The chief approved of Natalie, so they all did.

It wouldn't surprise Kelsey if the crew kept their distance. After all, she was only here temporarily. They had no reason to enfold her into their family.

When she removed the towel, redness formed where the mascara had been, thanks to the firm sweep to erase the evidence of her tears.

Part of her considered waiting around at the hospital for Natalie to wake up, but she'd be in the way when the lobby would already be full of firefighters. The last thing she wanted when her friend needed immediate medical attention was to be a distraction.

Instead, she'd focus on canceling the rest of Natalie's patients for the evening. A task she could complete without interfering or facing the disapproving looks of the crew.

Another onset of tears blurred her vision, and she propped her hands on the edge of the sink.

She didn't want to bring trouble to this amazing town. Some of the people here had even made her consider staying after the grant ran out.

But what would it cost Last Chance County if someone had it out for her despite the help she thought she provided for people? Would the grant program even continue with the sabotage against Kelsey?

With a swipe of her sleeve, Kelsey dried her tears then pulled out her phone. When Natalie's voicemail greeting came over the other end, she bit her lip to keep from crying again.

"Hi, Nat. I'm so sorry this happened." Her voice caught at

the end, and she paused for a minute. "I'm here if you need anything." Kelsey didn't know what else to say and hung up.

After fanning her eyes with her hands to compose herself, Kelsey left the bathroom and headed upstairs.

Dean's door stood ajar, so she rapped on the wood before stepping inside. His shoulders hunched over as he wrote something down. He paused, pen in the air, and glanced up. Kelsey bit the inside of her cheek.

Should she suggest they pause the grant program, or let him tell her? After today, he must be having second thoughts.

"I don't have any more clients on the schedule for this evening, so I'm going to head out." Although it came out as a statement, she still sought his permission. Like he would even want to be in the same room as her right now anyway.

"I think that's a good decision. Go home, decompress." He gave her a tight smile.

Tears threatened again and Kelsey sniffed. She read between the lines of what he didn't say. Dean was being polite. Buying himself time to remedy the situation. Amara probably stood ready to take over the program.

She wouldn't argue if that was the course he decided to take. But he needed to know how grateful she was for his swift rescue earlier. "I don't know what I would've done if you hadn't shown up to help. I—well, we're taught to remain calm in various circumstances, but I couldn't think. I panicked."

"I get it." Dean set his pen down and pushed his papers aside to give her his undivided attention. "I'm grateful I was in the office today to provide assistance. Now use those techniques and go relax for the rest of the day. I'll see you tomorrow."

"You will?" She furrowed her brow.

"It is a workday. There are still clients to see."

"Of course. Yes." She nodded, then excused herself.

On her way back home, Kelsey's windshield wipers beat back the rain that resembled the tears she wanted to shed.

She unlocked her front door and flicked on the light switch, mindful to survey the area and listen before entering. Just because her house had been broken into was no reason for paranoia. Whoever had broken in wasn't going to come back. And yet, she couldn't shake the feeling of being watched.

In a few minutes, she secured the rest of the house and tugged on the doors to ensure they were locked. She turned on her fireplace. She needed to distract herself with a cup of tea and a good book for a few hours.

The gray sky made the night sky even darker. She steeped a cup of chamomile lavender before grabbing a blanket, then settled in on the couch.

Next thing she knew, a bang sounded on her door and her eyes flew open. The knocking persisted, and Kelsey rubbed her eyes. She needed to find a weapon, but all she had was the book she'd been reading.

With the hardcover in one hand, she tiptoed to the entryway.

Her heart beat fast. Of course, her front door didn't have a peep hole. She put her hand on the knob, the book hidden behind her back, and she placed herself to the side in case they kicked the door in.

The knocking stopped, and for a minute, it seemed that the person had left. Until her phone began to ring and the knocking started again. Kelsey froze, unsure which to answer first.

One more glance at the door, and she walked back to her phone. Trace's name flashed on the screen.

"Kelsey. Where are you?" The tone in his voice sounded urgent, hurried.

The knocking stopped once again. "In my house. Why?"

"Could you open up your front door then?"

Her brows scrunched together. Trace stood on the other side of the door, phone still to his ear.

"Why were you banging on my door?" Did he have an update on Natalie? His stoic expression gave no indication as to Natalie's condition. "I thought someone was going to break it down and barge in."

"Well, when you didn't answer your phone the first two times I tried, I thought something happened to you."

She unlocked her phone and noticed the missed calls at the bottom of the screen. "Oh." She dropped her hand to the side.

Trace stood tall in the hallway, his arms crossed and feet planted a few inches apart. He had enough stubble on his face that it matured him a few years. He still wore his work khakis and black jacket, and his biceps bulged through the sleeves as if ready to swoop in and save the day.

Irritation bubbled to the surface. She didn't need anyone swooping in to rescue her. She could take care of herself. "I was taking a nap, for your information." She stepped back into the living room. "Everything is fine here." In a grand gesture, she swept her hand through the air.

No way she wanted him to know her nerves were more on edge now. Because that meant she needed protection. If he committed to it, eventually he'd realize what a hassle it was to guard her. She didn't want someone to have to put their life on hold because of her needs.

"No, it's not fine, Kels." His words came out in a husky tone, and her nickname dangled thick in the air. To her dismay, she liked the sound of it coming from his lips.

She shook her head to clear the thought. "What do you mean?"

He let out an exasperated sigh. "When are you going to take these threats seriously? Can't you see someone is out to hurt you? Whatever happened to Natalie wasn't an accident, and I'm certain it was meant for you." He took a step closer and pointed at her, his finger inches from her lips. She wished it were a sweet gesture. Instead, he might as well have just accused her.

"Do you have an update on Natalie?" The words tumbled out in a whisper, otherwise she might have broken down in tears again. It was her fault. He didn't need to come here and pile on even more guilt.

"They found chemicals in her blood stream after testing and they pumped her stomach. At least, that's the update I got from Macon."

Kelsey's hand flew to her mouth and she gulped. "That's terrible."

"It's not safe." He widened his stance. "Whoever's doing this has upped their antics. I waited at the hospital for you, but you never showed."

"You waited for me?" Her voice almost squeaked.

"I don't like the idea of you being alone." He frowned.

"I appreciate your concern, but I don't need you to keep tabs on me." He could get hurt instead of her, just like Natalie had been. If he stuck around, that made him a target.

She stood a little straighter in an attempt to match his height but still came up several inches short. Short enough, though, that she'd fit comfortably in the crevice of his shoulder.

She needed to get a grip.

Now was not the time to think about feelings for Trace. She had to persuade him she didn't need him. Given the fact his heart belonged elsewhere.

"You help all these other people, yet when it comes to yourself, you refuse it. What's your deal?" His cheeks reddened a shade.

All the memories flooded back into her mind. He'd struck the perfect chord.

It was easier to champion others on their journey toward recovery. But anytime she asked for help, she became a bother. A somebody who nobody cared about. Just like with her mother and her peers in school. She couldn't even call them friends.

Kelsey stared into Trace's eyes, their bodies inches from each other. The smell of peppermint enveloped his breath.

Unsure what to say, she swallowed, her mouth sucked dry of any moisture.

She wanted to tell him, but what if he responded the same way others had? With disdain and disapproval. Their close proximity made it hard to hide the truth. "Why would I want people's help when they end up holding it against me? I'm just a weight keeping them down."

Trace searched her eyes. "How can you think that?"

"I don't think it." Her breath hitched. "I know it."

He took her hands in his and rubbed them with the pads of his thumbs. "When your life is hanging in the balance, every precaution is important." He studied her.

It took everything in Kelsey not to avert her gaze. His brown eyes held her gaze, warm and inviting.

"What if I want to protect you? I thought we were at least friends."

His words took her by surprise. Did he want to protect her out of duty and a sense of manliness, or because he *actually* liked her? Oh, how she wanted it to be the latter. No way did he feel the same.

"Having friends has never helped me. I end up alone when things go wrong, and my friends get hurt."

"That's not true." He squeezed her hands. "You're the one your friends find solace in. They trust you to be there for them."

"They shouldn't, though." She shook her head. "Today terrified me, Trace. Natalie could be dead because of me, and there was nothing I could do to help her."

Trace swallowed. "I know what that feels like."

"Now here I am hurting you by bringing up that reminder,"

she cried. Kelsey stepped back from Trace's hold, then slid her hands along her head and tugged her hair into a ponytail. The pain from pulling her hair tight matched her forming headache. "I can't cause more heartache for you." Kelsey took another step back in the hallway.

"Please don't push me away, Kels." Trace extended his arm, but she didn't take it. "I've already lost so much. I can't lose you too."

"What does that mean, Trace?" Kelsey hung her head. It could mean so many things. He didn't want to lose her friendship. Or the reminder of his wife when he saw her. Or the chance at hope on the other side of the pain.

"I..." He cleared his throat. "I don't know."

"Let me know when you figure it out. In the meantime, I won't stand around dilly-dallying." Kelsey wanted to help him, but the closer he got, the more pain it caused. For both their sakes, she couldn't let that happen.

"Then let me protect you. So I don't have to figure it out the hard way."

"I have no idea who would want to do this though." A few tears trickled down her face before they ran in a steady, silent stream.

Trace wrapped his hands around her shoulders and tucked her into an embrace. He rubbed her back, and she laid her head in the crook of his neck and closed her eyes. His tenderness worked to ease the fears she had. Maybe she could find solace in letting people in and it wouldn't be held against her.

After several minutes, he said, "We'll find them. Whoever it is, we'll lock them up for good."

Kelsey shifted, looking up into his gaze, and her collarbone rubbed against something hard and circular underneath his shirt.

The engagement ring.

He still wore it. She'd seen Renee's ring at the basketball game the other night, where it dangled from his necklace chain.

She tensed up and pushed out of his hold. A few steps back provided the needed distance.

That ring was proof of the grief he still carried.

She took a strengthening breath. "Feel free to do whatever needs to be done to ensure the police can figure out who is targeting me." Kelsey wouldn't deny anymore the fact she needed people keeping an eye peeled for this person. "But I need you to leave. Please."

A flash of something crossed his face, but it disappeared as quickly as it had come. *Good.* Better that this hurt a little than he suffer more when he'd already lost so much.

"I want you to move forward in hope. But you can't do that if your heart is full of the past." Kelsey pointed to the ring around his neck. She bit her tongue and blinked. She wanted to help him heal, but she couldn't let her attraction to him complicate the situation.

And right now, she needed a reprieve from the onslaught of feelings this man stirred in her.

With shaking hands, she opened the front door and stared at the ground as Trace brushed past her and walked out.

17

L eaves crunched under his feet as Trace walked down Kelsey's front porch steps. He shoved his hands in his pockets to keep them warm amidst the changing fall temperatures. Each step took him farther away from the one thing he'd vowed to accomplish—keeping Kelsey safe. When she hadn't shown up at the hospital to check on her friend, Trace worried her attacker lurked nearby and had taken the opportunity to finish their work.

He couldn't lose her too.

But *why*?

Kelsey's question haunted him.

He'd taken note of how she fit in his embrace, his arms a shield around her. And just when he'd gotten close, she'd driven him away. He wanted to be a safe place for her to go in a world where she'd experienced others take advantage of that privilege. But given the escalating threats, it seemed futile. Except, he wouldn't stand around helplessly. He would incur whatever costs it brought if it meant Kelsey came out of these attacks unscathed.

He'd call in reinforcements and get people set up to take

shifts guarding her. The closer he stayed to Kelsey, the sooner the police could catch whoever was scheming these attacks. Eventually the assailant would slip and leave evidence behind.

For tonight, he would watch her house again.

Make sure no one tried anything stupid.

A few doors down, a black truck idled. Normally he wouldn't think anything of a parked vehicle, most likely one of the neighbors. But the muffler on this one made its presence evident against the quietness of the area.

The driver had the headlights off, running his truck while he sat there...doing what? Watching Kelsey?

He'd been a police officer in Washington state long enough to know he needed to check this out. Trace's nerves tingled along his back, and he changed his trajectory to intercept the driver. Time for the friendly, local EMT to make sure the person didn't need directions somewhere.

He slid his hand in the side of his jacket and touched the solid butt of his weapon. Of course, that would be his last resort. He could take the element of surprise and get in his car, drive around the block, and approach the vehicle from behind. No need to scare a neighbor if that's who sat in the car.

The direct approach would at least ensure his line of sight never left the truck or Kelsey's house. He pulled out his phone and texted Donaldson.

TRACE

I might need backup at Kelsey's house.

Aiden responded immediately.

AIDEN

You want a cruiser en route?

TRACE

Stand by. If you don't get a response in five, then yes.

He strolled over to the passenger side window and rapped on the glass.

The person let out a yelp, and the pen in their hand flew in the air along with the papers propped against the steering wheel. In the attempt to grab the floating notes, they hit the horn and it let out a loud, short blast. The man turned his face for Trace to get a full profile.

"Gerald?" What did he think he was doing here?

A scowl formed on the guy's face.

Trace reached the driver's side and tugged on the door. He wanted to haul the man down to the station himself, but he needed to give Gerald the benefit of the doubt. "You visiting a friend in this neighborhood?" The accusation in his voice still rang loud and clear.

"You can't. Can't. You're not allowed to question me." Gerald reached for the door handle, but Trace held the frame so he couldn't shut it again.

"You're avoiding an answer." Trace gritted his teeth.

"It's not your business. You can't do this." He waved his hands.

"You're right. It's not. But it'll sure be the police's when they get here and find you stalking Kelsey's place." He crossed his arms. His hand hovered close to his weapon, just in case. "And should we add breaking and entering, hit and run, and attempted murder to the list?"

"What?" The man jumped out of the truck. The quick movement made Gerald stumble. He gripped the side mirror. It snapped in his hold, and he began to fall.

Trace lunged forward and grabbed Gerald's arms to lift him back up.

Gerald's reaction was far too indicative of a guilty conscience. The tint of red in his cheeks and the clenched fists spoke volumes. Although Trace might have been bluffing with all those accusations and no proof, sometimes the guilty party took the bait and brought about their own confession.

"I did no such thing." Gerald's eyes roamed the street. "You made me break my car. My car. I worked hard for this." Gerald picked up the mirror from the ground then gripped the door handle.

"What in the world is going on out here?" Kelsey's voice echoed down the street.

Trace turned. She'd put on a beanie and had a wool coat wrapped around her shoulders. She hunched forward to stay warm. "I thought I told you to go home, Trace."

"But Gerald was in his truck a few doors down from you."

She stepped into the street and came around to Trace's side, but she positioned herself strategically behind him. *Good.* At least she understood the importance of staying guarded. The traumatic incident from the other day must have run through her mind.

"What are you doing here, Gerald?" She softened her tone.

Silence lengthened, and only the light rain against the streetlights indicated time passed.

"Why don't you answer her?" Trace dug his feet into a pile of leaves by the tire of the truck but never let his gaze waver from Gerald. "At least give her the respect of the answer you wouldn't give me."

"Trace." The way she said his name came with a warning, and if he turned around, those emerald eyes would be lasers.

He wouldn't apologize for the question. He'd met all types of people during his cop days. If it meant protecting Kelsey and stopping the threats on her life, he'd take the gamble and probe harder.

"I—" Gerald began then stopped. "I came to see you." He tilted his head to get a better view of Kelsey. "And say I'm sorry."

"For what?" Kelsey asked.

"A lot of things."

Trace opened his mouth to speak, but Gerald beat him to it.

"I shouldn't have yelled. Or scared the kids. I just..." He let out an exasperated sigh. "It's the emotions. I can't control it. Now this." Sobs wracked his frame, and he held up the shattered mirror.

Trace stood with his arms at his side, unsure how to respond to this grown man's distress.

"I'm so...so..." Gerald hiccupped. "So clumsy."

"That's not true, Gerald." Kelsey waved her finger. "You went through vision therapy and earned back your license. You did that. You worked hard for years to drive again. I remember when your other therapist, Amara, praised all your hard work in her reports before I came to the Ridgeman."

"I don't know." Gerald sat back in the driver's seat. "I want to do better." One foot dangled as he twisted and reached across to the passenger side for something.

Despite the perceived sincere attitude, Trace didn't buy it. He tensed. With Gerald's hands out of sight, anything could happen.

"And you are," Kelsey affirmed.

Gerald climbed out of the vehicle again and held the papers he'd tossed when Trace surprised him. "These are for you." He extended his arm to Kelsey.

She stepped forward and brushed against Trace's side. Her nearness sent chills coursing through him along with the urge to put his arm around her.

Trace peered over as she studied the documents. The streetlights framed her face and accentuated her freckles, adding a level of cuteness he hadn't realized she possessed.

Her nose reddened from the cold. They really needed to hurry up and make sure Gerald got home. Trace would personally follow him to his house to ensure he didn't stick around. Or he'd ask a police officer to do it.

Shoot. He'd forgotten to text Aiden back.

Trace pulled out his phone, but sirens broke through the night. Blue and red lights pierced the dark sky.

"Why are police here?" Gerald's voice went up an octave.

"Trace?" Kelsey turned to him, suspicion in her gaze.

He pivoted to see two cruisers pulling up to the side of the curb. Leaves crunched under the tires, and the bright lights illuminated the street.

"You called them. You did this," Gerald snarled. He ripped the papers from Kelsey's hands and stuffed them in his pocket. "I'm not going with them."

"If you can somehow prove you weren't the one stalking Kelsey, then I don't see why you'd be arrested. Maybe show them those papers." Trace nodded his head, knowing full well the police would take Gerald to the station for questioning.

"No way." Gerald slid into the driver's seat and went to close the door.

Trace held it open. "You can't get away that easily."

"Trace, what are you doing?" Kelsey moved so she stood between Gerald and Trace.

"Making sure this guy doesn't cause any more trouble." The officers made their way over. "Lieutenant Basuto and Detective Wilcox. Thanks for coming. This is the man who's been causing trouble for Kelsey, and I found him watching her house tonight." Trace pointed to Gerald.

"That's right. I came to apologize." Gerald planted his hands on the steering wheel.

"I'm not convinced." Trace scrunched his forehead.

Gerald let out a huff.

"Deep breaths, Gerald. We'll get this resolved, okay?" Kelsey spoke low, as if the words were only intended for Gerald.

"He can't bully me." Gerald slid out of the car and shoved Trace.

"Don't touch me, man." He stabbed his finger at Gerald's chest.

"Okay, back up, both of you." Wilcox stepped between the two men.

Basuto moved closer to Gerald while Savannah did the same with Trace. Treating him the same as a criminal?

Before Trace could ask, Basuto said, "Gerald, if you'll come with me." To Kelsey he said, "We'll question him at the station and figure out how to proceed."

He escorted Gerald to the cruiser, and Savannah followed. After the cars disappeared around the corner, Trace turned to Kelsey. "Let's get you back inside. It's cold."

"I'd rather freeze out here after such an embarrassing situation. What in the world was that?" Kelsey jutted out her arm and pointed to Gerald's truck.

"That man was waiting outside your house to make a move, and I stopped him."

"You had no right to do that." She laughed, but the sound contained no humor. "He was sitting in his truck."

"That's exactly why the police need to talk to him. To make sure he doesn't cause more trouble."

She crossed her arms and lifted her chin. "He seemed genuine about wanting to apologize. And after glancing at the letter, I think he was being honest."

"What did the letter say?"

"As his counselor, I'd say that's none of your business." She narrowed her eyes. "You should learn to give people the benefit of the doubt. Not everyone is a criminal."

Trace wanted to talk some sense into her. Not even an hour earlier, she'd admitted to the fact she needed protection, wary of what someone might do, and now she defended Gerald.

He folded his arms. "You don't know when to give up on people and accept the facts."

"Really? What evidence do you have that all this is Gerald?"

"That letter he took back might be proof." Trace huffed.

"I can assure you it is not." Kelsey shoved her hands in her pockets. "You can't go around assuming things just because you want to. Everyone deserves a fighting chance." Her eyes drifted to the ground. "When you give up on people, you leave them broken and alone."

Trace bit his tongue to refrain from saying something he'd regret later.

"I—need to go."

And with that, she turned around and stomped off.

Their fight sent a flood of images back to his mind of his last interaction with Renee before she died. He hadn't wanted her to share the news with her girlfriends that weekend at the beach. He'd suggested postponing the trip until after her appointment, until they got the test results back—given the difficulties they'd already endured. She'd told him she could keep a secret and he needed to have more confidence in her. Then she'd stormed off.

The same way Kelsey now retreated to her house.

A rock formed in his stomach. No, this wouldn't have the same outcome. He wouldn't lose her.

He'd find a way to watch her back. Because if she died, Trace would never forgive himself for failing not just one woman dear to his heart, but two.

18

K elsey walked up to the front desk of the police station first thing the next morning. Crystal, the receptionist was there. Kelsey drummed her fingers against the back of her phone while she waited for the woman to finish up. Two unoccupied chairs sat inside the entrance, but she didn't want to get too comfortable, so she opted to stand.

She wanted to know Gerald's status pronto. Sleep had evaded her last night, and she'd tossed and turned until her clock told her it was an acceptable hour to start the day. It had been one thing for Trace to be in protection mode for her but completely different to interfere with one of her clients.

When Dean got wind of this situation, he might think she couldn't even maintain a professional manner with her clients. Gerald sitting in a holding cell wouldn't look good from any angle. If he'd had to stay overnight, she'd truly have nothing to show for her competency as a counselor. If Dean hadn't already decided to make Amara the lead on the grant program, he could now.

Which meant Kelsey needed to straighten this out.

Crystal hung up and offered a smile. "How can I help you?"

The area behind reception bustled with cops huddled deep in discussion.

"I'd like to see Gerald Santos." She pushed her shoulders back and offered a smile in return.

"Ah yes. He's still in a holding cell. Give me one moment." She twisted around. "Junior, you got a minute? Ms. Kelsey wants to see Gerald Santos."

The uniform nameplate said *Ramble*. His dirty-blond hair was spiked, and his clean-shaven jawline gave him a slight baby face. He was a little younger than Kelsey but wore a warm expression. "Gerald's been talking about you. If you'll follow me."

Kelsey thanked Crystal and followed the officer past several cubicles and downstairs. The white cement walls amplified every noise, and their footsteps echoed in the hallway. Kelsey let out a cough, the air musty and cold.

The officer glanced at her. "Okay?"

"Did Gerald get arrested? Is that why he's down here?"

He shook his head. "Not yet. We're waiting on prints to come back."

As they continued, she noticed security cameras lined the ceiling. They approached a barred door in a row of more barred doors. Someone muttered at the end of the hall.

Gerald sat on a cot, his expression grim. The officer motioned for Kelsey to sit down on the bench on the other side of the door. "I'll be right over there if you need me. Take your time." He walked away.

Kelsey set her purse next to her.

She needed strength to be kind with her words but also get this resolved. She'd mulled over what Gerald had said in the letter last night too. He was tired of the consequences his actions had and wanted to take more proactive steps to get better. Starting with new hobbies that didn't involve dangerous gadgets—unlike hunting. He wanted to enjoy life again with his family, even if it involved new traditions.

"How're you feeling?" She leaned forward and propped her elbows on her thighs. "I want to help in whatever way I can."

He turned his head toward her. "Frustrated." He sighed, then sat up. "I want my own bed. They said they're waiting on evidence. I didn't trash your place. Promise. And I didn't hit your car. I am better. I'm trying to do better."

Kelsey could attest to that. The police wouldn't find a match. Whoever had run her off the road drove a gray pickup. And Gerald had a black F150. "There's nothing to worry about, then. I know you didn't do it."

"I really am sorry. This injury. I wish it never happened," he mumbled. "I can't blame my head. I *want* to do better."

Kelsey nodded. "Thank you for apologizing. You have made tremendous progress." They'd worked through a lot, and Gerald had done a good job of accepting his new normal. But something had caused him to regress. "What happened the night before you were supposed to go on your trip?"

"We had a lot to pack. And Alice forgot snacks." Gerald rubbed his forehead. "We went to the store."

"How did you feel after all that running around?"

"Tired. Too much to do all day."

From all the paperwork she'd reviewed when she'd gotten the position at the Ridgeman Center, Kelsey knew Gerald's personality before the injury didn't line up with the outburst he'd had.

"What did you do to rest?"

"We watched a movie."

"So you were up late?" she asked.

Gerald hung his head. "Yes."

Now the pieces were coming together. Too much stimulus and being up late were not a good combination. It would easily have set Gerald up for failure the next day as his body worked to compensate for everything.

"It's easy to become lax when you're doing better, but you still need to be proactive." Kelsey made a note to focus their next therapy session on this topic.

"I want to get past this."

"That's a great mindset to have." She could use some of that growth in her own life, navigating her need to prove herself and learning how to trust people with her feelings when they wanted to help. "You are a survivor, Gerald. We'll work through this together."

"Will you forgive me?" The words came out clearly despite his averted gaze.

"Of course, Gerald. What happened wasn't right, but all we can do is move forward."

It wouldn't do her any good to hold a grudge. The remorse in his tone seemed evident. She needed to forgive herself, too, and not stay focused on what others had done in the past. Sometimes she was her own worst critic, and it did no good if she wanted to be an advocate for helping others.

Conviction welled up inside her.

She needed to ask Trace for forgiveness as well. The way she'd spoken to him last night could fracture their friendship. And that was what he needed from her most right now. A small step in the right direction, because forgiving herself would prove to be harder.

"I promise I didn't do it. Nothing they say I did." He turned his head to peer into the hallway. "What your boyfriend is saying I did. I didn't."

Kelsey considered correcting him for misinterpreting her relationship with Trace, but that was beside the point.

She studied him for a moment, searching for signs that he was lying.

Everything about him communicated sincerity. She was certain they wouldn't match his prints to those in her house.

"So you weren't involved with the break-in at my house?" Could he possibly know who had done it? "Whoever it was wrote *home-wrecker* on my mirror." She studied him. "I can understand why you or your family might feel that way about me. After all, I was part of the reason you weren't able to go camping with your kids."

He'd spent a night in jail after the hostage situation, and now here he was again. Because of her—and Trace.

"I didn't know where you lived. Not until two days ago. Alice told me not to go. Not to go to your house." His brow furrowed. "But I wanted to give it to you. Give you the letter personally." He laughed. "Maybe I should have listened to her, and I wouldn't be in this cell."

Kelsey stood up so she could stretch her legs and get the blood moving. Maybe it would help her make sense of everything. "Clearly you didn't mail it, so who gave you my address?"

Gerald dropped his hands to his sides and inhaled. "I was at the Ridgeman Center. I saw you leave. So I followed you home."

"I see. Well, I appreciate your honesty." That might account for her feeling like she was being watched. But it didn't solve the mystery of who thought she was a "home-wrecker." Or might've tried to poison her and hurt Natalie instead.

"Will you get me out of here?" He did a full turn in the enclosed area.

"I'll see what I can do." She plastered on a smile and waved the officer back over to let him know she wanted to leave. She'd put a good word in for Gerald with the officer and see what else she could do to expedite his release.

As they walked back upstairs, Kelsey was certain about two things. She had a game plan for Gerald's next therapy session, and she'd confirmed he wasn't behind the personal attacks.

But when they could fully clear Gerald of any wrongdoing, it wouldn't explain who had run her off the road—or attacked her home. Which meant she had another enemy prowling around. One who'd blindsided her and demonstrated adeptness at staying hidden.

Were the signs there and she just wasn't seeing them?

Kelsey said bye to the officers and asked the receptionist to have Lieutenant Basuto call her. Then she called Jamie.

"Hey, girl, what's up?" Her friend answered the phone on the first ring.

"Gerald isn't the one targeting me. And now I'm back at square one."

"You want to brainstorm some names?"

"Bingo." Kelsey tapped the steering wheel but didn't make any moves to leave the parking lot yet.

"Is there anyone you're counseling who hasn't been happy?" Jamie asked.

"I don't have any stalkers or obsessive patients like Natalie did." She couldn't disclose names for confidentiality purposes, but talking it through could still be helpful. "There have been a few clients' family members who've complained to Wren." Including Alice, Gerald's wife. Apparently, she'd made a comment expressing her dissatisfaction with her husband's lack of improvement in the program and wanted to know if there were any other counselors to switch to.

Kelsey picked at her nail polish, and a section of the golden paint floated to the car floor.

Alice had never spoken with Kelsey about her concerns, so she'd written it off. She should follow up with Wren, see if any more complaints had come in.

"Could it be someone who didn't want you getting the grant? A runner up, perhaps, or someone on the committee?" Jamie rattled off speculations.

"Everyone on the committee supported the initiative.

Although..." Kelsey paused. Did she really want to accuse a fellow coworker?

"Yes...?" Jamie drew out the word.

"Amara is another counselor who works at the center. I overheard her in a heated discussion with Dean one day about why she should be on the family counselor team for the grant."

"Have you talked with Trace about this?"

Kelsey sighed. "We got into an argument last night when he confronted Gerald and I stormed off." She stared out the car window at the police station, wishing so much had gone differently.

"Girl, put yourself in his shoes for a moment. He gets a call that someone is seizing at the place *you* work, and there's speculation of foul play involved. He cares about you and doesn't want to see you get hurt."

"Every time I try to help people, they end up getting hurt because of me or abandon me."

"Has he ever blamed you for what happened in his life?"

She paused. "No."

"So don't blame yourself. The only person it's hurting is you."

"I don't know how to do that." Kelsey rolled down her window to get a breath of fresh air.

"Yes, you do, girl," Jamie said. "God delights when we're dependent on Him. Ask for help. You can't control how people respond, but those who truly love you will support you. And I have a hunch Trace wants to be there for you."

"Not after I pushed him away last night."

Jamie chuckled. "Don't make it complicated. Ask for his forgiveness. Tell him you're ready to accept his help. And in the process, you can give yourselves both grace."

Kelsey pulled out of the police station's parking lot and headed back to the office to get some paperwork finished. Tonight, she would talk to Trace and apologize. She wouldn't chicken out, either. If her clients could put in the hard work to not dwell on the hardships in their life, then she could try to do the same.

Cheers erupted from the gymnasium as she walked into the school and made her way down the hall. The timer buzzed for the end of the game, and each boy lined up to exchange high fives with the other team.

A couple stood off to the side in a heated conversation. The man's arms flailed, and his upper body extended forward. The woman propped her hands on her hips, her eyes narrow. Kelsey kept her eyes down as she passed, trying to give them space.

She found Trace as he offered a few handshakes to the players before the kids lugged their equipment bags on their backs to their parents. He held up his finger as she approached and headed in the direction of the passionate couple.

"This is not the place to argue." Trace raised his voice.

Kelsey whipped her head in their direction.

"If you did a better job teaching my child how to defend the ball, I wouldn't have to," the man scoffed.

"Clay, that's enough," the woman cried. "It's not about the points. You're so self-centered."

"I suggest you take this conversation elsewhere. Perhaps the parking lot or away from listening ears." Trace steeled his jaw.

A boy stood with his hand on his bag, tucked in the side of the bleachers with wide eyes and tousled blond hair. His gaze remained fixed on the argument several feet away.

Kelsey moved in front of him to block his view. "How long have you played?"

"This is my first year." He swallowed, his eyes on his parents facing off with his coach.

"What's your name?"

"Sam."

"Well, Sam, it's nice to meet you. I'm sure you did a great job during the game."

His eyes lit up. "Really?"

"Oh, yeah. If I had to run, track the ball, and watch the people around me, I'd trip and fall flat on my face." She let out a laugh.

"You just have to learn to dribble right." He unzipped the bag and pulled out a ball. "Like this." He bounced it a couple times. "Not too fast, not too slow."

"A pro-baller already." Kelsey clapped.

"Sam!" His mom called. "Let's go."

With a sigh, he picked up his bag and walked out of the gym with them.

"Thanks for getting Sam to smile," Trace said. "He needs all the encouragement he can get."

"And you have a way of sticking by people when they need it. I'm sorry for the way—" A ringtone interrupted her apology.

Trace answered his phone. "Hello?"

Kelsey waited and his expression changed. The flush on his cheeks disappeared.

"What's wrong?"

His hand dropped to his side. "That was Macon."

Suddenly her hearing dimmed, and she had to fight to listen to what he said. If something else had happened to Natalie...

"The toxicology report came back. Natalie's food was poisoned."

19

Kelsey's shoulders slumped and her expression crumpled. "Who would poison the food?"

Trace's hand shook. The reality slammed into his chest like the jolt of an AED.

He could have lost Kelsey for good.

She wasn't just someone to protect. He cared about her, and she was a friend who managed to point out the good in people and their potential.

She'd done it with him too. The way her eyes had lit up when she'd complimented his loyalty.

He'd stand up for the people in his life and those he invested in any day.

Just like with young Sam. That fight between Sam's mom and dad haunted him in more ways than one—reminding him of his parents' failures and his failure to protect his own wife. Yet Kelsey's encouragement made him want to do better.

She bolstered his strength in ways others didn't. Maybe she'd had the same effect on Gerald and he *had* wanted to sincerely apologize the other night.

But if not him, then who would want to hurt her so badly? Even to kill her?

"So, the seizure?" She motioned for him to continue.

"Right." He combed his fingers through his hair. "Induced by rat poison."

"Where would someone get rat poison?" She covered her mouth.

"Any garden or do-it center. But who would use it on you and what their motive could be is a different story." One that set Trace on edge. "Come on. Let's go."

The cold air froze his face the moment he stepped outside. Trace put his hands in his jacket pockets.

"The police are going to open an investigation, right?" Kelsey zipped up her coat.

"I'll make sure of it." He hit the button on his key fob and the engine spurred to life. Trace wanted her thoughts on the best plan for a protection detail.

It *would* have been Kelsey writhing on the floor if the food hadn't been swapped.

But he wasn't about to make her stand out in the cold to discuss details. "Let's sit where it's warm."

He guided her with his hand on the small of her back and opened the door. Once she'd climbed in, he made his way to the driver's side.

"How's Natalie doing?" She'd have a more recent report on her friend than the bits of information he'd gotten from Macon.

"Still weak and nauseous, but she's at home, according to what was shared in the group message." Kelsey cleared her throat. "All things considered, she's doing okay and resting."

"I'm glad." Trace had seen enough calls for poison or overdose to know the outcome could've been extremely different. Especially when the amount ingested was unknown. The risk for complications became greater.

With a push of his feet against the floor mat, Trace turned

EXPIRED VOWS | 157

in his seat. "You don't know who could have mixed in the poison in the Backdraft order?"

"I keep going over all of it in my head. Why it happened to Natalie instead. Somehow, I brought the trouble with me, but it hurt her."

The way she picked at her nail made him want to take her hands in his and ease her worries.

"I've made a list and triple-checked it. I don't know who'd be willing to go to such extremes measures."

He'd figured as much. Right now, he didn't need to push it and make her feel guilty for not having an answer.

"The PD doesn't know who ran me off the road or trashed my house either." She bit her lip. "The only thing everyone agrees on is that someone tried to kill me. There's no way to figure out when they'll strike again or how to stop this mess." She hung her head.

"Let me help." Trace leaned forward while his arm rested on the center console. Heat emanated from the vents. The blast tickled his hand, but the warmth added to the kindling fire in his heart.

He wanted to run his fingers through her hair and tell her how beautiful she was.

Her tender heart beat for others and their needs. She'd been through a lot herself and still stood strong.

And it was attractive.

He wanted to tell her whoever was scheming these attacks didn't see the worth she possessed. But no amount of affection or affirmations would change reality.

It could never work.

The moment he entangled himself in a relationship, his guard would be down, and the cost would be far too great.

Kelsey's life hung in the balance.

But the stakes were higher than that now. Kelsey had weaseled her way into his heart as more than an old friend.

He wanted to do whatever it took to protect her, but if he doubled down on his efforts, she could push him away for good. If not, he could lose her like Renee.

He rubbed the side of his face.

She let out a breath. "I haven't been able to shake the feeling of being watched. But there's never anyone there, and Gerald told me he was following me."

Her arm moved toward the door, and an ache formed in his gut at the idea of the seat across from him being vacant. Instead, she propped her elbow on the windowsill and narrowed her gaze. The scrutiny of her stare sent needlelike darts his way to prod at places in his heart he'd covered over like scar tissue.

This woman cut through all his defenses and left him reeling.

If he let her in, he would never be able to hide behind the walls he'd erected after Renee's death to guard himself from experiencing that pain again. He'd give her everything.

He'd gain it all with Kelsey, but in return she'd have to do the same and let him in.

Or it wouldn't work.

Was that a risk she'd be willing to take with him?

"What was the conversation with Sam's parents about? They seemed to take what you said well." She smiled.

Trace rolled his eyes. "It's a work in progress."

"Sam seems like a nice kid."

"The kid is great. Come a long way in a few months with his skills on the court and with the team. Although his parents put too much pressure on him."

"I'm sure they just want to see him succeed." Kelsey shrugged. "At least, that's how it is with some of my clients."

"That they do. But they can't do it in a way where Sam has to carry all the weight of successes and failures on his shoulders."

Kelsey propped her head on her hand. Her eyes never wavered from him.

Trace struggled to breathe.

For the first time in a while, they sat as two friends talking about life. And he wanted to scrape away at the plaque build-up around his heart that life had caused and show Kelsey what hid behind his defensive exterior.

"No child deserves to witness their parents fight. For any reason, but certainly not on their behalf. It already took weeks to build Sam's confidence. And in a few moments, his mind could shatter that. All because of what he saw."

"You can relate to his situation, can't you?" Kelsey's words hung in the air.

Trace gulped. "I was in his shoes once." His tongue dried and he licked his lips.

"How so?"

"My parents fought all the time when I was a kid. Nothing was ever good enough." His mind transported him back to those nights when he'd clutch his pillow and walk through the hallway after his parents believed he was asleep. He'd stand against the wall and peer into the living room, where they had their shouting matches.

Their raised voices echoed in his mind. "Somehow, I became the center of their problems. They never had enough time for each other because they were busy working and taking me to sports practice. My mom worked late and never made it to my games, and my dad lost his enthusiasm the more he had to drive around town for games and couldn't be at home."

"I can't imagine how hard that must have been." Kelsey reached across and squeezed his hand. Her fingers still held some of the outside cold and sent a tingle through his body. And in the same touch, it carried a furnace of heat that grew inside him.

"Eventually those arguments ended in the police being called. My mom stormed out. That was the last time I saw her."

A knowing look crossed her face.

"What?"

"You lost someone you loved."

It was one thing to talk about his parents, but it still felt too soon after his wife's death to talk about Renee. Maybe Kelsey needed to process more about losing her best friend during a traumatic time of her own.

The fact was her friends hadn't been there for her—because she hadn't let them.

Trace said, "I was the reason my mom walked out. She told me so herself."

Kelsey sat up tall in the seat and shook her head. "They were adults who had their own problems to work through."

"Yeah, well, they didn't do a great job of it."

"And the police?"

"I remember the one officer gave me a teddy bear and a cop star pin." Trace widened his lips. That man had given him something good to hold on to in one of his scariest moments. He still had that pin on the shelf over his mantel. "From then on I wanted to join the force."

Kelsey studied him but didn't say a word.

"I wanted to offer the same compassion to those who walked through similar situations."

"Like Sam," she said.

He nodded. "I couldn't just stand by and say nothing. Not when two grown adults can set a better example. They should know how to engage in healthy disagreements." He sighed. "Hopefully Sam doesn't get reprimanded at home tonight. Every time I try to fix something, it somehow finds a way to backfire."

"You don't have to try so hard." Kelsey focused her gaze in

the distance. Even though she shared the advice with him, did she realize she should preach it to herself too?

"I can't help it."

"Why's that?" Kelsey prodded.

"I hate seeing people hurt. If I can keep them from experiencing pain, it's worth it."

"Only God can control that, Trace."

"Yeah, well, if He loved me, then He would have stopped it from happening." Trace clenched his jaw and leaned back against the headrest.

"Often times our suffering is exactly what He uses. He's not a stranger to pain either. He became the God-man, so He's able to empathize with us in our heartache."

Trace put his hands on the steering wheel, the column locked in place, unable to move in any direction. Trace felt stuck like that too. Stuck in his past. "You don't understand." There was more to the situation than he'd shared.

"Try me." Her features softened, ready to take on whatever he said.

Silence lengthened between them. Trace couldn't muster the words. Because the moment they left his lips, the reality would be solidified. And it wouldn't fix the past. "What's the point? It won't change anything."

Kelsey stiffened. She clutched at her purse on her lap and reached for the door handle. "I should get going."

She slung her purse over her head so it sat like a crossbody satchel. "See you later, Trace." She stepped out of the car and shut the door.

The soft way she spoke tightened his chest. It'd been a long time since he'd heard those words from a woman. And he'd effectively pushed her away, creating distance he didn't want anymore.

Unless he decided to change it.

The thought created a gaping void in his heart.

If he wanted Kelsey to grow in confidence that he would be someone she could trust, he needed to support her first. Which started by opening up all the way. Not simply with the parts of his story that were easier to share.

It didn't only take time to heal. It sometimes required pain too.

Kelsey made her way across the parking lot. Each step took her farther from him. The tingling sensation in his fingers grew. She deserved to know. After all, she'd been Renee's best friend.

Trace slid out of the car. The cold gave him a renewed alertness. "Wait, Kels." He took long strides and closed the distance.

She turned around, a hopeful look on her face.

"I needed to protect Sam from his parents for another reason. Not because of my parents."

Kelsey didn't say anything but simply cocked her head and waited for him to continue.

He shoved his hands in his front pockets and pulled in a deep breath.

"Kelsey, if my wife wasn't dead, I'd have a child almost Sam's age."

20

His words pierced the air and stung Kelsey's face more than the wind that nipped at her skin.

She'd walked halfway across the parking lot and thought for sure Trace had shut down. Put his walls back up. Kelsey had become his friend, not a therapist, in that brief moment in the car, and she'd savored every second. Hearing his heart and being close to him made her want to learn more. And let him into her life a little more.

Renee had been pregnant?

Kelsey shuffled her feet. The ground underneath gave her comfort while everything else spun around her.

Regret and shame bubbled to the surface, and she hung her head. The man who stood in front of her was not the same person she'd known as a freshman in college. He carried the weight of the world on his shoulders.

The life he'd dreamed of had shattered.

She'd almost jumped on him over his approach with the parents, not even knowing the truth. He would have been a dad now, starting a family of his own. "I didn't—"

The feather light touch of his fingers brushed against her skin as he lifted her chin. "You don't need to say anything."

She stared into his gaze and searched the depth of his dark eyes. He'd matured over the years. The stubble along his jawline added to the effect. But the crinkles on his forehead told a different story—one of someone who'd seen more than their fair share of pain. There'd been more hidden under the surface. Kelsey just hadn't realized how much pain he'd been carrying.

"It was finally time I told someone, and I wanted it to be you."

Kelsey's lip quivered. "She called me to say she had something to tell me in a few days. That she could barely contain her excitement."

"No one knew except us." Trace's eyes glistened. "She was so excited to tell you first."

She blinked several times as tears welled in her eyes. "I would have liked to have shared that with her."

Renee and Trace would have made a beautiful baby, but that hadn't been the plan for them. Just like it hadn't been God's plan for her to have both legs. With everything she'd lost in life, it could be easy to forget all that God had done.

She'd helped many people because of what she'd experienced. It might not be so bad to ask for help herself.

The lampposts illuminated the dark sky around them. It was getting late, but there was so much she needed to apologize for.

So much left to say to Trace.

"Can we talk more? Maybe somewhere warmer?"

"You want to get that coffee?" Trace gave her a weak smile, and the door to her heart cracked a smidge.

Except now was not the time to act on her growing affection for him. He'd gotten vulnerable with her. And for now, the only distraction he needed was a friend.

"I'd like that."

"I'll follow you."

Trace walked to his car, but he waited until she got in hers before he followed suit.

He pulled into the parking spot next to her, and they headed inside. Bridgewater Café was already closed for the night, so she opted for the diner.

Kelsey glanced over her shoulder as Trace held the door open. LED lights shone back at her from the 24/7 sign that alerted customers the store was open for business.

Only a few other patrons sat inside. A young couple, clearly on a date, held hands. The only drinks they nursed were each other's gazes while their coffee cups sat untouched. Another woman sat at a booth, her nose glued in a book held by one hand, while the other hand held her mug.

"What can I get you?" The waitress twirled to their table, pen and pad poised.

"I'll take a hot chocolate with almond milk, no whipped cream." She entered the numbers into her food tracker on her phone and set a timer to check her glucose levels in case she needed to adjust her insulin.

Would Trace make a comment about her sugar intake again? She glanced over.

The barista said, "And you, sir?"

"Grande coffee with caramel, please." Trace said it all without taking his attention from Kelsey, his lips curled up in a slight smile even with the grief close to the surface of his expression.

Kelsey wrinkled her nose. "You know, you'll be up all night with a buzz after that."

He looked down at his wrist. "My shift starts in a couple hours, so it'll keep me alert."

A few minutes later, steam rose from the cups the waitress

set on their table. Kelsey tasted the hot chocolate. The milk added a creamy layer to the top.

Now that Trace had opened up about his past, she had a better gauge of what she was dealing with. She wanted to help him release the bottled-up emotions and work through his thought process.

"Why did you become a medic?" She wrapped her hands around the cup.

Trace rubbed the bridge of his nose. "Most of the time, I tell people I'd been an officer for six years and needed a change from what I encountered every day." He grinned. "But I know you won't accept that answer."

"You're right about that." Kelsey laughed, then quickly sobered. "I want to support you, whatever that looks like. And I'm sorry for how I responded to you the other night with Gerald."

"Thank you. I appreciate that. Although I didn't handle the situation the best either. But I can assure you my intentions were for your safety." Trace took a sip of his coffee. "I just couldn't bear the thought of being too late to save someone again."

"Is that why you became an EMT?" Kelsey circled back to her original question. She nursed her drink and waited for Trace to share more.

"We were called to the scene of the crash, and I had to stand back while my wife died in the arms of another EMT. There was nothing I could do to help her. By the time I got there, it was too late." Trace cleared his throat. "I never got to say goodbye or tell her I was sorry."

"Sorry for what?" The bell over the door clanged, and Kelsey jumped. Her drink sloshed and spilled hot liquid onto her hand.

Trace handed her a napkin and gave her a quizzical look.

"I'm fine." She dried her hand. Her eyes followed the man

who'd entered as he walked to the counter before she focused back on Trace. "Will you tell me more?"

He closed his eyes like he was reliving the events. "We had an argument. She found out she was pregnant and wanted to tell her girlfriends about it on the beach trip, but I wanted to wait until our first doctor's appointment to make sure everything was okay with the baby. I was concerned Renee wouldn't be able to keep the secret, so I suggested she postpone the trip. We'd had a series of callouts that day, and I was abrupt with her in the car with my partner listening. I didn't want to deal with personal stuff on the job. The next thing I know, a call comes through for an accident with a yellow Kia."

Renee had always been obstinate. When she put her mind to something, it was futile to convince her otherwise. In that way, she and Kelsey were a lot alike—enough that Trace would never fall for her. Why would he if she'd be a constant reminder of his wife?

Instead, she said, "I can't imagine what it must've been like pulling up to the scene."

Trace held up his hand before she could continue. "Don't get all introspective on me, okay, Ms. Counselor?" He paused and his eyes flitted back and forth assessing her. "I need my friend, not a therapist."

Kelsey nodded. "Okay, fair enough. I failed you as a friend when you needed it most, and for that I'm sorry." Kelsey stretched her hand across the table.

"What do you mean?" He furrowed his brow.

"By not making it to her funeral." The words came out in a whisper, and Kelsey's mouth dried.

She'd failed herself and those around her. Each day after the surgery, she'd poured out her anguish in tears. Even making a sandwich became a chore as she'd teeter off balance, despite her crutches. Managing the physical pain had been one thing, but being unable to call Renee in the midst of it had proved even harder. She hadn't even been able to work up the courage to call Trace and explain why she hadn't shown up. If the doctor had scoffed at her inability to prevent her amputation, surely the response would have been echoed by Trace.

"It's okay." Trace shrugged.

"No." She shook her head. "I let my medical issues get in the way of being with those I care about. All because of my stupid leg."

"That's not something you can control." He placed his hand on top of hers.

"I wanted to come, but I couldn't postpone the surgery." She swiped a tear from her cheek.

In the end, she'd been alone. Swallowed in a kind of grief of her own over the leg she'd lost. Figuring out what her life would be after the worst had happened.

Through her time counseling, she'd come to learn everyone's journey with trauma was different. One person's sorrow could never be compared to another. And that was the beauty of pressing forward. All her clients learned to cope with a new normal and find hope in life again. A story unique to them and their circumstances.

Trace pulled his chair closer. "Just because I was hurting doesn't mean I didn't want to know how you were doing. Your diagnosis isn't something that could have been prevented. And even while you're capable of managing it, it still has a mind of its own. Your doctor should have been the first one to remind you of that." He frowned.

Kelsey blinked several times to ward off more tears.

Trace's compassion unraveled her fear of failure. He'd managed to comfort her while they were talking about his hardship. "I couldn't add more to the heavy load you carried."

Trace shook his head. "You were an important part of our lives. I called a few times after the funeral to check in on you. But you never answered."

"I was embarrassed I let my diabetes get so bad. And I didn't know how you'd respond. We were grieving in our own ways, Trace. We wouldn't have been able to be there for each other, regardless of how much we think we could have now. And that's okay."

Trace pinched his lips.

The reality of it was sad. They'd both been searching for light in a dark pit. And it wouldn't have done any good to try to console each other then.

"Well, neither of us are alone now." Trace squeezed her hand.

"I'm grateful for your friendship, Trace." Kelsey finished off the last of her drink and wiped the foam from her lips.

Movement outside the window caught her attention. A figure walked past the sidewalk and to a gray truck that sat idle under the blanket of the dark sky, away from the lights of the diner. Kelsey gasped. "That's the truck that ran me off the road." She braced her hands on the table ready to jump up.

Whoever they were, they'd purposefully concealed themselves in the shadows.

"Where?" Trace whipped his head to the side, and the chair squeaked against the linoleum.

"Right hand side of the parking lot. Gray truck bed." The back of the vehicle faced them, but she couldn't see a license plate anywhere.

"Stay here while I go investigate." He stood up and squeezed her hand.

Even if she wanted to move, she didn't think her legs would allow her. She glanced around and took note of everyone's innocent bliss. No one appeared worried. Maybe she was overreacting.

Trace walked across the parking lot, his hand at his hip. Her breath hitched as he approached the vehicle. Each step shrouded him further in darkness.

Rear lights flashed. The truck's engine roared to life and the tires squealed on the pavement. Trace began to jog after it, and a loud pop resounded.

Kelsey let out a scream.

Her knees connected with the table. Both mugs tipped over and clattered against the wood. Her leg went numb as she tried to stand.

"Those old cars backfiring is ridiculous if you ask me." The girl who'd been engrossed in her book earlier walked over. "Let me help you." She grabbed a wad of napkins and dabbed at the mess of remaining coffee from Trace's cup.

Backfire? No, it had sounded like a gunshot.

All eyes in the room stared at her.

She braced her hands on the edge of the table to stop the shaking in her fingers. "Thank you." Kelsey grabbed the wet napkins and limped out the door.

Trace stepped back onto the sidewalk. Her shoulders loosened at the sight of him. Kelsey ignored the spider web of pain in her leg and closed the distance between them, nearly tackling him to the ground in an embrace.

"Whoa." Trace grabbed her forearms and steadied her.

"Are you hurt?" She pulled back to fully assess him but didn't see any injuries.

"That I couldn't keep pace with the truck and they got away? Yes."

"But that loud bang. It wasn't a gunshot?" Kelsey inspected him once more, afraid she would see a pool of blood.

He brushed a strand of hair away from her face. "The car backfired. That's all." He stretched out his arms. "See, I'm fine."

Kelsey gulped. He was fine all right. But now wasn't the time to think about that. "Nothing can happen to you, Trace Bently. Especially not on my behalf."

"Why's that?"

"Because I care about you too much." Didn't he know that already?

"Care about me as..." He left the sentence unfinished.

"More than friends." There, she'd said it. Out loud. "Since way back in college, actually." At least now the truth was out. Even if nothing transpired, she'd been honest about how she felt.

"Why didn't you say anything back then?"

Kelsey cocked her head. "My best friend had a major crush on you. I wasn't going to stand in the way of that. Then you and Renee started dating, and..."

"And what?" Trace took a step closer, and the warmth of his breath heated her cheek.

"I was dealing with my health issues." And Renee had been healthy. Beautiful. Better than Kelsey in every way, and perfect for Trace. She'd been so happy for them. "On top of caring for my mom after my dad died. I wasn't about to put those burdens on someone else."

"You're always ready to help people but rarely let anyone help you."

His words sank deep, like a scalpel that scraped at the build-up around her heart. "No one's ever stuck around to help me. Or it's just been the wrong time." She didn't blame him for not being there for her when he'd lost Renee. How could she? "Why burden someone who doesn't want to be there? People need to live their own lives."

"That's not true." Trace ran his thumb along her hand. "There are people who care about you."

Kelsey opened her mouth to protest, but before she could, Trace leaned in and cupped the base of her neck in his hand. He pressed a kiss to her forehead, then the tip of her nose.

Shivers shot down her spine and sent a flood of warmth through her whole body that negated the frigid air. She surrendered to the feel of his lips on her skin and drank in the tenderness he exuded. His strong arms held her close. He rubbed her back, and with each circular motion, she relaxed.

All her worries faded when she was with Trace.

When she pulled back, the smell of caramel lingered on his breath, and she was wrapped in a sense of warmth, connection she'd never experienced with anyone else.

He took her hand in his and whispered in her ear, "I care."

21

The buzz that coursed through Trace's brain was from one thing only. And it was most definitely not that pre-shift caffeine jolt. Even if Trace wanted to take a power nap in the sleeping quarters, his thoughts wouldn't let him.

Instead, he tapped his finger on the chess piece while the firehouse hummed with activity around him.

He'd let his guard down and kissed Kelsey on the forehead. A woman who constantly went above and beyond for others. Those actions had been evident in college and compounded even more so now.

She'd braved a hostage situation and saved lives. She'd made a beeline straight for a scared kid to console him. And she believed the best for people. Enough to confront the pain he'd stored up the past five years.

Trace cared about her.

It was the most terrifying and relieving thing he'd told her. After he'd followed her home to make sure she got there safely, the only thought that consumed him was her. He'd opened up to her, and now he could only hope she'd grow in trust toward him.

Her cuteness didn't help matters either—those freckles. The way she'd let him hold her while she rested her head against his chest. She'd let him in, and he never wanted her to feel alone again.

"You going to keep your finger on that pawn all night?" Logan raised an eyebrow.

"Just thinking about my next move." Trace gave him a tight-lipped expression. Bringing his personal life on shift with him was a bad idea. He needed to stay sharp and professional, but the urge to share with a friend—kind of like the way he'd shared with Kelsey—made him wonder what that would be like.

"Your move with this game or something else in your life?" Logan leaned back in the chair and crossed his arms.

"Both." Trace let out a sigh. What would Renee think about him kissing Kelsey? Was it a disservice to the love he'd professed for her?

'Til death do us part.

Trace let out a groan and moved his knight.

"Clearly you're preoccupied today." Logan let out a whistle.

Trace's king stood isolated on the board, and Logan slid his pawn to secure his victory.

"I want better competition next time."

"Deal." Trace slapped his hand, then walked to the counter and grabbed a slice of pumpkin roll.

With fall now in full swing, the baked goods had started to make an appearance. Mrs. Crawford had made this one.

"Tell your mom this needs a tiny bit more nutmeg." Trace licked some cream cheese off his finger.

"Last time I gave her feedback, she told me I needed to be your sous chef and learn a thing or two myself." Logan wrinkled his nose.

"The kitchen's open for lessons." He leaned his hips against the counter. "What would you do if you liked someone but it meant betraying someone else?" He stuffed another bite in before he said too much.

"Oh boy, that's a tightrope to walk." Logan poured himself a cup of coffee that had been there for a few hours and was probably lukewarm. "It's hard to say. Being blindsided once makes me stay clear of women. Focusing on my career now is the easiest way to go."

"Not the most rewarding, though, when you find the one you want to be with." Allen maneuvered into the kitchen area on his forearm crutches and winked. "The right woman is worth whatever it takes."

Great. Now Allen knew Trace had a woman in his life. That meant more questions from the other firefighters as well and more back-slapping from Charlie if it didn't work out.

The sound of the alarm blared over the intercom. "Rescue 5. Ambulance 21. Child trapped." The dispatcher read off the address.

Trace raced through the hallway and checked the back of the truck before he buckled in. The rescue squad truck pulled onto the street, lights and sirens going.

The thought of a child alone and scared sent a chill down his spine.

"These calls always break my heart." Andi snapped in her seatbelt.

"I know." Trace flicked on the lights and mentally prepared himself for what they'd encounter. He pulled out of the ambo bay onto the street behind the rescue squad truck.

Andi grabbed the radio on the dash. "Ambo 21 is en route. ETA five minutes."

"Copy. Officers are on their way too."

They pulled up in front of the house, and Andi grabbed the

bag. Rescue squad jogged over to the side of the house, and a cop car pulled up behind the ambo.

Trace headed for the rescue lieutenant, Logan's twin brother Bryce, who stood with a woman in her sixties with graying hair. "Where's the child?"

Her hands wrapped tightly around a sweater. Mascara trailed down her cheeks. "She's in the treehouse out back."

They made their way around to the yard where a man, retirement age, stood at the base of the playhouse. His lanky frame didn't add any intimidation despite his hands in the air. "Get down here, little lady. This is no way to treat your grandpa." He slammed a fist against the trunk.

Trace winced. "That's enough." He stomped over, unable to believe someone would treat a child that way. "That's not how you speak to anyone, let alone your granddaughter."

The man hooked his fist and took a swing. Trace ducked, then went to grab for the guy, but a hand on his arm held him back.

"Don't." Logan got in his face. "Not worth it."

Officers rushed past Trace and pinned the man to the tree. Handcuffs clicked before he was escorted off.

"Eddie, I want you and Logan up there. Figure out what's keeping that door shut and get it open," Bryce's voice bellowed.

"Yes, Lieutenant." Eddie grabbed his gear and started the ascent, Logan right behind him.

Trace stepped over to the woman, who'd made her way to the back. "How long has she been out here?" They needed to know the chances of hypothermia setting in. "Is she injured in any way?"

"I don't know." New tears formed in her eyes. "Her poppa hit her pretty hard on the arm and she ran off. A door closed, but I assumed it was to her room." Her breath hitched. "When I went to find her, she wasn't there."

"Chrissy!"

Kelsey jogged across the lawn to the woman. She wore a featherdown jacket and a scarf. Her hair fell in waves around her shoulders. The tan color brought out the freckles on her ivory skin.

Trace looked back at rescue squad, breaking open the door to the treehouse. Now was not the time to get distracted.

Kelsey touched his arm. "What's happening?"

"Client?" Trace said.

"Yeah."

"They're getting the girl out." And Chrissy would be in good hands with Kelsey here to help her through it. If he was going to stay focused on his job and not get wrapped up in last night, he needed to create some space between them.

Trace made his way back to the base of the treehouse. He shielded his eyes and tried to locate the girl through the windows.

Eddie's foot slipped on the rung. It connected with Logan's jaw and sent him tumbling back to the ground. Trace held his breath and, out of instinct, stretched his arms forward. Logan's deadweight collided into his chest and knocked them both to the ground. Eddie dangled for a moment. His forearms held his weight, and he regained his footing on the slippery rungs nailed to the tree.

Trace rolled over. The air whooshed from his lungs, and he let out a grunt. "You okay?" he wheezed. It took a moment for him to regain his breath.

"I'll be fine." Logan pushed himself up. He straightened and pinched his eyes shut.

"You sure about that?"

"Yeah." Logan waved him off. "Thanks for breaking my fall, genius." Logan limped off to the side, and Trace stood there, unsure what to do. Logan could have been more appreciative of Trace's help.

"Bro, we can't have you injured too." Bryce walked over to him.

"I didn't want him to get hurt."

"We're trained to let someone land on the ground if it's only a few feet. It prevents them and anyone else from getting hurt."

He'd just been trying to do the right thing. "I see," he mumbled.

"It's never worth it to get hurt trying to rescue someone, man. Otherwise, your help is no good to anyone." Bryce held out his hand. "We'll do the rescuing and let you know when we need you to do your job."

"The doorknob's broken," Eddie yelled down. "We're going to need to saw it open."

Bryce cupped his hands and spoke. "Get it done. We're losing time."

Eddie directed the child to get into the far corner and turn her back so the sawdust didn't get in her eyes. The whir of blades cut through the air, and wood chips flew every which way. He handed the saw back to Charlie and ducked inside the space. "Blanket!"

Trace handed it to Charlie, who climbed up and leaned in. Bryce had them hook up a rope to secure their descent. Eddie scooted to the edge, a little girl in his arms, her blonde hair pulled into pigtails visible above the folds of the blanket.

"Mee-maw?" the girl whimpered from the firefighter's arms. Her head turned in each direction and scanned the array of people from her perch.

"Lucy, I'm over here, baby." Chrissy waved her hands to get her granddaughter's attention, Kelsey by her side.

Bryce directed them, and they got the child to the ground.

Charlie climbed down the ladder, careful to avoid the spot Eddie had slipped on. Each step slow and calculated. The moment her feet touched the ground, the child broke into a sprint over to her grandma, dragging the blanket with her.

Andi made her way over to them.

Trace let her take the lead. Lucy would be more comfortable with another woman—especially after the trauma she'd endured from her grandfather. The whole situation left a bitter taste in Trace's mouth.

How could anyone treat their own flesh and blood in such a vulgar way?

Trace shut his thoughts down. If he didn't, his mind would take him to the place of what-ifs in fatherhood and what it would be like to have a child of his own. A role he might have welcomed a second time by now if it hadn't been for Renee's death.

He witnessed tragic things happen to people every day. Most nights he wrestled with how God could allow such heartache. Sure, God hadn't withheld pain from His Son on the cross. But why had He allowed it? *So you could have freedom.* Trace shook away the thought. It was still hard to reconcile the hardships he and others endured.

Trace moved to stand by Andi.

"Vitals are good." Andi glanced over. "Temp hovering at 96.9."

Lucy's cheeks glowed red, but at least they'd gotten to her before the condition got worse.

"No, I want to talk to my granddaughter." The old man struggled against the officer and the cuffs.

Lucy curled inward and looked up at her grandma with wide eyes.

Trace knew what it was like to cower when the people who were supposed to take care of you fought. Thankfully, he'd never experienced any abuse. But the lack of love he'd seen had been just as unbearable. If the Lord ever decided to give him children of his own, he wanted to set a different precedent. One of support and genuine affection.

Kelsey made her way over to the men, and Trace followed.

Lucy was in good hands with Andi, and Trace didn't want Kelsey getting stuck in the crosshairs of any more aggression.

The old man continued to struggle. "Lucy. You listen to me."

"Now's not a good time, Thatcher." Kelsey squared her shoulders.

"And I'm supposed to be in a jail cell? That's where they're taking me." He writhed in Officer Olivia Tazwell's grasp. "Like I'm some kind of common criminal. Chrissy's not even pressing charges." He raised his voice. "Are you, Chrissy? You're not pressing charges on me, right?"

Kelsey turned toward Tazwell and noticed Trace. "Please don't talk me out of trying to get him help."

Trace said, "I'm not here to argue. Just to have your back."

Kelsey looked at Olivia. "A holding cell is not going to do him any good. He needs treatment."

"That's for the district attorney to decide. This is child endangerment, not a simple domestic," she said. "Whether the wife presses charges or not, he's going to jail."

"He needs medical care. At a hospital."

Tazwell gave her a skeptical look.

"I'm his counselor. Without disclosing confidential information, assessing him at the hospital is what he needs so we can figure out how to heal this family."

Kelsey narrowed her eyes at Olivia like she'd stepped into another mama bear's territory. Right, she thought she could handle everything on her own. Except Officer Tazwell was only trying to help. And if they could come to a compromise, everyone would be happy.

An officer's first priority was always to ensure safety for all involved. "We'll make sure he's fully checked out by a doctor. If there's any suspicion of retaliation or those girls being in jeopardy again, he's at the station." Tazwell crossed her arms and steeled her gaze. "We take it seriously when a child is in danger."

"You won't regret this." Kelsey extended her hand to Tazwell, who slowly unfolded hers and shook Kelsey's before leading Thatcher away to the patrol car.

Kelsey blew out a long breath. "Thank you."

Trace shrugged.

Andi confirmed that Lucy was stable, but she complained of pain in her arm, and a welt had begun to form, so they needed to take her to the hospital to get it checked out.

As Chrissy was escorted to the ambulance to ride with Lucy, Thatcher started screaming again. He pushed against the patrol car and swung at Tazwell, who held firm to the edge of the roof. "You will not get away with this, Lucy. You need to understand the meaning of discipline," he snarled. More officers made their way over to contain the situation.

Lucy's eyes misted with tears, and she trembled in her grandma's embrace.

Trace turned his back to the commotion with Thatcher and positioned his body to block Lucy's view from her grandpa's outburst.

Just like a cop had given him a glimmer of hope all those years ago, now was the time for Trace to focus on his patient and do the same.

22

The confrontation with Thatcher set Kelsey's nerves on edge because one wrong move and someone else would need actual medical attention.

She walked over to the waiting ambulance and exhaled at the sight of Trace talking to Lucy. A smile formed on the girl's face, and she snuggled in next to Chrissy. Trace had made Lucy his top priority, and clearly the girl had already begun to forget the shouts from her grandpa.

He would make an excellent dad one day. Between his compassion and quick action, his kids would know their dad loved them.

Goosebumps prickled her skin, and she wove the scarf tighter around her arms. She'd gone over her confession and their kiss a hundred times already. And she still needed to pinch herself.

Trace cared for her.

She'd half expected him to push her away when she'd come forward with the truth of her feelings. Yet it had somehow drawn them closer together. He hadn't scoffed at her either. Which made her long to share more parts of her life with him.

His protective mindset was truly because he cared and wanted her to stay safe. Even when it rubbed against every independent bone in her body.

And she liked it because she witnessed the real Trace. The man who sent her heart fluttering.

She moved closer to Andi and Trace. "What's the plan?"

"We're going to get Lucy triaged at the hospital. Make sure she doesn't have any broken bones." Trace relayed the information while Andi finished splinting the girl's arm.

"I'll meet you over there." She turned to Chrissy. "I'd like to spend some time with Lucy and debrief with her about this situation. Walk her through what she's thinking and feeling."

"That sounds perfect. Thank you." Chrissy gave a weak smile and rubbed Lucy's back.

Kelsey followed the ambulance until they pulled into the hospital. She found a visitor parking spot, then made her way over to the ambulance bay.

Chrissy held Lucy's uninjured hand while Trace and Andi wheeled her inside.

Once Lucy was settled in a room, Kelsey observed the girl's expression. Her eyes darted around the area while her finger remained gripped in Chrissy's hand.

Kelsey took a step forward, but Trace beat her to the girl's bedside.

He handed her a plush dog. "Here's a friend to keep you company while you're here. Anytime you need a reminder, just squeeze his ear."

Lucy pressed the dog's right ear, and the animal broke out singing "I'm so glad you're my friend."

"He's my bestest friend!" the girl exclaimed. "Thank you, Mr...uh, Mr..." Lucy scrunched her forehead. "Mr. Doctor."

Kelsey grinned. She wanted to wrap her arms around Trace and tell him all the ways she was thankful for him. If she wasn't careful, she'd be his next cardiac arrest patient from the way her heart flipped.

A knock sounded on the door, and Sergeant Donaldson stepped in with Tosha, the CPS woman Kelsey worked with occasionally when situations like this arose.

"Ms. Long, I'm Sergeant Donaldson." The officer smiled.

"And I'm Tosha Willis, CPS." The woman extended her hand to Chrissy.

"We need to ask you a few questions. Do you mind?" Donaldson pointed to the hallway.

Kelsey didn't want to leave Lucy alone. It could trigger an emotional response.

Trace picked up on her hesitancy and said, "I'll stay with her."

Out in the hall, Donaldson leaned in. "I know this has been a challenging day for you, but we need to know if you want to press charges." He spoke to Chrissy in a low tone, guarding her privacy as much as possible.

"I really don't want to." Chrissy shook her head. "He's not like this all the time."

"I understand how hard this is for you. I need you to think about Lucy too," Tosha added. "Considering Thatcher used physical force, is Lucy in danger at home?"

Chrissy rubbed her eyes. "I wish it hadn't come to this. Every day brings a new learning curve."

"I think we can all agree we want what's best for you, Lucy, *and* Thatcher." Kelsey smiled. "My goal is to keep you intact as a family as much as possible." The eight-year-old had been through so much already after losing her parents, and now her grandparents remained her sole guardians. She needed a steady, safe family unit in her life, and Kelsey was determined to make sure she got that. "Has Thatcher gotten abusive before?" Chrissy had never mentioned anything to Kelsey about a prior history, but she still needed to ask.

"Not with Lucy." Tears sprang to Chrissy's eyes.

"I have a family Lucy could live with. The Cunninghams are very sweet." Tosha pulled out a clipboard.

"I don't want to put a restraining order on Thatcher." Chrissy folded her arms.

"Are you sure?" Donaldson asked. "He was still agitated when we got to the station."

"He's my husband, and I will stick by him through thick and thin."

Skepticism furrowed Donaldson's and Tosha's brows. Kelsey had to find a compromise to ensure everyone's safety. "Chrissy, I'm going to refer Thatcher to the inpatient clinic for sixty days at the Ridgeman Center. This will give us time to work through the mood swings he's experiencing and give you and Lucy space at home to rest. You can still visit him in the wing. But I think this will be best for everyone."

"I think that's a fabulous idea." Tosha scribbled on her paper.

"Donaldson?" Kelsey lifted her eyes.

"We can work with that."

"Chrissy, you're here!" A woman with red hair and bright green eyes hurried down the hall. With a gold-colored jacket, her array of colors added brightness against the sterile white walls.

"Maggie, what're you doing here?" Chrissy smiled and enveloped her in a hug. "This is Maggie Filks, owner of Hope Mansion."

Chrissy made introductions, but Donaldson and Tosha already appeared to know her. Kelsey had heard about Hope Mansion and the safe haven Maggie created for women there but had never formally met the owner.

"I had just finished a batch of gingerbread cookies when I heard what happened, so I boxed some up and made my way over here."

Donaldson and Tosha thanked them for their time and left while Kelsey, Chrissy, and Maggie headed back into the room.

Lucy's mouth widened at the sight of Maggie. "Ms. Maggie. You're here."

"You bet I am, darling. And I brought some gingerbread with me."

"Those are my favorite." She pushed herself up with one hand on the bed, and the blanket she'd been wrapped in fell to the floor.

"Well, then, here you go," Maggie said.

Kelsey bent down to grab the blanket at the same moment Trace reached for it.

"Here." She handed him the other half. "Thanks for looking out for Lucy."

"I was happy to help." Trace folded the blanket.

"I should get over soon to see Thatcher." Kelsey hefted her purse strap higher on her shoulder.

"All of you need a cookie for the road." Maggie extended the tin of cookies stacked high with the gingerbread men.

"If you insist. I won't make you offer twice." Trace grabbed two cookies.

"I'll pass, but thank you." Kelsey didn't want to have to adjust her insulin needs at the moment.

"This is amazing." Andi closed her eyes.

"I'll let you in on my secret." Maggie winked. "Coconut sugar. Adds the right amount of sweetness without all the harsh effects of refined sugar."

"We might just need to make use of your services at the station. Show the rest of the crew the best cookies in town," Andi said.

"Hey now." Trace winced. "I thought I was the master chef at the station."

"A little friendly competition never hurt anyone." Andi winked.

Maggie laughed. "Let me know when, and I'll whip up a batch."

"I'll be in touch. But if you need anything in the meantime, you have my number," Kelsey assured Chrissy.

"Thank you for everything," Chrissy said.

Another knock sounded on the door, and a doctor came in.

Yes, Lucy would be in good company with Chrissy, Maggie, and her new stuffed animal.

"She's in love with that dog," Kelsey said as she, Trace, and Andi made their way outside. "Where did you get it from?"

Andi made her way to the back of the truck to organize supplies. "He always has a secret stash on the ready." Andi popped her head around the corner.

Trace's cheeks matched the red stripe on the ambo. "You never know when you'll respond to a call with a child who needs a little comfort."

Kelsey's heart skipped a beat.

He'd taken the hardest moments in his life and found simple ways to impact others. "It certainly made a difference." She cleared her throat and averted her gaze from his.

Her ears grew warm underneath her hat. She liked his tender side. And if she wasn't careful, she'd fall into the trap of fantasizing about what could be.

In the distance, a gray object sat in contrast to the Douglas fir trees that lined the edge of the staff parking lot, just before the main road.

She squinted and noticed the truck. Was it the truck that had run her off the road and had also idled in the diner parking lot? Butterflies formed in her stomach. She hadn't seen the vehicle earlier. Then again, she'd been too preoccupied with Chrissy and Lucy to pay much attention to anything else. So why did it make her nervous?

"Can guests park anywhere on the premises?"

Trace gave her a quizzical look. "Anywhere that's not designated as staff or emergency vehicle."

"Right. Makes sense." Lots of people drove gray trucks. But something about it rubbed her the wrong way. Her phone buzzed before she had a chance to say anything more about the sighting. "That's my reminder. I have paperwork to finish for a client before I go visit Thatcher."

"Of course." Trace shoved his hands in his pockets and walked her to her car. "Are you doing anything tonight?"

There was the question that made her heart speed up. "Only dinner and plans with my couch and TV." She chuckled.

"Let's grab something at Backdraft. That is, if you're not too set on a night in with the only interactions being with people on the screen." He smirked.

"That makes it sound depressing." Kelsey laughed. The thought of not being alone tonight was even sweeter than Maggie's gingerbread cookie. "In that case, I'll see you then."

Kelsey's hands tingled as she climbed into her car. She gripped the steering wheel to steady them. Trace had actually asked her to dinner. She couldn't believe it. Even if it was just as friends, it reminded her of the days when she, Trace, Renee, and Maeve would grab food after class.

She made her way out of the parking spot and eased her foot on the brake to make a left onto the road. Except nothing happened. The car continued to gain momentum on the down grade.

She pressed down on the brake harder and stared at the speedometer. The number didn't change.

Kelsey pumped the brake.

The car wouldn't stop.

Kelsey whipped her head around and scanned the area for a place to exit. Sweat broke out on her palms.

Trace waved as she sped past the ambulance. She banged her fist on the window, and Trace began to jog after her car.

She slammed her foot against the pedal once more before rolling out into traffic. There was no way to stop without hitting something. Kelsey screamed.

23

Kelsey's car careened onto the street. Trace raced after her and watched as a delivery truck narrowly missed slamming into her. More than one person honked their horn.

Kelsey's scream pierced the air, and he pumped his arms harder.

The pure terror in her eyes propelled him farther. He couldn't let anything happen to her. Not when he'd just gotten his friend back.

Dear God, I cannot lose someone else to a car crash. His mind uttered the words in desperation. *Show me what to do, please.*

An ambulance sped up the street, its siren blaring. Cars moved off to the shoulder to give it space.

Except Kelsey had nowhere to go.

Her tires gained momentum, and Trace couldn't breathe. His eyes narrowed in on both vehicles as they came closer to colliding. Horns blared and people yelled. The sounds grew muffled to Trace as his feet pounded on the sidewalk. Despite his efforts, each step landed with more distance between himself and Kelsey.

He cupped his hands and yelled, "Watch out!" Except he could do nothing to stop it. The ambulance clipped Kelsey's mirror and sent it shattering to the ground. She veered into a grassy area on the other side of the road.

A fence snaked around the perimeter to a construction zone. Several bulldozers sat at the bottom of a mound of dirt.

Right in Kelsey's path.

With traffic still stopped, Trace sprinted across the street.

He whipped out his phone and dialed 911.

Her brake lights didn't come on. Her car continued to bounce on the uneven ground toward the fenced-in area. The vehicle jerked back and forth like Kelsey couldn't maintain control. Was she having a mechanical failure and her brakes were shot?

It didn't make sense, though. Rental companies had to have their loaner vehicles inspected.

"Where's your emergency?" The dispatcher spoke in his ear.

"She's going to hit the dozer," someone to his left hollered. A few bystanders stood by the road and pointed.

"Across the street from the hospital. At the construction entrance," Trace said between gasps for air.

He pinched his eyes shut for a split second. He needed to think of something. Except his hands were tied. He couldn't do anything until the car came to a stop. Then he'd work to save Kelsey.

If it's not too late.

This was Renee all over again. Her car would be a crumpled mess, and they'd extract her body too, just like...

His thoughts taunted him. *Haven't I experienced enough pain? Save her, Lord. Please.* No, it wouldn't be too late.

Suddenly the door flew open, and Kelsey's legs jutted out before her whole body tumbled onto the ground.

"Renee!" Trace tore through the grass.

The car bounced a few more feet, then pummeled into the

fencing. Another screech filled the air as it came to rest at the base of the bulldozer.

Trace grabbed Kelsey's arm to stop her from rolling before she hit the fence.

He collapsed onto the ground beside her to catch his breath. Her hand clasped his. The touch of her skin against his was a tangible reminder that she wasn't in the crumpled car.

Kelsey pushed herself up next to him and stared.

Tremors wracked her body, and he pulled her close, unwilling to let go. He combed his fingers through the ends of her hair and repositioned her scarf that had fallen off her shoulders.

"You're safe." He pressed a kiss to her forehead.

"Don't kiss me, Trace." She pushed back on her hands and winced. "I'm not your wife."

He opened his mouth, then shut it, unsure what to say. He hadn't meant to overstep any boundaries. "You did the right thing by getting out of the car." He stood and extended his hand, except she didn't take it.

"Hey." He crouched down. "You're safe." Although, those words were meant more for him.

Tears welled in her eyes, and Trace had to choke back his own.

"Does it hurt anywhere?"

Her hair was matted and tangled. Her jacket had added a nice cushion to the fall at least.

He took her hands in his, and she hissed. Her palms had a nasty rash, and blood trickled from a few cuts where grass and pebbles dug in.

"My leg and side are sore."

He helped her to her feet and wrapped her arm around his shoulders. Kelsey grunted as she put her weight on him and limped through the grass.

Kelsey stopped moving.

"What's wrong?" he asked.

"My leg."

"Let me look."

Kelsey waved him off and rolled up her pant leg. "It's the prosthetic."

He watched her press a small button on the back that released the mechanism and allowed her to reposition it.

"That's better," she said.

A man ran toward them, and his white medical coat flapped behind him. "Let me help you guys."

"Thanks, Jack." Trace had much respect for Dr. Jackson Welch. He was one of the best in the field and had even taught some professional development courses for their crew.

The doctor shouldered Kelsey's left side as they made it to the street.

Drivers stood outside their cars haphazardly parked in the road.

"I've wasted my entire lunch break now," one woman huffed.

"I could have died with her reckless driving," another man shouted, his face beet red.

"Excuse us. Coming through," Trace barked. "Make room." Trace held his tongue and focused on getting Kelsey back over to the hospital parking lot in one piece.

Officers had the road blocked off and swung their light flares as they redirected traffic down a side alley.

Andi jogged over to meet them. "Rescue squad is on their way to clean up the scene."

Trace blew out a breath. "I'm glad they'll only be pulling out the car." He squeezed Kelsey's arm.

"What happened?" Andi surveyed Kelsey.

"The brakes wouldn't work." She turned toward the parking lot. "Where's that truck?" Her voice rose a notch.

"What truck?"

"The gray truck I saw." Kelsey pointed to the staff lot. "It's not there anymore."

The squad truck squealed to a stop. Bryce hopped out and slammed the door shut.

"Where's it at?" Bryce asked.

"Across the street by the construction zone. Entangled in the fence in front of the bulldozer."

"We're gonna need the pulley and jaws," Bryce shouted to the rest of the crew as he climbed back into the driver's side.

Trace, Andi, and Dr. Welch escorted Kelsey inside. Andi typed in her security code, and the doors to the ER swung open.

Charlotte Duncan wheeled a computer cart past them.

"What room do you have for us?" Andi asked her nurse friend.

Charlotte clicked a few buttons. "Head down to room six. I'll be right there." She turned to Dr. Welch. "Patient in room two is ready for you."

"On it." The man saluted and rounded the corner.

"I see we've made a habit of meeting under less-than-ideal circumstances." Officer Tazwell stepped into the room.

"It's a habit I want to change." Kelsey grimaced and shifted on the bed.

"Walk me through what happened."

"My brakes wouldn't work."

"Have you had your car inspected recently?"

"Yes. But that wasn't my car. It's a rental until I can find a replacement for the one that caught on fire."

"Was there anything else that seemed out of place?" Tazwell jotted down notes.

"I noticed a gray truck parked in the staff lot earlier when I went to leave. I think it was the same one that ran me off the road."

"The one I chased at the diner?" Trace added.

She nodded. "When I came back over here, it was gone."

"Someone's not messing around." Andi let out a whistle.

"Because they want me dead," Kelsey muttered.

"I'm not going to let that happen." Trace clenched his jaw. "I wonder if security cameras caught anything." He wanted to search every nook and cranny until whoever had done this was found and held responsible.

"It's worth a shot to see if it pulled something," Tazwell said. "Whoever this is needs to be stopped."

Charlotte walked into the room and squirted the hand sanitizer before donning a pair of gloves.

"We'll check out the footage and let you know if anything comes back." Tazwell closed her pad.

"I'm coming with you." Trace stepped forward.

The officer raised an eyebrow.

"While she's being treated, there's no reason for me to stay here. Plus, I witnessed the entire thing. You can take my statement while we're at it." He crossed his arms.

"All right." She beckoned for him to follow. Tazwell flagged down a security officer whose nameplate read *Louis Turner*. "We need to look at your security footage." She flashed her badge.

"Certainly. Right this way." The dark-haired man led them to the room.

Trace and Tazwell hovered over the man, who pulled up the video and rewound it to fifteen minutes prior.

"There's the truck." Tazwell pointed at the screen.

If he hadn't known where to look for it, Trace would have missed it completely since it was on the edge of the frame. Although, it was visible enough to make out some features.

"Can you rewind some more to see when it appeared?"

"Stop. There," Tazwell said.

Sure enough, their vehicles pulled into the ambulance bay when they dropped off Chrissy and Lucy. A few minutes later, the truck pulled into the staff area.

"Someone followed you here." The words hung in the air as the seconds ticked by on the screen.

"And whoever it was knew to avoid the cameras. Look," Trace said.

The figure made their way to Kelsey's car in the visitor lot. They ducked below the car before re-emerging a minute later. A bulky, hooded coat covered their body and prevented their features from being seen. He couldn't even tell if it was a man or woman. Before long, the person climbed back in their vehicle and drove off.

"Pause it right there." Tazwell leaned forward. "Can you zoom in?"

Louis complied.

Trace squinted at the screen and made out the grainy image.

A license plate number. *KPR2001.*

The year his parents got divorced. At least it wouldn't be hard to remember the combination.

"Did anyone know you were coming here?" Tazwell asked.

"No, except for the people at the scene of the entrapment. We followed standard protocol to have the patient looked at." Trace didn't like all the missing pieces. He'd told Kelsey he wouldn't let anything happen to her, but how could he ensure that if there was no telling what he was up against? Gerald hadn't broken into her house. Thatcher was in custody. So who had painted a target on Kelsey?

Someone who thought she was a "home-wrecker."

"Either the person was involved at the scene of the call, or they were watching in the shadows." Trace paced back and forth in the tiny room.

"Does Kelsey have any names of people who could be targeting her?" Tazwell stepped back from the screen.

"She didn't share names with me."

"I'll need a copy of this footage to review at the station."

Tazwell thanked the officer, and they headed back to Kelsey's room.

Kelsey sported a bandage on the palm of her left hand, and her legs dangled off the side of the bed. Andi stood in the corner of the room by the counter.

"Any luck?" Kelsey and Andi asked in unison.

Tazwell nodded. "We got some time stamps."

Kelsey's shoulders loosened. "Good."

"I know you've already thought this through, but we've got to start thinking about people close to you who might be targeting you, even if you don't like the idea. Because if we don't, we may miss a vital piece of this puzzle." Trace didn't want to sound harsh. It was the unknown that killed him and made him want to get the upper hand here. "Otherwise, next time you could be dead."

"I know." She shuddered.

"Can you give me a few names to start running through the system?" Tazwell clicked open a pen.

"I don't like the thought of any of these people wanting to hurt me. But Alice Santos, Gerald's wife, and Amara Lyn, another counselor I work with, might have motive. Neither of them have been happy about my work as a family counselor and have expressed their frustrations. And Maeve Wells." Kelsey shrugged her shoulders. "She's a sweet friend. Although, I've noticed her take a liking to Trace, and she might not be happy with all the time he and I have spent together." Her cheeks turned pink and masked her freckles.

Trace swallowed a laugh and grinned. So Kelsey had noticed Maeve's advances.

Clearly, Kelsey had more thoughts about him, and Trace wanted to learn all of them. Hopefully over dinner.

"Thanks. This gives us something to work with," Tazwell said. "We'll be in touch soon."

Trace's phone rang, and Bryce's picture filled the screen. "What's up, man?"

"You're not gonna believe this. Are you sitting down?"

Trace slid a chair to Kelsey's side and sank into it. "I am now."

"Kelsey's brake lines were cut."

Blood rushed from Trace's face, and the temperature in the room dropped. "How'd you figure that out?"

"Intuition, I suppose. Plus I noticed no skid marks had torn up the grass, so I checked to confirm it."

Breath whooshed from his lungs as if Trace had been knocked back by the impact of the car hitting the fence.

No skid marks.

He swallowed. His jaw went slack.

No skid marks.

No, it couldn't be.

"Tazwell, wait." Trace disconnected the call.

The officer paused in the doorway.

"Rescue said they inspected the brake lines on the car. They'd been cut."

"I'll go check it out." Tazwell lifted her radio and left.

"Were you fully checked out?" Trace scooted his chair against the wall.

"Yes. Just waiting on the discharge papers."

"I'll be right back." Trace needed to talk to Bryce and Logan. See the car for himself. He jogged out of the hospital and across the street to the scene.

Kelsey's rental hung at a forty-five-degree angle, held by a tow hook, while Tazwell talked to Bryce.

"Can I see the brakes?" Trace walked over to Logan, who spoke with a tow truck driver.

"Officer Tazwell is going to take pictures."

"Someone tampered with Kelsey's car, man. I don't like it."

"None of us do. The police can worry about the details, though."

"What if they miss something? Like with Renee's accident?" Trace rubbed his jaw.

"You can trust them to do their job. Where's Kelsey?"

"Getting checked out. Andi's with her."

"Kelsey needs your support, bro. Not for you to work this case like a cop. She just needs you." Logan stuck his finger in Trace's chest.

Trace stood taller. "There's a lot at stake here. Her life is in the balance."

"Exactly why you should go help her."

Trace crossed his arms. Tazwell continued to snap photos, so he headed back over to the hospital. They needed to catch this person before Kelsey ended up dead. Which meant after work, he would have to visit a place he never imagined he'd go to, because of the incident today.

Trace got back to Kelsey's room, where she stood with papers in her non-bandaged hand, ready to go.

"When my shift is over, I've got to check something, but I'm not letting you out of my sight." Trace stood in the doorway.

"What do you mean?" Kelsey's wide eyes stared back at him.

"I'll explain soon."

A few minutes later, they climbed into the truck, and Trace prayed his instinct was wrong. But there was only one way to find out.

24

They hadn't exchanged a single word on the ride in the ambulance back to the station.

Kelsey still couldn't believe Trace had called her Renee. His response stung.

She'd thought she was more to him than simply a reminder of his late wife. And the way he'd freaked out about her brakes being cut added to her already frayed nerves. Someone had deliberately taken note of the rental car she'd been driving and decided when they could get their job done.

Outside the truck window, trees and signs flew past. Kelsey gripped the door handle with her non-injured hand. "Slow down, Trace. Please." The speed made her head swim, and bile rose in her throat.

The most important function in a car had failed, and Kelsey had almost been squished amidst a pile of metal.

"We're back." Trace eased on the brake and turned into the firehouse.

"I need a bag." Kelsey turned to Andi, who'd been kind enough to sit in the back. Andi opened a drawer, but it was too late. Kelsey hopped out the passenger side and threw up.

The cool air eased the rest of her nausea. "I'm so sorry. That's disgusting." She leaned against the ambo.

"I should have been aware of how fast I was going. Considering." Trace grimaced. "Here." He handed her a few napkins.

"Thanks." She dabbed at her mouth. "Now, would someone please tell me what's going on?" Kelsey huffed.

Trace flicked his wrist. "I've got three hours left on shift. Then I need to go look at something with you."

"Okay..." Kelsey drew out the word. He still wasn't giving her much context. "So why am I here and not able to wait at home?" They made their way inside past the conference room and Macon's office.

Trace stopped walking. "Because if my instincts are correct, the whole playing field has shifted."

"You're talking in circles and it's scaring me." Kelsey tapped her foot and leaned up against the wall. Each muscle ached from the fall. She needed some ibuprofen and a good nap.

Kelsey's phone rang, and Jamie's name popped up. "I need to take this. May I?" She pointed to the conference room.

I'll be in the gym, Trace mouthed and gave her a thumbs-up.

"I saw the news report. Are you okay?" Jamie didn't even give Kelsey a chance to say hello.

"I'm okay. Thank God. A few bandages and sore muscles, but that's the extent of it." Kelsey eased into a chair and winced. Her side hurt. "If you want to come pick me up, I wouldn't complain."

Jamie said, "I can be at the hospital in ten." Keys clinked in the background.

"I'm not there." Kelsey squeezed her eyes shut. "I'm at the firehouse."

"You know I can't show my face there, girl."

"It's been long enough. Please." Kelsey put her phone on the table and hit the speaker button. "They're out on a call, so he won't be here. And"—she lowered her voice—"Trace is acting weird."

Jamie sighed. "Fine."

Fifteen minutes later, Kelsey met Jamie at the front entrance. "A few bandages?" Jamie raised her eyebrows.

Kelsey gave a sheepish grin. "It's just my hand and cheek." And one on her side, which she didn't need to worry Jamie with.

"I'm ready to go home." Kelsey hooked her purse under her forearm.

The intercom system blared. "Ambo 21. Woman with stroke-like symptoms."

Trace barged into the hall and almost collided with Kelsey.

He looked between Jamie and her, then put his hands on Kelsey's shoulders. "Please do not leave." Those chocolate eyes pleaded with her. "I won't be gone long. I haven't shared the whole story, but if my hunch its right, you could be in more danger than we thought." He turned to Jamie. "Please don't go."

"Trace, we gotta move." Andi clapped.

Jamie swallowed. "I'll stay here with her."

Trace disappeared around the corner.

"Jamie." What was her friend doing? Kelsey wanted to get home and sleep. And there was no way Jamie wanted to stay a second longer in this building. Her tense shoulders said it all.

"Let's get some tea and sit down. If I'm going to jeopardize my reputation by staying here, then you can at least tell me why you're ready to jump ship when Trace is trying to help you."

Kelsey followed the signs to the common area. Amelia sat at a table in the lounge, reading a book about effective leadership. "I see you're quickly becoming part of the clan now," she said and set her book down.

"I guess so. I hope you don't mind me being here." The last thing Kelsey wanted was to be a burden. Especially when everyone at the station had other demanding duties to take care of.

She stood off to the side while Jamie grabbed teabags and mugs.

"Are you kidding? You're welcome here anytime. Seriously." She shifted her seat. "Don't tell the boys I said this, but it's nice to have another female around. You can only handle so much testosterone, you know?"

Kelsey laughed. "I appreciate the reassurance." She went to pick up both drinks and winced. The bandage on her left hand rubbed against the raw skin.

"May I?" Jamie extended her hand.

"Thanks." Kelsey smiled.

With drinks in hand, Jamie followed Kelsey to the conference room and shut the door.

"What happened?" Jamie set her cup on a coaster and gave the other to Kelsey.

"He called me Renee." Kelsey paced. "When I jumped out of the car, he freaked out and yelled her name. It was like I didn't exist."

"Renee died in a car accident, right?" Jamie propped her elbows on the table. "So of course he would be thinking about her. *You* almost died in a car accident today too."

Kelsey bit her lip as images flooded her mind of the car headed toward the construction site. "I just don't want to be one more reminder of what he lost."

"Do you realize how much courage it took Trace to go after you today? To not withdraw from fear but fight through it to protect you? That takes bravery."

Kelsey sipped her peppermint tea. Trace had stayed by her every step of the way. Despite all the mayhem that had followed her in Last Chance County, Trace hadn't complained about her being the problem.

He cares.

What if his actions were proof of those words?

Goosebumps pricked her arms. It was a good thing she still had her jacket on, because the thought created a shiver of delight.

"God brought him into your life for a reason. Was it for you to fix him or to love him?"

Jamie's words invigorated her senses more than the smell of the peppermint. "You're right. I can't change him. Only God can do that. But I can show him Christlike love."

Kelsey could encourage Trace. Show him patience. And call him out when the need arose—because she wanted what was best for him. And she, too, cared very deeply for this man who'd shown her he'd stick by her side.

Jamie finished her tea and stood. "I should get going. Before, you know..." She nodded to the closed door.

"You are incredibly wise, but sometimes I think you need to take your own advice." Kelsey shrugged.

"That's different."

They made their way outside just as rescue squad pulled into the drive.

Jamie groaned and averted her eyes to the ground. The garage door screeched open, and the crew hopped out, bantering.

"Hey, Kelsey." Bryce waved. "Trace gave us a heads-up. He should be back in thirty."

"Jamie?" Logan shielded his eyes from the sun. "What are you..." He pinched his lips.

"Don't worry, I was just leaving," Jamie huffed.

"What was that about?" Eddie whispered as Kelsey walked inside with the guys.

"Don't ask." Kelsey hung a left and settled into the common area, then pulled out her phone. She could catch up on a few client emails until Trace and Andi got back.

"You stayed." An hour later Trace's voice pulled her from her work. He braced his arm against the doorway.

"I did." Kelsey got up and closed the distance between them. She really wanted to kiss this man. And if he made a move, she'd reciprocate the gesture. At the same time, her mind told her to take things slow, so she wrapped her arms over his shoulders and hugged him. "Thank you for having my back this morning."

He leaned back. "I'm glad the outcome wasn't worse."

Before she gave herself permission, Kelsey glanced down at his chest. Was he still wearing the silver chain with Renee's engagement ring? With his medic scrubs and jacket on, it was hard to tell. Her best friend had deserved to be treasured, and Trace did just that. But maybe now he was healing in the process.

A flutter worked its way through her veins.

"Me too." A smile danced across her lips.

No more calls came in on his shift, and an hour later, Kelsey sat in Trace's car en route to an undisclosed location.

"Will you tell me now where we're going?" She stared ahead as they merged onto the highway.

"My storage unit."

"For what?"

"It has some, uh, of my stuff," he said.

Once they arrived, Trace entered the lock combination to the compound and pushed open the garage door. The door squeaked on its hinges, and light streamed into the space.

Kelsey sucked in a breath at the sight.

A hunk of yellow metal sat in the area, mangled and distorted. She could make out the KIA logo on the front, but as she walked around the vehicle, she could see the mirrors dangled off the side and the front hood crumpled in on itself while the doors bent inward.

The sight made her insides twist.

The realization that she could have been trapped in her car earlier in the middle of a construction zone gripped her with a wave of nausea. She put one hand on her thigh to steady herself.

She stared at the yellow paint. Trace had lost his wife and their baby to this accident. And he might never get over Renee. Her muscles relaxed a fraction as she realized that was okay.

He'd always have a special place in his heart for his first wife. Yet, he'd also had the courage to care about someone else again, and that took bravery. After that kind of loss, he could have sealed his heart and not let anything penetrate it, considering Kelsey had been Renee's best friend and a reminder of his past.

But he'd pushed past the grief and had her back.

Trace must have been terrified when he'd pulled her farther away from the car today. Afraid she might die the same way Renee had.

Which made the heap of Renee's car sitting in a storage unit confusing. Why would he want to relive that tragic event? "Um, Trace? Why do you still have Renee's car?" She furrowed her brow.

"Her accident never sat right with me. Something always seemed off. So I have the evidence along with the police report in case new information ever surfaces." Trace had a blank stare on his face and didn't make eye contact with her.

"It's deeper than that, isn't it?" He had solid cop instincts, and Kelsey didn't doubt for a second his keen sixth sense. But he could have easily taken pictures of the vehicle to file with the police report.

Trace rubbed the back of his neck. "I let my own fears get in the way during our argument. I tried to fix things with Renee, and this is what it cost me. It serves as a reminder to never fail again."

Kelsey rubbed her forehead, trying to make sense of the scene in front of her. Trace stood several feet away, his hands hidden. Closed off like he didn't want her support.

Despite that, Kelsey wanted to love him. To carry the burden with him and stand by his side the way he'd done for her. Trace had shown her time and time again he wouldn't leave.

Now she wanted to do the same.

Kelsey took a step toward him. Before she reached his side, he said, "I'll be right back."

He walked back in with a tire jack. "Could you shine a light under the car?" He cranked the handle and raised one corner of the car and added a few pieces of wood on the other corners to hold it steady.

She pulled out her phone and turned on the flashlight with her good hand while he slid under the car.

When he rolled back out, grease covered his fingers, and he had a smudge on his chin.

"Did you find what you were looking for?" Kelsey turned off the light.

His face was grim. "Yeah." He stood up and wiped his hands on a towel.

"When Bryce called, he said they found your brake lines cut." The color in Trace's face disappeared.

"And *you* made sure Officer Tazwell investigated it." Trace continued to take care of her. Even when she didn't know what to be aware of, he did. "Did you find anything on the cameras?"

"Someone pulled into the staff lot like you suspected and took an interest in your car while we were inside." Trace raked his fingers through his hair.

Kelsey's hands grew clammy under the bandages, and it made them itchy.

She had been followed.

But how were they tracking her? Responding to Thatcher's incident hadn't been part of her normal routine.

"So my brakes malfunctioned," she stated.

"Exactly. And there were no skid marks."

"That was evident when I couldn't stop." She blinked. Her head ached, and it hurt to think. At least Trace was thinking clearly, because she didn't have much energy left.

"Your accident made me think of Renee's."

"It was a hit and run, correct?" Kind of like her, being run off the road by that truck. But it wasn't like the accident tonight. "Not mechanical failure."

"They could never confirm anything." He tapped his foot against the floor. A soft sheen of sweat covered his brow.

Kelsey could imagine the terror Renee must have experienced in those moments, considering she'd almost endured a similar fate. What she couldn't fathom was the terror Trace endured from Renee's death, then watching it unfold again today.

"I left that accident with more questions than answers as a cop. The one part of the report that bugged me was that there were no skid marks."

"Just like Bryce said."

"Yeah. If anyone knew they were about to crash, they'd hit the brakes hard."

"Unless they couldn't."

"The police report said the brake lines appeared frayed. But given the significant damage to the vehicle and the various factors, there was no way to determine what actually caused her death. It was deemed a horrific tragedy." Trace pulled in a breath. "Renee didn't have a car accident. Someone intentionally targeted her." He swallowed.

"Trace, I'm so sorry." Kelsey pinched her eyes shut.

"Don't be."

"Why's that?" Kelsey cocked her head.

"Now we have another piece to the puzzle." Trace gulped. "Renee was murdered, and now whoever killed my wife is after you too."

25

"Can you call Jamie, please?" Trace focused on the road as they drove back to Kelsey's house, to make sure they didn't have a tail.

For years, Trace had buried the idea of someone murdering Renee. He figured someone could have cut deep to create a flesh wound and the pain wouldn't hurt as bad as his discovery. Someone sabotaging Renee's car, killing her and their child, was a deafening blow. Like a thousand air missiles that needed to be dodged.

But now whoever sought vengeance wanted to destroy another part of his life.

He cared about Kelsey. Probably too much. Her tender heart, the way she encouraged him. How she persevered through difficult things in life. Even her love for the Lord. It made him want to wrestle with God through the pain He'd allowed Trace to face and find joy again. "Tell her to meet us at your house."

"This changes everything," Kelsey muttered and pulled out her phone.

"You're right." He grated his teeth. "Now it's personal."

Which meant there was only one thing he could do: step out of the picture. He'd make sure Kelsey was safe under Jamie's watch, then he'd leave. If he stayed around, Kelsey would be murdered too. He couldn't let his growing affections put her in more danger.

"What do we do now?" Kelsey leaned her head against the window.

"Stay far away from me." Trace grimaced. He wanted to protect Kelsey, but not if it cost her life. He'd work the case from the background. If whoever was after Kelsey realized he'd backed away, they might stop their attempts on her life.

"What?" Kelsey twisted in her seat. "I thought you had my back." She placed her hand on his shoulder, and it took everything in him not to pull off to the side of the road and hold her tight. To pepper kisses along each one of those freckles and never let go.

"This is for the best. I can't let you get killed at my expense." Trace turned down the street to her house.

Jamie's white sedan sat in Kelsey's driveway.

"You won't. You're the one who's stayed with me. Even when I didn't want it at first." She let out a sad laugh.

"I'm sorry." He unlocked the car. "You need to go. Jamie's got you covered."

Trace stared straight ahead, refusing to catch a glimpse of the hurt on Kelsey's face. Otherwise, his resolve to do this might break.

Kelsey slid out and shut the door.

And with that, he backed out of her driveway and drove off.

Trace got home and flicked on the light in the foyer, then set his keys in the bowl on the entry table. The beige walls and empty space mocked him. Only a couch and TV stood ready to welcome guests.

He'd never been much of a decorator. Renee had enjoyed adding a touch of coziness to their place in Benson,

Washington. Once he'd moved back to Last Chance County, attempting to make the place homey had seemed wrong. With his work hours, it wasn't like he was here much anyway.

A knock sounded at his door.

Logan stood on his porch. "I brought some wings." He held up a Backdraft to-go bag.

"Thanks for coming over."

"You kidding? I'd rather be productive on my day off than sit around by myself."

"Let's get to work then." Trace grabbed two plates from the kitchen and led Logan to his office down the hall on the left. "I want to go back to the drawing board. Figure out how Renee's accident is connected to Kelsey."

He opened the door, and Logan whistled.

"You have quite the list of information."

Trace shrugged. "Cop instinct."

The space was covered with papers and notes. A whiteboard hung in the corner that had his most recent thoughts scribbled on it. Other information was tacked to a bulletin board, and files lay piled high on his desk.

"You sure you don't want to go back to patrolling?" Logan set three wings on a plate and licked his fingers.

"Positive. But I'd be happy to dust off my skills if I'm able to close this case once and for all." Trace followed suit and grabbed some wings.

"Where do you want to start?" Logan asked.

"From the beginning," Trace said as his mind wandered back to that day. The scene he'd pulled up to as an officer.

"Okay. Walk me through it." Logan bit into a wing.

Trace spent the next several minutes relaying everything, showing him relevant pictures and notes from the report.

"It was concluded that she lost control and, due to a frayed brake line, couldn't stop until she hit the tree." Trace sank into the chair at the desk and leaned his head back.

"There were too many variables, so the report was inconclusive."

"Did anything seem odd to you about it?" Logan tapped the chair arm rest and stared at the board.

"Yeah. There was paint along the metal rail for a good quarter of a mile."

"Almost as if she'd tried to regain control and get back on the road?" Logan asked.

"Exactly. Like someone was on her tail and wouldn't let her stay in her lane."

"I didn't know it was that bad." Logan paused, wing in hand. Sorrow and pity filled his eyes.

"Don't. There's no going back and fixing it."

"So there were no skid marks either, like Bryce noted with Kelsey," Logan continued.

"Right." Trace still remembered asking Gage Deluca, one of his officer buddies, for the files when they'd been finalized. Would he be willing to make a request to reopen the case with what Trace had discovered?

"This happened five years ago, right?"

"It might as well have been yesterday." Trace swallowed and swiveled in the chair, not wanting to think about it.

"Which means whoever did this had a connection to you back then too."

"Renee and I lived in a different city. So how does this person know where I am? Let alone Kelsey?"

"I don't know. But you shouldn't have left her high and dry, man. Something crazy is going on."

"She has Jamie." Trace didn't want to argue with his friend. He'd done the right thing. "I'm protecting her by solving this case and letting someone else cover her back. If I get too close, she'll die."

"If you want a relationship with someone, you have to get close. The best way to protect her is to stand by her. Trust me, you don't want to make the same mistake I did." Logan leaned forward in the chair and propped his elbows on his legs.

"With Jamie?"

"That's not the point. Right now, it's about you stepping up to keep Kelsey out of harm's way. You have the skills and heart to care for her." Logan waggled his eyebrows. "I've seen the way you light up when you talk about her."

Trace had brushed off his feelings for Kelsey. Logan had tried the same tactic with someone he cared for, but it hadn't worked for him.

If Trace got close to Kelsey, he risked losing another woman he loved. Being responsible for failing to save two lives was more than he could fathom.

"If I don't know who's after Kelsey, I can't control what will happen to her."

Logan shook his head and stood up. "You don't have that power. You can't control the outcome. Period. But you can do your part and trust God to work it out."

"And if I don't like the outcome?"

"Then you still trust. And run to Him as your refuge. He cares about you and has your back too." Logan slapped him on the shoulder.

Trace shifted in his seat, and his eyes landed on the Bible that sat on his bookshelf in the corner of the office. All the books collected dust because he rarely had time to sit and read.

If you want a relationship with someone, you have to get close.

Logan's words echoed in his mind.

Kelsey had found solace in the Lord despite her pain. And Logan seemed confident in trusting God. Maybe he needed to crack open the book himself. It had been a while since he'd studied Scripture. After everything that happened with Renee and their baby, what if Trace had a wrong view of who God really was?

"What else do you got?" Logan walked over to the whiteboard.

"A license plate. Tazwell got it when we watched the security footage at the hospital."

"Now that's something." Logan wrote down the letters and numbers with a marker.

"Let me see if one of my buddies can track the plate down." Gage picked up on the first ring, and Trace put his former cop friend on speaker.

"Can you run a plate number? It's KPR2001"

"Let me see what I can find." Gage clicked away on the other end.

Trace tapped his fingers against the desk. If they got a hit, they could catch this person before they struck again.

"All right. I think I found something." Gage came back over the line.

Trace sat up and grabbed a pen. "Okay, I'm ready," he said.

"The last registered owner was a Noah Riner."

He couldn't believe it. They had a solid lead. "Thanks, dude. I owe you one," Trace said.

"Do you know who Noah Riner is?" Logan asked.

"The name rings a bell. Although I'm not sure why."

Trace pulled up a web browser and did a quick search of the name. Several articles popped up, and he clicked on one from the local newspaper dated back nine years ago.

The headline read *College Student Goes Missing Weeks After Graduating.*

Trace skimmed the article and noticed two things. First, the kid had no family who seemed distraught over his disappearance. At least the article made no mention of any family comments. And second, Trace had seen the guy around campus when he'd been in school.

Trace rubbed his chin. "I recognize this guy from college." He showed Logan the picture.

"If you recognize him, he probably knows Kelsey." Logan wrote down the name on the board. "You've got to tell Kelsey, stat."

"I know." Trace scooted forward in the chair to study the image of the man on the screen. Where had Noah disappeared to, and why was his truck in Last Chance County?

26

The descending sun peeked from behind the clouds, sending rays of oranges and pinks across the sky. Kelsey wrapped herself in a blanket and stretched her legs across her couch. God had never left Kelsey. And Jamie had stuck around too. But the hurt of being abandoned by others she cared about—dare she say loved—stung. How could Trace walk away so easily after all he'd done for her and how adamant he'd been about her safety?

"I just don't understand." A tear slid down Kelsey's cheek, and she brushed it away. She refused to cry over this.

The mirror in the room taunted her. The red ink had been scrubbed off thanks to some rubbing alcohol. But the message still screamed at her.

Home-wrecker.

She destroyed people's lives.

Alice didn't like how slow Gerald's progress was in his recovery. Natalie had almost been killed because of Kelsey. And now someone hated Kelsey enough to target her like they had Renee.

"Give him some time, he'll come around." Jamie sank into the loveseat next to her.

As if on cue, Kelsey's phone dinged with a message from Trace.

TRACE

Do you remember a Noah Riner?

She set her phone on the coffee table. As much as she wanted to reply, Kelsey had no mental capacity to do so.

"Does the name Noah Riner sound familiar to you?" Kelsey shifted to face Jamie.

"Wasn't there some big news story about him?" She pulled out her phone.

"I think you're right." Sure enough, an article popped up on his disappearance. A young Noah covered the screen, the man's black, curly locks accentuating his olive skin tone. Yet his eyes appeared empty. Kelsey gasped. "I do remember this. He went to college while I was there."

She hadn't engaged with him much because he'd been a man of few words. Although, he might have joined their friend group for a few sporting events, like when their football team made it to the championship round.

"Do you have any yearbooks?" Jamie asked.

Kelsey went to her bookshelf and found the one from the year she'd graduated and set it on the table. She opened the front cover, and a collage of images splattered the page. Each face smiled back at her, memories of another time.

The good times.

Except oh, how much she'd learned in the following years about what the good life actually meant—especially when it was ladened with hardship.

Jamie slid onto the floor, crisscross applesauce style, and leaned over.

Kelsey flipped through the pages and stopped when she

spotted Trace and Renee together, smiling faces aglow. They were both dressed up, and Trace had his arm around Renee as they stood next to the emblem for the Criminal Justice Honor Society.

"I remember that day," Kelsey whispered. She'd stood on the other side of the camera, proud of her friend and cheering him on with his accomplishments while in her heart, she'd longed to stand by Trace's side.

What she wouldn't give now, though, to have Renee next to her in the flesh while her laughter filled the air. Even if that meant laying down her dream to be with Trace. She'd do it in a heartbeat.

Little had any of them known the curves life had up ahead.

No longer could her best friend come over whenever a girl's night was warranted.

"I miss her so much." Kelsey's voice cracked.

Memories of all their adventures and shenanigans circled her brain. From their monthly waffle and ice cream late-night hangouts to the intermural volleyball games. Time was precious, and it had been stolen from them all. She could still remember Renee's squeals as she'd barged into their dorm room doing a happy dance. *He asked me on a date,* she'd exclaimed.

Kelsey stared at the young Trace in the photo. Yes, the two had complemented each other well. "I never realized how fast things would change." She'd helped Renee get ready to walk down that aisle and make a lifelong commitment. A life cut too short.

"I'm sure it feels like a lifetime and only a day ago all at the same time," Jamie said. "I'm sure she'd want you and Trace to find joy in life. Whatever that looks like."

"I want him to find joy too. Even if that means only staying friends. Except he doesn't want to be around me." She sighed.

And now she had a killer on her heels who didn't want her in the picture either.

"That's not true. He's scared. There's a chance he could lose you too, and he doesn't want to risk it."

"How can you be so sure?" Kelsey flipped to another page.

"He could barely keep his eyes off you long enough to back out of the driveway when he dropped you off."

Kelsey had already admitted to Trace how she felt, so now it was up to him to decide what to do.

But what if they never found the person responsible for Renee's death? What if whoever wanted Kelsey dead succeeded as well?

She wanted answers. But they appeared elusive.

Many of her clients experienced the same challenge. Although, closure provided the ability to move forward, to accept the new life and rhythm they found themselves in and make the best of it. Call her selfish, but Kelsey wanted a reprieve as well.

Kelsey's finger trailed down the alphabetical list of names for the senior class under the *R* section.

"Right here. Noah Riner," she said.

"He seems depressed," Jamie said.

Kelsey agreed. His face remained stoic, no smile evident.

"We might have had a general education class together in the lecture hall. But if I barely remember him, what is the likelihood he remembers me?" Kelsey asked.

"Those who keep to themselves tend to be more observant of their surroundings," Jamie added.

She made a good point. Just because Kelsey hadn't been close with Noah didn't mean he hadn't had his eyes on her and Renee.

The thought sent a shiver up her spine. Although, it begged the question why.

"What about me caught his attention?"

"You're a catch, Kels. Inside and out. It's not hard for someone to notice that." Jamie smiled. "People shouldn't do it in a creepy way, though." She wrinkled her nose.

"Look. That's Noah." She pointed to a photo.

She, Renee, Trace, Noah, and Maeve all stood mid-laugh with ice-cream bowls in hand on the lawn by the residential area of campus.

"I wonder if Maeve remembers him," Kelsey said.

"It's possible."

There was one way to find out. Kelsey grabbed her phone from the table and waited as the line rang.

It went to voicemail, and Maeve's upbeat voice told the caller to leave a message.

"Hey, Maeve, it's Kels. Let's find a day to hang out soon and catch up. I also have a question for you, so give me a call back when you can." She hung up and folded her hands on the table.

"Are you hungry?"

"I could use a pick-me-up." Kelsey stood up and stretched her legs.

"Why don't we head to Backdraft? See if Maeve is on shift."

Kelsey grabbed her bag and climbed into Jamie's car.

Cars filled the parking lot when they pulled in, and music filtered its way through the restaurant as they walked inside.

A line of people waited to be seated as waiters and busboys shuffled around the tables, cleaning and seating parties. Kelsey turned to Jamie and raised her voice above all the chatter. "Let's check the bar first."

"One carbonated lemon water please." Kelsey held up her finger to the attendant.

"And one Sprite," Jamie added. The bartender took their order and went to get the drinks.

"Do you see Maeve?" Kelsey searched for her friend's blonde hair.

They stepped off to the side to let another couple sit at the bar.

"Over there," Jamie said into her ear. She pointed toward the other corner of the bar area, where she loaded pizza boxes in a delivery case.

Kelsey's stomach rumbled as a waitress passed by with a tray of loaded burgers and fries. "Let's see if we can catch Maeve before she leaves to make a delivery."

"Let's get our drinks first, then we can go over."

"Good idea."

Kelsey turned toward the TVs above the seating area as images flashed from a football game.

"Here you go." A few minutes later, the bartender set their drinks down.

"Thanks." Kelsey chugged the cold liquid and let the tangy lemon zest coat her throat. She licked her lips. "That was sweet."

"You think so?" Jamie licked her lips.

Kelsey finished off her drink and grabbed a napkin to wipe the condensation from the glass off her fingers. Maybe they added extra sugar packets with the lemon. She needed to find out so she could change her insulin intake if necessary.

Kelsey flagged down the bartender. "Excuse me. Is the lemon water sweetened or unsweetened?"

"Unsweetened." The bartender took a rag and wiped down the counter. "We just add lemon slices."

"I see. Thanks." So then why had it tasted like tablespoons of sugar had been mixed in? Kelsey recorded the drink in her phone and set a timer to check her blood sugar in half an hour.

"I still want to talk to Maeve." Kelsey shifted on the stool to face Jamie.

"Let's wait awhile. When she has a break from putting orders together, we can chat. Plus, they have a football game going right now." Jamie pointed to the TV.

Maeve was still busy when Kelsey's timer went off.

Jamie stood up to stretch. "I need some fries. That smell is making me hungry. I'll go grab a menu."

Jamie walked off to the hostess station. Kelsey headed to the restroom off to the side of the front entrance.

With each step, Kelsey's legs grew weak.

The bell overhead jingled, and Trace and Logan walked in. Kelsey's mouth dried at the sight of Trace, who walked in, shoulders back. His eyes scanned the area like he was on a mission. Were they here to talk to Maeve?

Kelsey raised her hand to get her friends' attention, and her world tilted on its axis as the ceiling came down to meet the ground.

Her vision tunneled, and in one last attempt to save face, she reached for the barstool only to have her legs go limp. Her hand slipped off the fabric, and the world cascaded to black.

27

"Kelsey!" Trace rushed past customers waiting to be seated for dinner. Her frame crumpled, and Trace dove to grab her arms. He'd dropped her off with Jamie so that she wouldn't get hurt at his expense.

So why had she passed out? Had she not eaten enough and watched her blood sugar?

Maybe Logan was right. He needed to be near Kelsey to have her back. If it wasn't a glucose issue, then Noah might be here somewhere—hidden—and he'd taken the chance to catch Kelsey off guard. Whether Trace stayed with Kelsey twenty-four seven or not, he couldn't stop something from happening. Sweat formed at the nape of his neck. He needed to trust God. But how?

Trace eased Kelsey to the ground. The last thing he wanted was her head slamming into the tile floor. He patted her cheek. "Kelsey, can you hear me?"

"She just drank a carbonated lemon water." Jamie knelt beside Trace. "She said it tasted too sweet." Jamie's voice rose a notch.

"Where's her purse?" Trace searched the ground. People

continued to walk around them, and someone brushed against his back.

"Someone had too many drinks," a woman commented to Trace's right.

"Logan, can you clear the area? We need space."

"On it." He gave Trace a thumbs-up.

"Here." Jamie handed him Kelsey's bag.

"Kels, can you hear me?" Trace leaned near her face—close enough he could smell her vanilla perfume. In any other circumstance, when she was conscious, he would have kissed those lips and drunk in her sweetness.

"I need her glucose monitor, Jamie."

Seconds ticked by and Trace almost reached for the bag himself.

"I found it." Jamie handed him the kit.

"Is her insulin in there too?"

The monitor beeped, and the number made Trace wince.

"Here you go." Jamie gave him the bottle. Trace measured it out, then pinched a fold of Kelsey's skin on her arm and injected the medicine.

"I need a cup of cold water and a towel." Trace flagged down Logan, who held people at bay.

Within seconds, Logan handed him the glass.

Trace dipped the towel, then placed it on the back of Kelsey's neck.

The sudden cold did the trick, and Kelsey's eyes flew open.

"What's going on?" she asked.

A tremor worked its way through her hand.

"It's okay. You're going to be fine." Trace rubbed his fingers along hers.

Her gaze drifted around the room. "I don't understand." She swallowed and pushed herself to a seated position. Her face remained pale, and the harsh indoor lighting didn't help. "What happened?"

"Did you eat enough today?"

"Of course." Her forehead wrinkled. Tears began to slide down her cheeks.

With her non-bandaged hand still intertwined in his, he couldn't tell anymore whose tremored. "You need to get checked out at the hospital. Make sure your levels come down to a safe zone."

More tears filled her eyes. "I don't understand. I'm doing everything I'm supposed to."

"You tracked the sugar content in your drink and put it in your food journal, right?"

"Of course." She narrowed her eyes and used her forearms to push herself up. As she straightened, Kelsey swayed to the side, and Trace held out his arms ready to catch her. "I take my health seriously. All I ordered was a fizzy water."

What if someone had spiked her drink?

"How do we know someone didn't do something to her drink?" Logan stepped forward.

He'd read Trace's thoughts.

"How? Jamie and I were at the counter the whole time." Kelsey took a step forward but tripped. She grabbed a handful of Trace's shirt to stop herself from falling.

"Let me help." Trace bent down and scooped her up. "Excuse me." He maneuvered his way through the narrow aisles.

"I can walk perfectly fine by myself, you know," she said, even while she gripped his arm.

He headed for the door. "You just passed out, for goodness' sake." Out of his peripheral vision, all eyes were on them. One child at a table stared while he gripped his straw with his teeth.

Trace repositioned his hand under Kelsey's knee, and his thumb jabbed against something hard.

"What did you—" Kelsey's eyes widened, and she leaned forward. "It's going to fall—" She reached for her leg.

In a swift move, Trace used his back to push open the door. As he shifted back around, Kelsey's legs stretched past the entrance and slammed into the doorframe.

A screech escaped her lips and something thunked on the floor. Kelsey's prosthetic leg lay on the ground. He stared. "Uh..."

Kelsey squirmed and broke free from his hold. Jamie helped her prop herself up against the wall. The hostess rushed forward and retrieved the leg, wide-eyed at the scene.

He moved in front of Kelsey to block patrons' view from inside. The least he could do with the mess he'd just created. His pulse thrummed in his ear.

Kelsey's cheeks filled with color as she lifted her pant leg. Her fingers shook and it took a few minutes for her to press the black button to reconnect her prosthetic. She wrapped her arms around her body and went to sit on the bench before changing course.

"I—" Kelsey turned in a circle. "I need to go." The door shut in Trace's face as she walked out to the parking lot.

"She's all yours, man." Logan dipped his head and sat down on a bench by the hostess area.

"I've got her purse. I'll just wait in my car until you've talked with her." Jamie brushed past him and went outside.

Trace followed Jamie outside. "Kelsey. Wait, please."

She stopped marching and spun around. Her skin paled once more, and for a moment, Trace thought she might fall over again. Instead, she planted her feet. "I think you've done enough damage for one day, don't you think?"

"Kelsey, I know you can take care of yourself, but I think you might've—"

She spun around. "Jeopardized my life? I don't know what happened in there." She swung her hand to point at the entrance. "But it's humiliating. I work hard to take care of my body, and it keeps betraying me."

She started walking again along the sidewalk, and he followed. "Where are you going?" he asked.

"Away from prying eyes right now, thanks to you." She waved her hand in the air and let out a huff.

"You can't just walk off."

"Why not? It's not like you care."

"That's not fair." He did care. More than he probably should. And it wasn't because she was a damsel in distress.

"Did you watch them make your drink?" he asked.

"I didn't think I needed to. It was just water. Plus, Jamie was right there."

Which meant someone could have easily added something to it.

"You should be more careful because of your health." He extended his hand.

She ran her fingers through her hair. "My whole life I've been told that. From my mom and doctor. They thought I was a silly girl who didn't understand my own body. Couldn't take care of myself. But I have been. Between medicine, appointments, exercise, and food, I don't know what else I'm supposed to do." She stumbled backward and bumped into the curb.

Trace wrapped his arm around her and eased her to the ground. He wanted to take her frustration away and carry it himself.

She pulled in a shallow breath, and sobs shook her body. He tucked her head against his shoulder and let the tears soak his shirt.

A family climbed out of their car and headed for the entrance, parents and two kids. All four heads turned to watch their drama unfold.

"Could you be a little quieter?" Kelsey said into his ear. "Can't this wait for a more private setting? Not in public?"

"This is important, Kels. I think someone spiked your drink.

You said it tasted extra sugary, right?" Trace leaned his head back to face her.

"I don't understand. I'm not careless. I would have seen if someone tampered with my cup."

"That's not what I'm saying. I believe you, Kels. You know what to do for your health. Although, you should have a good team of medical professionals." He used his thumb to wipe away a smudge of mascara under her eye. "But I think Noah might be behind this—lurking in the shadows. Or got Maeve to do it."

"But Maeve's my friend." Kelsey rubbed her forehead.

"Then we need to consider Noah as a suspect. I found an article about his disappearance. No one's heard from him since."

"I read that too. Do you think he's been here the whole time?"

"I don't know. It's possible."

"But why?" Kelsey echoed Trace's thought.

"Whatever his reason, we will find him. I don't want to see you get hurt. When I walked in and you wilted to the ground, I freaked out."

"You'd just left me at my house. Said you couldn't be around me."

"I was wrong." Trace rubbed his thumb along her hand. "I should have stayed by your side. Whoever is targeting you will have to go through me first. I'm falling in love with you, Kelsey."

His words hung in the air like thick smoke, and for a minute it appeared that Kelsey had stopped breathing with how still she stayed.

Then Kelsey sighed. "Trace, you caught my eye a long time ago. But I can't do this. Not now." She scooted back on the curb a few inches. "Not with all my health issues." She pointed at her leg.

"I can help you. I know a thing or two about medicine." He clasped his hands.

"I won't put that burden on you. My doctor was right. I can't take care of myself. So why should I expect someone else to? You deserve better, Trace." Kelsey stood up and tucked her hands in her pockets.

Trace opened his mouth, then clamped it shut. He'd expressed his interest in her as more than a friend. She'd already shared her feelings. So why did this feel like a breakup?

The streetlights flicked on and cast a spotlight on them as the sky grew darker.

"I need to go." Kelsey started walking.

"Where?"

"To the hospital. *You're* the one who said I need a team of medical professionals."

"Right." Trace pinched his lips.

"Where's Jamie?"

"In her car," he said.

"Great."

"I can drive you." Trace followed her.

She shook her head. "Go see if Logan needs something."

"You can always call if you need something." He took a step back.

"Right." She nodded, then turned her back to him.

As Kelsey slid into the passenger seat of Jamie's car, all Trace could see was Renee as she headed to her vehicle and drove off. Moments after their last fight. The last time he'd held her before he'd planned her funeral.

And the same feeling he'd had then snaked its way up his spine now.

He was falling hard for Kelsey.

But it didn't matter. Because he stood in the Backdraft parking lot, helpless.

A failure who couldn't do anything right or fix what was broken.

And all he could muster was one simple prayer. *Don't let the outcome be the same, Father. Please.*

Because the thought of losing Kelsey was a fear that threatened to pummel him and left him gasping for air.

28

Of all the things that could send her into diabetic shock, Trace Bently topped the list. His sweetness sent shivers of delight down her arms, and Kelsey wrapped herself in the hospital blanket the nurse had given her.

Kelsey wanted to love Trace. Especially after hearing him say that he loved her—something she'd desired for a long time.

Her mind traveled back to the restaurant the moment her leg had fallen off. A stark reminder to everyone that no matter how hard she tried to take care of herself, it backfired. She couldn't be the woman Trace needed. In her current state, she wouldn't complement him and help him flourish. She'd only hold him back with her constant health issues.

Ones she'd be scolded for again soon by the doctor and nurses. She could tell them until she was blue in the face that she took her health seriously—didn't want to live every day feeling sick and unable to have a normal life—but the test numbers and her leg told a different story.

That she hadn't learned the consequences that came with poor health.

Warmth crept into her cheeks as the *beep, beep* of the heart monitor increased. The only noise in the room.

She leaned back against the pillow. Where was Jamie? Her friend said she was just going to park the car, then she'd be in.

Thankfully, Kelsey hadn't needed to wait long, and she'd been triaged and brought back in ten minutes. An IV had been started and fluids pumped into her system. Already she could tell her body was leaving its fight or flight response.

Kelsey pushed the blanket they'd given her off to the side to let the cool air circulate.

She wanted to believe her friends would come. They'd shown that they cared. Even when she was a mess and insisting on being independent, they'd stuck around.

But how long would they be willing to do so? Especially after her attempts to keep them at a distance and given her body continued to betray her time and time again and couldn't function properly on its own.

God, I don't understand why I can't handle this. I help other people on their healing journey but can't even find healing myself.

Tears soaked her face, and she reached for a tissue to blow her nose.

Kelsey let out a humorless laugh. She was a snotty mess.

The adrenaline from the last few hours dissipated, leaving fatigue in its wake. Before she knew it, Kelsey was startled by the crinkle of paper. Her eyes flew open.

She turned to the side and the pinch of a needle squeezed the crevice of her arm.

A man in a white coat stood with his back to her at the sink, where he disposed of a paper towel in the trash.

"How long have I been out?" Kelsey shifted her legs under the blanket, trying to untangle herself. She wanted to get out of here. She didn't need another doctor peering over his glasses and chastising her for failing to take care of her body. It might be their job to assist sick people, but it wasn't like they actually cared about the patients. They checked on too many of them in such a short timespan to develop any sympathy.

The doctor turned around and glanced at her chart. "Not long since I got here." The gray stubble along his jawline and the creases under his eyes told her he had been in the practice for a long time. "I'm Dr. Welch. You had quite the adventure." He extended his hand.

Kelsey remembered him from when she'd had her car accident at the construction site. He'd rushed over to help.

Kelsey shook his hand and nodded. If only he knew.

"How long have you had diabetes?" The man raised his eyebrows, and Kelsey gripped the edge of the bed. Prepared to be scolded.

"Twenty years. Long enough I know what I'm supposed to do."

"I see." The doctor stayed silent. "Then you're a pro who knows your body and when something's off."

"I try to be." Kelsey pushed herself up in the bed. "But somehow things went haywire today."

Dr. Welch pulled out a stool and sat down. "We all have rough days. Things won't always be perfect, and that's okay."

His response reminded Kelsey of her own dad. He'd never berated her. Instead, he'd encouraged her to work hard but to remember it didn't all depend on her.

"So you're not going to chastise me for not doing a better job with my health?"

"You're not a child." Dr. Welch's kind eyes never wavered from hers. "You're capable of knowing your body's needs."

Kelsey's jaw went slack. That was not the response she expected to hear. "Thank you."

Guilt rose at her cynical thoughts from earlier. There were people who cared about others, just like she did for her clients. Like Trace and her friends did for her.

"I just don't understand." Kelsey scratched her forehead.

"Everything was fine before I went out to eat."

The doctor flipped through her paperwork. "The police called. Indicated you might have been given a hefty amount of glucose against your will." He glanced at her monitor. "If that's the case, it would explain the sudden spike in your numbers."

Trace had mentioned the same suspicion. Kelsey swallowed. She was glad the doctor had listened to the police and hadn't blamed it on her.

If they were right about her drink being spiked, who had done it? Was Noah really hiding in the shadows somewhere, stalking her every move? Or could Maeve have done it, like Trace insinuated?

No. She barely knew Noah, and Maeve was her friend.

"Your numbers look much better now than when you first got here, so I'm going to write up your discharge papers and you'll be on your way."

"I appreciate it." Kelsey grabbed her phone and texted Jamie.

KELSEY

Where are you? The doctor is releasing me. Can you give me a ride home?

Jamie must've gotten tied up somewhere, and Trace was probably busy searching for leads, so Kelsey had no ride home. *Why does it always go bad, Lord?*

The doctor exited the room and nearly collided with someone as they barreled through the doorway.

"Oof. I'm so sorry." An apology rang from the woman's lips.

"Maeve!"

Her old friend shuffled into the room and let out a huff. "I came as fast as I could after what happened." She tossed her purse on the chair and walked over to Kelsey. "How are you doing? Is everything okay?"

"I'm fine. Just too much excitement for one day." Kelsey

sighed. "How did they let you in?" Kelsey half expected a nurse to come in and say she couldn't have visitors in the ER.

"I might have told them I was your sister." Maeve gave a sheepish grin. "So they gave me a badge since there were no other guests back here already." She held up her wrist that had a yellow band wrapped around it.

"Well, I appreciate your concern." Jamie still hadn't texted her back. At least Maeve had been kind enough to show up. "I'm just waiting on the doctor to give me my discharge papers."

"Oh, good. Is Trace here?" She twisted in a half circle around the room, like he might be hiding.

Kelsey pursed her lips. "Ah, no. He had to meet up with Logan and take care of a few things."

"Do you need a ride home then?" Maeve asked in a high-pitched voice. Her eyes lit up with anticipation. "I can take you."

Kelsey forgot how animated and passionate her friend could be. It had been too long since they'd hung out and intentionally caught up.

Maeve couldn't be behind things like Trace suggested. Not when she'd shown up to check in on Kelsey. Now would be a great time to hear how Maeve was doing and also ask about Noah. See if she had any helpful tidbits of information as to what had happened to their other friend and what might be happening to Kelsey now.

"Actually, that would be wonderful, if you don't mind." Right now, her mental energy was as depleted as her physical.

"It would be my pleasure." Maeve waved her hand.

"And we can catch up at my house if you don't have anything else going on this evening."

"Sounds great." Maeve clasped her hands together. "You want anything while we wait for the discharge papers?"

Kelsey ran her tongue along the roof of her mouth, and it scraped like sandpaper. Maeve was a delivery person. She was probably used to getting things for people. She wanted to say no, so that Maeve didn't have to fetch for her, but she was also thirsty. "A bottle of water would be great." If she wanted to practice letting people in and helping her, now was the time.

"You got it. I'll be right back."

Kelsey pulled up the notifications on her phone for any missed messages.

A few work messages displayed on her home screen, but nothing urgent. And nothing from Trace or Jamie. She hated how she and Trace had left their conversation, but maybe it was for the best. It would give them both a chance to blow off steam, and she could do some of her own research in the meantime. Where Jamie had gone, Kelsey didn't know.

A knock sounded on the door. "Come in."

Maeve sauntered back in with a water bottle in hand. She twisted the cap and handed it to Kelsey. "Here you go."

"Thanks." Kelsey took a long drink. "That's refreshing."

A couple minutes later, Charlotte walked in with papers and disconnected the IV. "You're all set to go. We recommend following up with your family doctor if you have any questions or concerns."

Kelsey thanked the woman. Maeve walked beside her to the parking garage. Her legs began to move slower as they walked, and Kelsey took slow steps as they walked down the stairs to the parking level.

She'd only been sitting for a couple of hours max, and she'd taken a nap, so why did her legs seem like rubber again? Her calf muscle screamed with each movement, and she put extra weight on the handrail to assist her. Both their footsteps echoed against the concrete and made her head thrum.

She needed to get home. Take a nice long shower and get some sleep. Kelsey fought the panic. "Maeve."

Her friend pushed through the door into the parking level. Kelsey followed, but Maeve let go of the door. It slammed

Kelsey's shoulder, and her phone cracked against the concrete. "Oh no!"

"Oh, I'm so sorry." Maeve fished her keys out of her purse. "At least you can buy a new one."

Kelsey blinked, trying to make sense of what her friend had said. She bent down to grab the phone, and a shard of glass from the broken screen nicked her finger.

Her surroundings tilted as she stood. She needed to sit.

A beep sounded and headlights flashed yellow against the cement pole.

A gray convertible sat between the two white lines.

The gray paint was so similar to the one she'd seen idling by her house and at the hospital. She'd thought it was a truck, but had she been wrong?

But it couldn't be Maeve. That was too unbelievable to imagine. She'd done nothing to Maeve to warrant this woman trying to kill her.

No.

This was her old friend.

She climbed in the car. When Kelsey closed the door, the noise reverberated loudly enough that it made her wince. What if the doctor had missed something and her sugar levels weren't okay? Maybe something else was wrong with her.

"Maeve—"

Her friend climbed in. "Let's get you home."

Right. Home. "Thanks for driving." Kelsey leaned back against the headrest and closed her eyes, fighting off sleep. "I need a nap."

"I'm happy to get you where you need to go."

Now was not the time to fall asleep. Kelsey needed to ask Maeve what she remembered about Noah. She propped her arm against the windowsill, but the movement took too much effort, and her elbow slid back down to her lap.

"Do you remember Noah Riner from college?" Kelsey

leaned her head to the side, against the cool glass of the window. It took everything in her to think of what she was saying and form a coherent question.

"Noah?" Maeve huffed. "He wasn't much of a talker, and he kept to himself mostly."

Kelsey stifled a yawn. "I heard he disappeared after graduation."

Why couldn't she think straight enough to carry on a conversation? Her head spun and her eyes refused to focus. The lines on the road blurred together as cars flew past.

Kelsey said, "Something is wrong."

"He got what he deserved." Maeve sputtered the words.

"What...mean?" The question came out garbled and inaudible. She managed to get out the word "Water."

Maeve shoved the bottle at her without taking her eyes off the road. Kelsey downed more of the liquid, willing it to help her feel better. *Lord, what is going on?*

A few seconds later, nausea rolled her stomach. Kelsey focused on the mirror to keep from upheaving. She tried to shift in her seat, but her muscles refused to move, and she gagged.

"What's wrong?" Maeve rubbed her hand on Kelsey's forearm. "Not feeling too well, huh?"

Kelsey used the last of her strength to turn her head toward Maeve. A smirk formed on her friend's face.

Kelsey tried to speak, but her head pounded and dizziness encircled her.

"Don't worry, it'll all be over soon," Maeve said in a singsong voice. "You'll be a memory, just like Noah."

Kelsey tried to grope for her purse and locate her phone. She needed to alert someone. Except her phone was broken. Whatever Maeve had put in her drink worked fast. Unable to fight the effects, Kelsey let her body drift into unconsciousness once more.

29

"I need you to get me the information, stat," Trace growled into the phone. He paced the length of the conference room at the fire station.

After Kelsey drove off with Jamie to the hospital, Logan had urged him to come back to the station, where they could run ideas off each other—get Macon's or Andi's input too. It was better than staring at all the notes in his home office by himself.

Kelsey might see herself as a liability, but Trace wasn't willing to accept that view. Someone had proven the lengths they were willing to go to get Kelsey out of the way. She might not want him by her side at the hospital, but he would have her back here.

And it started with the information Gage might be able to give him.

"Aye, aye, grumpy," Gage's voice echoed through the phone in response. His friend had been a cop when they'd worked together in Benson, Washington. Now he ran the SWAT team there. Gage had witnessed the tragedy of Renee's death and the impact it had on Trace. But he'd also been a great partner on the force, and Trace had trusted him with his life, literally too many times to count.

Logan leaned against the wall, his eyebrow raised. *Take a deep breath, man,* he mouthed.

"Sorry. Something's not adding up and it's driving me crazy." Trace ran a hand down his face and massaged his jaw.

"I'll do my best to get something back to you, stat," Gage said.

"Thanks, man, I appreciate it." Trace hung up and groaned. The way he'd left things with Kelsey grated on his nerves.

He cared for her as more than a friend. And the reality that he was falling in love with her gave him pause.

He chewed on the words. Yes, he was. And he would do anything for her.

Several times in the last few hours he'd wanted to rush to Kelsey's side. He'd called twice, but she hadn't picked up. She'd been adamant about leaving her alone, yet his gut churned with uneasiness.

What if something else happened and he wasn't there to stop it?

Or he could be overreacting and she was safe at the hospital. He wanted to respect her wishes to have space, but he wouldn't leave her if she was in trouble. There was only one way to confirm Kelsey's whereabouts and safety.

"Have you talked to Jamie?" Trace paced the room.

"No." Logan folded his arms. "Why would I have?"

"To make sure Kelsey's okay." He'd texted Jamie for an update, but she hadn't gotten back to him yet. Trace chewed on his pencil. "There has to be a connection somehow."

"We need to find out where Noah is. If we can pin that down, we might have a solid lead." Logan tapped his knuckles on the table.

"You're right. The biggest question right now is why his car would be in Last Chance County so many years after his disappearance." Trace drew a question mark on the white board next to Noah's name. "Did you catch Maeve while I was outside with Kelsey?"

"She'd already left to make a delivery." Logan frowned.

A rap sounded on the door, and Zack poked his head in. "Pizza's here if you want some."

"From where?"

"Only the best place in town." Zack's expression beamed.

Trace dodged past Zack. He got outside just as the delivery person opened their car door.

"Wait," he yelled. He needed to talk to Maeve.

The person turned around, and Trace's shoulders sank. A teenage boy had made the delivery. "Is Maeve Wells still working tonight?"

"Nah. She took off almost an hour ago. Said she wasn't feeling well." The guy tossed the empty insulated bag in the car. "Left the rest of us to handle the hungry crowd."

"Thanks for your help. Have a good night." Trace kicked a pebble on the pavement and made his way back inside.

"Any luck?" Logan met him in the hall.

"Nada." Something needed to give. Trace hated the fact he was walking in circles right now like a hound dog that had lost the scent on the trail.

"I've got to figure this out before it's too late and this person strikes again." The thought that a killer might plan their next move and attack while Kelsey was left unattended punched him in the gut. He didn't like that Jamie hadn't touched base either.

Kelsey was capable of watching her back, but Trace wanted the privilege of protecting her. He wanted her to need him. And her response earlier screamed the opposite, like her needing him was a bad thing.

But she didn't realize he needed her just as much.

"Why is God making me go through this all over again? It just seems cruel." Trace stopped and stared at the ceiling.

"You've got to get close to Him, man. Doesn't mean you'll have all the answers, but You'll see Him more clearly."

"How can you be so sure?" Trace squinted at Logan.

"When you hit rock bottom, He has a way of showing up. Doesn't matter what it is. If you trust Him, He'll use it for your good and His glory."

"Yeah, well, I'm not a huge fan of whatever route He's taking to do it."

"Doesn't make it easy. I've been there. But He's more concerned with this." Logan tapped his chest, right above his heart. "Often times the pain is a chance to run to God. To find refuge in and compassion from Him. He understands sorrow and hardship. That Bible you have..."

"Yeah."

"Try opening it more often. Maybe turn to 2 Corinthians 1. You'll be surprised with what you find."

Even when life pummeled him with waves that attempted to hold him down, Trace wanted to have a firm foundation. Logan appeared so calm in the midst of the chaos.

"Okay." Trace nodded. "Let's do it together sometime."

"Deal." Logan slapped him on the back. "You don't need to solve this alone either." Logan pointed to the conference room. "I pulled Andi and Macon in. They're ready to help."

"Fill us in on what we need to know." Macon reclined in a chair at the table.

Trace sat down across from him. "Kelsey passed out, and Jamie took her to the hospital." He inhaled. "We had a fight. Now she doesn't want me around."

Macon leaned into the table and clasped his hands. "We're here for you. If we work as a team, we can split up tasks and hopefully get answers faster."

He filled Macon and Andi in on their findings about Noah

and the tampered brakes. How he was concerned about Noah hanging around or getting Maeve to dose her with something.

The door opened and Natalie walked in with a smile.

"I'm glad you're feeling better," Trace said, considering the state he and Andi had found her in after the seizure.

"It's good to be up and moving." She pulled up a chair next to Macon and wrapped her arm around his. "God was certainly gracious. No long-term effects. *And* I can eat real food again."

"How'd you know we ordered pizza?" Macon gawked.

"I have intel." Natalie laughed.

Trace appreciated how the crews had enfolded Natalie in like one of their own.

"What's this meeting for?" Natalie looked around the room.

They filled her in on what happened, and she frowned.

"Have you heard from Kelsey today?" Trace asked.

"No, but I'll text her right now." Natalie grabbed her purse.

"If she's in danger, you can call the PD. Get an officer posted on her door." Macon pulled out his phone.

"That'll make her more furious." Trace paced a couple of steps. "We should alert hospital security at least."

Macon made the call.

"Kelsey's not answering her phone." Lines creased Natalie's forehead.

"Maybe they took her for tests." Trace let out a slow breath.

"Negative." Macon shook his head. "The hospital said she was discharged already too."

"Maybe she's on her way home." Trace tapped his foot.

"Go check on her." Logan waved his hand. "We'll cover things here and find Maeve."

Trace stood just as his phone rang. Gage's name lit up the screen, and Trace hoped he had some helpful information. He swiped with his thumb. "What did you find?" Trace put the call on speaker.

"Noah Riner was found dead, burned in a car."

Andi gasped.

"And no one wondered where he was?" Trace couldn't imagine family or friends not caring about their loved one's disappearance.

"Apparently not. His case was considered a John Doe until they were able to salvage a print to put through the system."

Trace let out a whistle. "What else?"

"The car he was found in belonged to Max Wells, a mechanic in Idaho."

"Nowhere near Benson or Last Chance County," Trace said. "So who reported the stolen car?"

"The owner, Max Wells."

Trace ground his teeth.

Logan said, "How does a dead guy's car wind up in Last Chance County?"

"Your guess is as good as mine," Gage added.

Trace said, "Do you have a number for Max or a shop website?"

"Sure do." Gage rattled off the phone number and web address.

"Thank you for everything. I owe you." Trace hung up.

Macon already had his laptop out and typed away. Trace moved behind him to glance at the screen.

"I'll try Kelsey again," Andi said in a hushed voice.

"I've got Jamie," Logan added.

Trace dialed the shop and listened to it ring. He stared at the antiquated webpage. Max Wells clearly hadn't taken time to stay on top of the technological advances with the small print and minimal information.

"Well's Autobody Corner. How can I help you?" The man's voice sounded hoarse and out of breath, and Trace pictured him rubbing grease off his forehead.

"May I speak with Max Wells, please?"

"You're talking to him," Max said.

"I'm investigating a report you filed a few years back on a missing vehicle. A Cadillac Escalade."

The man grunted on the other end. "That was a nice car, ruined from what the police told me. Melted to the ground. It was such a shame."

"Any idea who would have stolen it?" Trace drummed his fingers on the table.

"People are always looking for a way to get their hands on a luxury car. Serves me right for buying it. But if I had to take a guess, it was probably my deadbeat daughter."

Macon scrolled down the homepage screen.

"Why do you say that?"

"She always wanted to live a picture-perfect life. The moment anyone messed up, they were replaceable in her mind."

Trace couldn't imagine living with that mentality. Especially with how often he messed up. Like he'd done with Kelsey. He hoped she would forgive him.

"I couldn't get ahold of Jamie." Logan tossed his phone onto the table and rubbed his face.

Trace took a deep breath. He wouldn't panic. "Does the name Noah Riner ring a bell to you?" he asked Max.

"That girl was always bringing home a new man; I could never keep track," Max said. "Still emails me every week about some guy these days. Whatever his name is."

Trace pointed to the About tab so Macon could pull it up. He wanted to put a face to the person he spoke with.

Andi waved to get Trace's attention, her eyes wide. "Kelsey didn't answer either."

Macon tapped Trace's arm. He turned back to the screen. About halfway down the page, Macon's finger froze and hovered over the mouse.

Trace gulped. "You've got some nice pictures of your family on the website." He squeaked the words out. He rubbed his eyes as if that would change what he saw.

"Yeah, well, I don't have time to update a website, so it'll stay like that for now." Max's voice drifted into the distance. "Excuse me, but I have a customer to take care of."

Before Trace could respond, the line went dead.

"You know who that is?" Trace's voice quivered. A young face smiled back at him in the photo, the person's eyes taunting him like they were the star of the show and he was only a pawn.

In the picture, a spitting image of Maeve stood next to her dad, holding a wrench.

Trace pushed back the chair, and it slammed onto the floor with a clang. How had he missed the signs? "She's been behind this the whole time," he hollered.

"We'll find her, Trace." Macon closed his laptop and stood.

"Kelsey's not answering her phone. Jamie is nowhere to be found." He clenched his fist. The veins in his arm bulged. "What if it's already too late?" Perspiration trickled down his forehead. "How did I not pick up on this?"

"You had no reason to." Natalie used her calm counselor tone. Except it did nothing to soothe his turmoil.

"Actually, I did. She's been obsessed with me for a while. I just never thought anything of it." Her advance the other day when he was cleaned the ambo. Even when he'd broken up with her in college, she'd never accepted the fact they weren't together anymore.

"You've got to trust God," Logan said.

"I can't lose Kelsey." Trace spun around and grabbed his jacket. He pulled out his keys and sprinted down the hall.

"Where are you going?" Logan raced after him.

"Wherever I need to in order to find Kelsey." He opened his passenger door and unlocked the glove box.

"Let us help you find her, Trace." Logan came up short beside him. "You don't have to do this alone."

"This is my fault. I'm the one who's going to save her." He pulled out his backup Glock and shoved it in his waistband.

Maeve had seen the whole escapade when Kelsey fainted. And she hadn't been at Backdraft later. She'd gone home sick.

Trace could only imagine what her real reason for leaving early had been.

"I'm going to Maeve's house. I want answers, and she's the one who has them." He climbed in the driver's seat and rolled down the window. "If you find out anything in the meantime, call me." Trace peeled out of the lot.

"Come on, Kelsey. Pick up." He slammed his hand against the steering wheel. After another ring, the call went to voicemail again, and Trace pressed harder on the gas.

He had to find Kelsey.

Had Maeve killed Renee the same as she'd killed Noah?

If so, was she going to kill Kelsey now as well?

30

K elsey's pulse pounded through her temples.

She moaned and turned her head. The motion sent a wave of dizziness that crashed over her, and she shut her eyes so she wouldn't throw up. The effects of the drug Maeve had given her tricked her mind into thinking she was on the worst amusement park ride ever, and Kelsey wanted off.

"Maeve." The word sounded slurred to her ears, barely a moan.

A putrid smell of rotten eggs and car exhaust wafted through the air to invade her nostrils without permission. She went to lift her hand to cover her nose, but her wrists clung to each other and wouldn't move.

Ever so slowly, she opened her eyes.

Brown rope was wound around her hands, which were tied to the steering wheel. The frayed edges stuck out and made her skin itchy, but she had no way of scratching to relieve the sensation.

"Maeve." Where was that woman?

She rested against the headrest. A light bulb dangled in

front of the car from the ceiling. The storage space was cluttered with tools, and a rack of old clothes was shoved in the corner. If this was Maeve's house, it needed major cleaning. Cobwebs lined the crevices along the wall, and crickets chirped somewhere.

Kelsey stifled a yawn, a reaction to the stress and all the adrenaline in her system fighting with the drug that made her drowsy. How long had she been knocked out? There was no way to determine how late it was.

Her mind began to piece the events of the last few hours together. The fight she'd had with Trace, and Maeve picking her up at the hospital. Her "friend" had offered to drive her home, and then...

Whose garage was she in? Where was Maeve?

Kelsey strained to hear, but only silence greeted her.

She used her elbow to hit the unlock button. Now all she needed was a way to free her hands so she could find a way out and call for help. She lifted her upper body and tilted her head to the side to turn on the overhead light.

If Maeve was flying solo, Kelsey had a greater chance of taking her out. But if other people were involved—she shuddered at the thought.

Kelsey shuffled her feet along the floorboard in an attempt to locate anything that could be used to get out of these ropes. A credit card, tweezers, something. Except her shoes only swiped the air.

She let out a groan. With her phone broken, no one could track her location either.

How had Maeve fooled Kelsey for so long? Her friend was broken and deceived. Kelsey's heart ached for Maeve. But at the same time, she was terrified of her.

She'd trusted Maeve. And what had she gotten in return? Betrayal.

Kelsey had walked away from Trace. Jamie was nowhere to

be found. She hadn't even talked with Natalie since she'd been poisoned.

Lord, I have nowhere else to turn. I need You.

Tears trailed down her cheeks, but she couldn't wipe them away. With her hands bound, she wouldn't get out of this mess in her own strength.

I'm so sorry, God. Kelsey dipped her head. She'd done everything to help others while pushing away those who wanted to help her. Including God. She hadn't cast her burdens on Him.

Jamie and Savannah Wilcox had been right. It wasn't wrong to ask for help. It didn't make her inferior or less capable.

In the midst of the unknown and what lay ahead, the verse from Matthew 11:28 came to mind. Peace washed over her. Kelsey lifted her head and closed her eyes. God would help her find strength and rest. All she had to do was come to Him.

There were people who cared about her. She wasn't an inconvenience. Trace had put aside his own needs to protect her. Wilcox and Tazwell had spent hours of work sifting through evidence.

Most importantly, Jesus cared.

He had been with her every step of the way. Keeping her safe. Giving her a community of true friends. And He would strengthen her and never abandon her. All she needed to do was call upon Him. Depend on Him.

Lord, whatever happens, show me that You're enough. That I'm not a burden to You but loved by You. I need You.

Footsteps descended into the garage. Light streamed from the doorway.

Kelsey shivered.

"It'll all be over soon. She'll get what she deserves," Maeve muttered to herself.

The light illuminated a plethora of tools that hung on the wall to Kelsey's left.

At least a wide variety of self-defense weapons stood at the ready—If she could find a way out of the car without Maeve noticing.

Her former friend approached the tool shelf, and Kelsey shut her eyes. No need to alert Maeve to her consciousness. It could give Kelsey an advantage, and she could kick Maeve if she got close, since her legs weren't bound.

Clangs resounded in the small space, and Kelsey did her best to not wince.

She focused on breathing in and out the way she always told her clients to do.

Don't focus on what isn't or what could be. She had to ground herself in the present moment. Find ways to stay alert to what was happening now. Otherwise, her body would shift into fight or flight response.

Her pulse quickened, and she fought the urge to let panic set in.

The smell of gasoline tickled her senses again. This time, Kelsey opened her eyes and peered out the rearview mirror. Maeve hunched over the back of the car with a giant red bottle that gushed liquid from its spout.

Kelsey jerked forward in her seat. She wasn't going to be burned alive. Or even stick around long enough to find out if that was Maeve's intent. *God, I need a way out of here.*

She rubbed and twisted her wrists together against the rope.

"C'mon," Kelsey whispered and trained her eyes on Maeve.

The bandage rubbed her raw skin, the area already tender and dry from the fall air. A sharp prick sent pain through her hand, and blood trickled along the side of her thumb. The same shade of red as her cold fingers.

Tears welled in her eyes, and Kelsey blinked them away.

Her muscles still moved slowly, and her body protested the change of pace from the stupor she'd been in. She shifted in the seat to give more leverage to her wrists and propped her elbow on the window ledge. Another twist, and her right hand slid halfway out of the bondage.

A shriek pierced the air, and Kelsey's heart skipped a beat. She dropped her hand to her lap and froze. In her peripheral vision, the gasoline canister soared through the air and slammed into the tool bench. The force sent a wrench and hammer tumbling to the concrete floor.

"Where is that stupid lighter?" Maeve shouted.

The woman wasn't concerned about anyone else hearing her tantrum. She stormed past the car without a second glance and walked back into the house. The door shut with a resounding thud, enough that it shook the car.

Kelsey sat up straight and jerked her other wrist until it came free. A cry of relief escaped her lips. There were only seconds to spare before her window of opportunity would shrink into a black hole.

She pushed open the door and almost slipped in the liquid. It took her a moment to steady her wobbly legs, and Kelsey held her breath.

The smell of gas enclosed the space, and she let out a cough.

Without hesitation, she grabbed a hammer off the tool bench and clutched it against her side. She spun around in search of the best exit.

With the top up on the convertible, the Chevy SSR trunk created the appearance of a truck bed. A *gray* truck.

Kelsey gasped.

Maeve had been the one who'd run her off the road. And sat in the parking lot of the hospital waiting for a chance to cut her brakes.

Maeve had premeditated all of this.

Kelsey needed an escape.

Her shoulders drooped when she realized the only way out was by opening the garage door.

A window on the other side of the garage was blocked by a stack of pots and metal boxes. It would take too long to get everything out of the way.

The button for the garage sat mounted by the door that led into the house—the same door Maeve had disappeared behind. Kelsey gingerly took steps toward the wall. Her body ached, and her sluggish limbs didn't want to move. Each footstep made her muscles tense. It was only a matter of time before she was caught red-handed.

She reached for the door and slammed a hand down on the opener. *God, help me.*

The pulley system screeched as the door began to lift. A blast of cold air swirled into the space. Kelsey spun around to sprint toward freedom.

Her prosthetic foot hit a patch of gasoline and slid out from under her. Kelsey slammed her hands down on the door frame. She caught herself before she fell, but the hammer clattered to the ground. The door rose far too slowly, but it was enough she could roll underneath.

A thud came from the trunk of the car. Kelsey stopped. The sound grew louder. She turned back, ducked under the still rising door, and unlocked the hatch.

"Jamie!" she whispered. Her friend tumbled out, gagged and hands bound in front of her.

The door swung open behind Kelsey.

She made the mistake of looking back when she should have grabbed Jamie and dove for freedom. Maeve hit the door opener, and the door whined back down. She wore a stone-cold gaze, her eyes lethal. A lighter dangled from her hand. "Where do you think you're going?"

Kelsey dove for the partially open door, but it thudded shut.

A hand clamped down on her ankle. Kelsey kicked and screamed, trying to shake off Maeve's grasp. "Let go of me."

"Not a chance," Maeve shouted back through clenched teeth.

Kelsey rolled and kicked at Maeve, but the weight of her prosthetic leg didn't break the woman's grip on her ankle. She stretched her arm and managed to grasp the hammer. Kelsey slammed it down on Maeve's hand.

She screamed and let go of Kelsey's ankle. Kelsey scrambled away and positioned herself on the other side of the car. Maeve now stood guard between her and the door to the house. The garage door was down.

How was she going to get out of here?

Jamie stayed crouched by the trunk, out of view.

"You will not get away with this." Maeve stood up and took a step toward the vehicle.

"Get away with what? What did I ever do to you?" Kelsey spoke between breaths. Her lungs burned from the gasoline fumes, and all she wanted to do was collapse on the ground.

She needed the strength to get out of here.

Lord, I don't have any. I need Yours.

"You don't know?" Maeve scoffed. "Clearly you turned a blind eye."

Kelsey inched closer to the garage door while Maeve's gaze darted around the room. "I don't know what you're talking about."

"Stop." Maeve flung the lighter in the air.

Kelsey froze.

"You took what belonged to me." Maeve's red face stood in contrast to the blonde hair now mussed and knotted. The expression was one Kelsey had never witnessed before.

This woman hadn't ever been her friend.

Kelsey didn't know who she was.

If she was going to get out of here, she had to convince

Maeve not to burn both of them alive. She had to get this woman to see reason. That killing Kelsey wasn't the best course of action for her.

"Let's talk this through." Kelsey softened her voice and held up her hands. If she treated this like a client situation, there was a chance she and Jamie would make it out alive. "Tell me. What did I take from you?"

"Everything. My life, my dreams, my man."

"What are you talking about?" Kelsey focused on Maeve, whose finger hovered too close to the ignition on the lighter. One flick and the entire garage would go up in flames.

"Trace." Maeve let out a huff. "You took Trace from me."

None of this made sense. Kelsey wasn't in a relationship with Trace and she never had been. "I think you're mistaking me for Renee. I don't understand. I haven't taken Trace from you."

"Don't call me a liar." Maeve slammed her hand on the hood of the car. "You'll regret it. Just like the rest of them."

Kelsey retreated back and collided with the wall. She held up her arms. "No one's calling you anything. Why don't we take a deep breath and figure this out. Like friends."

"You were never my friend," Maeve spat. Her saliva landed on the windshield. "You clearly didn't learn the first time."

"What do you mean?" Kelsey had to get to the root of this problem in order to understand why Maeve thought her actions were justified. "Because I thought we were friends. All of us. You, me, Trace, and Renee."

Maeve screamed. "Don't say her name to me! She betrayed me. Whisked him away without even a second glance at me. Took my life. My future. But I took care of her. She took everything from me, so I took everything from *her*. Then you sauntered back into the picture."

"I was never in the picture with him." Kelsey's breath caught, and she thought she might hurl. Someone she'd trusted as a friend had murdered one of their group—and possibly Noah as well. Now she'd been trying to kill Kelsey. She balled her good hand into a fist, wanting to say something. Words wouldn't form on her lips.

"You liked him in college," Maeve growled. "I thought I could take care of it. But it didn't change. I see the way he looks at you now," Maeve screamed. "Like you're more to him than just a friend. Once again, Trace left me on the sidelines. After the way I've loved him all these years?"

"I think you..." Kelsey didn't finish.

"You are a home-wrecker," Maeve snarled.

"You broke into my house." Kelsey stood taller. She needed to hear the confession from Maeve's lips.

"Clearly it didn't deter you. Neither did the car accidents. I thought for sure the spikes in your blood sugar would send you to an early grave."

"What are you saying?" Kelsey narrowed her eyes and propped her hand on the car's exterior mirror.

"I spiked your drinks and food. I wanted to make you suffer for the pain you've caused me. I thought for sure Trace would turn to me for consolation after all the devastation he's been through."

The garage space grew hot, and Kelsey couldn't breathe. No wonder her insulin needs had been unpredictable lately. Her chest tightened. She blinked to clear the haze from her eyes.

"I don't—"

Maeve lifted the lighter. "Enough. Soon this will all be over, and the grieving man will only have eyes for me when I sweep in to comfort him from two devastating losses."

"You don't have to do this," Kelsey pleaded. "There's always another way."

In the mirror, Kelsey watched Jamie inch forward. With her bound hands, Jamie held up a finger to her lips.

"Not this time." Maeve stretched out the hand with the lighter.

A knock sounded on the door.

Maeve froze.

Was it friend or foe? Before Kelsey could decide what to do, Maeve twisted and slammed her elbow into Kelsey's back.

Kelsey rolled on her ankle and fell.

Gasoline soaked through her clothes. If Maeve lit the fumes, she and Jamie would be gone. She had admitted her failings to God. Only He could rescue her now. But she hadn't been able to make things right with Trace.

Now it was too late.

31

Trace pounded on Maeve's front door again. With his hand raised, his jacket caught on the edge of his gun holster and tugged. The weapon provided little comfort. He wouldn't be able to defend Kelsey if he couldn't find her. He'd let her walk away, and for all he knew, she could already be dead.

God, how can I trust You and live with that again?

Maeve's duplex sat at the end of a row of homes. A porch swing beckoned for visitors to sit down for a while. A single light mounted on the siding illuminated the evening hour. The pristine house stood in stark contrast to what hid inside. Maeve was deceptive, playing the role of friend while she breathed murder.

Trace groaned and laced his hands behind his neck.

He hadn't been able to control the outcome then, and there was no way to control the outcome with Kelsey now.

Logan was right. He needed to trust God. He couldn't put the pressure on himself to save everyone. He'd only end up disappointing himself. He had already added an undue burden to his job.

God, I don't know how You could use this for good, but give me eyes to see. Right now, there's no way I can be the hero. I want to rely on You. I need You to deliver us.

Trace hit the door once more.

If his incessant pounding didn't alert someone inside, it would certainly draw the neighbors' attention.

If Maeve didn't answer, he'd call Basuto and get a warrant to search the place. They were losing time they didn't have to find Kelsey.

"Coming." Maeve's sultry voice echoed inside.

She opened the door and smiled.

Her feigned enthusiasm did nothing to hide her disheveled appearance. Her blonde hair was knotted and tangled. Her face had streaks of dirt, and caked blood covered her chin.

Trace took a step forward. "I need your help." He brushed past her into the entryway. "To answer a few questions." Trace had to act like he didn't know she was behind the attacks. Otherwise, he might not get any information out of her on Kelsey's whereabouts.

"I'm so glad you're here." She put her hand on his bicep and winced. She lifted her hand away. Her fingers were red and swollen, and blood oozed from a cut on her palm.

"What happened?" Had she used that hand to strike Kelsey? He steeled his feet on the hardwood floor.

"Oh, this?" She waved. "It's nothing. I dropped a hot pot. Went to catch it and it hit my hand." She laughed. "Silly me."

"Why don't I take a look at it for you?" Trace followed Maeve into the kitchen and scanned each room on their way. "Have you heard from Kelsey at all?"

Maeve pouted. "Why worry about what she's up to? I'm the one who's hurt." She laid her hand on the counter.

Trace ripped a paper towel off the roll and soaked it in water. How could this woman be so self-centered? "She got sick, Maeve. Had to go to the hospital."

"That's right." Maeve gasped. "She did pass out at Backdraft."

"I wanted to run some questions by you, but I couldn't find you afterward at the restaurant."

"You were looking for me?" Maeve smirked and a slow smile curled on the edge of her lips.

Trace refrained from rolling his eyes. "A coworker said you went home early."

She pouted. "Because of this stupid burn."

From a brief inspection of the wound, Trace could tell it was not a burn incident. She'd lied to him. From the way it was swollen and red, she'd jammed it in something.

"Hold this on the cut." Trace handed her the wet cloth. "Kelsey's not answering her phone, and hospital staff said she got discharged. I'm afraid she's hurting and alone."

Maeve's forearm stiffened. Her blue eyes turned to ice. "I'm the one who's been alone." She scooted closer to Trace. The smell of gasoline wafted from her clothes.

He wrinkled his nose. "What's that smell?"

A clang sounded. Then a thud.

Maeve shot out of her seat. Trace reached into the side of his jacket. His hand clamped down on the weapon.

"Don't worry about it." She tossed the paper towel on the counter. "I'll be right back. Please don't go anywhere," she pleaded. "I'm so glad you're here."

Maeve walked down the hall and slipped through the door. It slammed shut.

Trace followed behind, ready to investigate the sound himself. Was Kelsey here and trying to signal for help? He hadn't gotten anything out of Maeve—yet. But God would help him find Kelsey. He had to trust Him.

A glare glinted off the doorknob to another room in the hall. Trace pushed it open. The door squeaked on its hinges.

"Hello?" He peeked his head inside.

The streetlight shone through the cracks in the window blinds. Trace flicked on the light switch and stumbled back.

Pictures covered the room and made his blood pressure soar.

On one wall, his name was written in marker. Under it, Renee's, Kelsey's, and Noah's names were listed with giant red X's.

Trace ran his finger along the images. Maeve had a section dedicated to his wedding day. Except she'd plastered her face over top of Renee's. Underneath it were images from the car crash, which hung next to articles about the tragic incident. What was pinned right below it made him want to hurl.

A picture of Renee's headstone hung with a note: *Until death did them part.*

Trace bit down on his finger. Was he in a dream? Bile rose in his throat.

Maeve had killed Renee.

Trace slammed his fist against the wall.

She'd been behind the hit and run. She'd tampered with Renee's brakes. The nerve of that woman to show up at Renee's funeral and offer her sympathies.

Now she wanted to take out Kelsey. But so far, her plan hadn't succeeded.

Trace wanted to handcuff that woman himself and haul her down to the station.

He had to trust God for justice though. Surely there was enough evidence here to prosecute her.

Trace examined the rest of the room. Several shots of Kelsey were tacked to the wall. Each one had a red X through it. Images taken unbeknownst to her, including when she'd been reading in the park. And when she'd played tennis with Jamie.

Another section displayed photos of Noah next to a printed-out text conversation. Trace skimmed the messages and exhaled. Noah had professed his love for Maeve. That he could make her happy. Told her to move on from Trace. At the bottom of the sheet, she'd written *paid for* with a check mark. A picture of the car where Noah had been found in flames.

Trace whipped out his phone and snapped several images of the room.

TRACE

You've got to see this.

Trace texted Logan before hitting the call button.

"I think I might've found Kelsey," Trace gasped. "Did you see the images?"

"Dude, this is sick. I'm sending them over to Wilcox right now."

"This is enough proof to warrant her arrest," Trace spat. If this weren't evidence, he'd take every last one of those pictures and rip them to shreds.

A scream pierced the air, and Trace nearly dropped his phone.

"What was that?" Logan hissed.

"Kelsey!" Trace shouted. "Get the police here stat. Whatever Maeve has planned, it's not good." He rattled off Maeve's address.

Trace raced from the room and barreled into someone.

"Oomph."

Trace staggered back and pulled his gun. "Jamie?" His brow furrowed.

"She—she's going to kill her." Jamie's hands shook. "She told me to run and get help."

"Where is she?" Trace whipped his head around.

"The garage. Over there." She pointed as best she could with her hands bound in front of her. Jamie took a step toward the front door.

"Wait. Let me help." Trace pulled out a pocketknife. "Give

me your hands." He slit through the ropes and tossed them to the ground.

"Thanks." She rubbed her wrists.

"Go. Get out. Cops are on the way." Trace sprinted for the door Maeve had disappeared behind earlier.

He whipped open the door and stepped down.

Maeve's finger hovered over the button that would ignite the flame on the lighter.

Kelsey stood over in the corner by the closed garage door, cradling her arm. Her cheeks were flushed, and wet clothes clung to her body. No water appeared evident. Which meant…

The smell of gasoline permeated the space. If they stayed in here much longer, they'd all pass out from the fumes.

Dear God. I have no way of protecting her. Please watch over her. Over us. If Maeve lit the garage, Kelsey wouldn't stand a chance. Her clothes would combust immediately.

Maeve spun around. "I told you I'd be right back."

"And let you murder Kelsey too? Not a chance." Trace stepped down onto the cement floor. One wrong move and the flame in Maeve's hand would kill them.

"She doesn't deserve you," Maeve shrieked.

"Neither did Renee according to you." Trace held his gun pointed down. He couldn't get a clear shot in this space without risking a bullet ricocheting and hitting Kelsey.

"Which is why I took care of her."

Kelsey gasped and let out a cry.

"Get back inside the house, Trace," Maeve yelled.

"You set fire to this place, we're all going with it." He focused his gaze on Kelsey and gulped. Right now, the outcome didn't appear favorable.

Even if Kelsey died like Renee—

Trace tried to pull in a breath. The smell was too strong.

Even if Kelsey died like Renee, God would sustain him. Somehow. He had to believe it.

Whatever the outcome, Lord, I trust You. God would be Trace's comfort, just like Scripture said.

Maeve held a steely gaze on him, waiting for him to comply with her orders.

Trace refused to leave without Kelsey.

In the corner, Kelsey pointed to the garage door and lifted her finger.

In his peripheral, the door opener was mounted to his left. All he had to do was extend his hand back. If Kelsey could escape, it didn't matter what happened to him.

Thank You, Lord.

Trace whipped his hand back and slammed the button. The garage door groaned and lifted on its hinges.

"What are you doing?" Maeve raced at him.

"Run, Kelsey!" he shouted.

"No. She will not get away." Maeve swung around, and Trace grabbed her arm. She took her other hand and punched him in the jaw. The sudden blow disoriented him for a second.

Cold, fresh air filtered into the space. The added oxygen helped him regain composure.

But it was too late.

Maeve flicked open the lighter.

Before he could grab it, she tossed it on the ground.

"No!" he yelled.

Kelsey scrambled toward the moving door.

Maeve reached behind him and pushed open the door to the house. Trace tackled her to the floor inside.

A rush of air and fiery flames rose behind them as the garage ignited in a ball of fire.

32

Kelsey raced down the driveway of Maeve's house. The force of the blaze rippled heat across the yard. She stumbled forward and her legs hit the pavement. Kelsey pushed herself up and brushed off the pebbles embedded in her palm, the skin under the bandage on her left hand burned from the impact. A cough escaped her lungs, and it took everything in her not to bend over and heave. To call it quits.

Her leg muscles screamed in protest, and her head swam. Beads of sweat trickled down her forehead.

The flames rose high in the night sky.

Trace.

She turned around. The garage was engulfed with flames. She could make out part of the Chevy SSR where the gasoline added more fuel to the fire. The heat sent a ripple of waves over her vision and made it difficult to make out anything else.

She couldn't see Trace. Or Maeve.

Kelsey collapsed on the grass several yards away from the burning house and sobbed. This is what it must feel like to lose someone you love. To never get the chance to say one more time that you love them.

In her stubbornness, Kelsey had pushed Trace away. She'd lost him. All because she hadn't been strong enough to be the woman he needed her to be. Hadn't wanted him to bear her burdens.

Kelsey wiped her nose along her sleeve. But that was love. Walking with someone through thick or thin. Just like God, who'd never left her side. Now she'd never get a chance to tell Trace the truth. She wanted him close. To have the chance to love every part of Trace Bently.

"Kelsey." Someone called her name.

Kelsey turned around in the yard. Jamie waved her hands above her head and raced toward her.

"Jamie!" Kelsey tried to push herself up but collapsed back onto the ground.

"You're alive." Jamie crouched and enveloped her in a hug. "The explosion. And flames," she whimpered. "I thought..."

"Trace." She hiccupped. "Trace is still in there." Kelsey pointed to the house.

Jamie took Kelsey's arm and hoisted it over her shoulder to help her stand.

Sirens cracked the silence of the neighborhood street. The fire truck horn blared as the truck rolled to a stop in front of the house. Lights flashed and bounced off the dark sky. If anyone had turned in early for the night, they were awake now.

Help had come. *Thank You, Lord.*

Amelia hopped out followed by Zack, Izan, then Ridge. "Let's get the hoses hooked up, guys." She clapped her hands and jogged over to Kelsey. "Do you know what started the fire?"

"It's in the garage." Kelsey licked her dry lips. "Maeve doused it in gasoline. Trace is still in there." Her voice quivered.

Amelia cupped her hands. "Ridge, you're with me. We need to get foam at the base of the fire, pronto."

More lights mixed into the commotion as the ambulance pulled up. Jamie tugged on Kelsey's arm. "Let's get you checked out."

"Go wait with Andi." Amelia offered a smile. "Zack, Izan. Suit up. Trace is in there and we need to get him out."

Kelsey positioned most of her weight on Jamie. Her muscles burned with each step. Thankfully, her friend had a firm grip on Kelsey's arm as they walked.

"That gasoline is strong." Andi took Kelsey's other arm and guided her. "I have an extra change of clothes from the gym in the front that should fit."

"Thanks." Kelsey changed out of her wet clothes and inhaled the scent of vanilla from the ones Andi provided.

"What happened?" Andi tapped the edge of the truck and took Kelsey's hand to change her bandage.

Kelsey sat down. Her eyelids grew heavy. She wanted to take a nap. Instead, she said, "Maeve's in there with Trace. She tried to kill me." Tears streamed down her face, and Andi squeezed her forearm.

Radios squawked and firefighters ran in all directions to fight the blaze. The amount of lights and noise made Kelsey's head pound. Police cars screeched to a halt on the pavement and added to the commotion.

Basuto hopped out and made his way over to the ambo. "Any idea of Maeve Wells' whereabouts?" He shoved his hand to the butt of his gun.

"She's in there with Trace." Kelsey grimaced. If she had to be reminded one more time that Trace still remained MIA in the burning building, she might scream.

"We need eyes all around the perimeter. She's still inside." Basuto spoke into his radio.

"Look out! There's someone over there," one of the guys yelled.

Kelsey shifted her focus to the front of the house where people pointed.

Out walked Trace with Maeve at his side.

Kelsey jumped up and grabbed the edge of the truck to steady herself. Trace was alive. She lifted her hands to her mouth and a cry escaped.

"Nobody move!" Maeve's voice tore through the air. She held a gun to Trace's cheek.

Every muscle in Kelsey's body stiffened.

"We've got a hostage," Basuto radioed.

Maeve shoved Trace down the front walk, then stopped halfway. He held his hands in front of him.

His gaze connected with Kelsey's for a brief moment, but he didn't give any indication as to how he felt.

Officer Tazwell jogged over to Basuto. "We need a negotiator here stat," Basuto yelled.

Kelsey stepped forward. There was no time to waste. By the time a negotiator arrived, Trace could be dead. Maeve wasn't thinking rationally, and anything could set her off.

"We don't have time to wait." Kelsey pulled in a shaky breath. "I'll go."

"You can't do that," Jamie shrieked.

"You still need your injuries assessed," Andi added.

"Trace doesn't have that time." Maeve hadn't moved from her spot on the sidewalk with Trace. Everyone else remained frozen, waiting for orders. It was Gerald's house all over again.

If Kelsey never got to see the fruition of the grant program, so be it. At least she'd die helping the one person she prayed would experience healing. If God used this situation to open Trace's eyes to the hope he could have in life, then her job would have been worth it.

"We can't put you in a hostile situation like this intentionally." Basuto rubbed the stubble along his jaw.

"Please. It's the only chance we have." Kelsey tilted her head. "I'm the one she wants."

Basuto raised his brow at Tazwell, who grimaced.

"Position yourself so we have direct sight to Maeve. One wrong move and she's gone. I'm not going to let you or any other innocent people die. Got it?"

"Yes, sir." Kelsey nodded. This crew had her back. She could trust them. More importantly, she could trust God. He'd given her people who rallied around her. And if He chose to take it all away, she would still bless His name.

Tazwell handed Kelsey a vest and she slid her arms through it.

Trace's life depended on her doing her job.

Lord, guide my words. I need You.

Kelsey brushed back her hair and slipped the earpiece in. "All right." The last time she'd stepped in to help Gerald, it had backfired. She wouldn't focus on the past though. It wouldn't change anything now.

"We've got your back," Basuto said again.

"And I have yours." Kelsey pulled in a deep breath and walked over.

"You don't have to do this, Maeve." Kelsey stopped five feet from her and stood in front of Trace.

"Of course I do." Maeve cackled. "No one is getting out of this alive."

Trace sealed his lips and gave a slight nod. Like he trusted her to get them out of this mess.

"Everyone knows it's you. If you put the weapon down, things will go much easier." Tremors claimed Kelsey's hands. It was a good thing it was dark so Maeve couldn't see. "You might not be my friend, but I want to help." Yes, it hurt to say that. Maeve had never been a friend. But Kelsey wanted justice. For herself. For Noah. For Renee.

"You ruined my chances. It's too late."

"Chance for what?" Kelsey asked.

"My happily ever after. The only thing that stood in my way was you." Maeve stabbed her finger in the air. "But Trace doesn't love me. So now he dies."

Kelsey's legs shook. Her rigid stance sent a wave of dizziness over her. She bent her legs. She needed to relax. It wouldn't do any good if she let fear take over.

Lord, I'm calling out to You. I am not alone. You are right here with me. Give me Your peace, Jesus.

"What good would that do?" Kelsey asked. "I'm the one you wanted out of the picture. Take me. Let him live."

"If I can't win, then no one wins." Maeve wrapped her finger around the trigger.

Maeve's mind was set.

If this didn't end well, Kelsey needed to get something off her chest first. She'd already made the mistake once. Trace had to hear the truth. *I love you,* she mouthed.

Trace smiled. *Me too.* He raised his eyebrow and wiggled his finger to the right.

Kelsey didn't second-guess him. "Maeve." Kelsey shifted to the right.

"Don't move!" Maeve screamed.

Trace swung his hand up.

Maeve fired the gun.

Kelsey's scream mixed in with other shouts. She dropped to the ground to avoid being the next target.

A hand clamped down on her wrist and jerked her to a standing position. The momentum pulled at her shoulder, and pain seared through her neck and down her arm.

"Let me go." Kelsey tried to move out of Maeve's grip, but she could barely stand without support. Except she had the Lord's strength to lean on.

Where was Trace? Was he okay? If he managed to escape, then she'd done her job.

The muzzle of the gun dug into her neck as Maeve dragged her backward.

"I'm afraid your time has run out." Maeve's lethal words trailed through Kelsey's eardrum and pounded against her skull.

So, this was how she would die.

33

Time stood frozen as Trace watched a horror scene unfold before his eyes. He could do nothing to stop it. No director to yell cut. No way to pinch himself and realize it was a nightmare.

Trace pushed himself off the ground, and pain pierced his shoulder. He blew out a breath and touched his fingers to the area. Blood came away from the wound.

Maeve had shot him.

He prayed it was only a graze. Right now, he couldn't focus on that. Because the woman who'd said she loved him was trapped.

Officers raced past him, but it wouldn't do any good. Maeve held her gun snug against Kelsey's neck.

"Hold your fire," Basuto yelled.

Trace had been wrong about Kelsey in so many ways. She solved problems with care and strength. She fought hard and well, even when the odds were stacked against her. She persevered for the sake of others, willing to give up her life to save his.

The love he'd seen in her eyes—for him, what's more. And

now she stood in the line of fire instead of him.

If only he had grabbed the gun from Maeve earlier. The outcome would have been drastically different.

You don't know that, his mind screamed at him.

When you hit rock bottom, He has a way of showing up. Logan's words replayed in his thoughts. He couldn't change what had happened, but Trace would rely on God.

He flexed his hand a few times. "Doesn't mean I have to like it," he muttered. Trusting God in the pain required a lot of work. And it wasn't instant. He'd much rather learn when the stakes weren't impossibly high. Like the situation in front of him.

Maeve pulled Kelsey closer to the house. Smoke still billowed out of the windows, even as the firefighters fought the blaze.

Trace walked up to where the group of officers had stopped. Guns trained and ready. They just needed Kelsey out of the way. "Give it up, Maeve." Trace cupped his hands.

"Certainly you're joking, darling." Her voice rang out in a singsong tone.

He took a few steps toward them, careful to shuffle his feet to obscure his movement in the dark. "Does it sound like I am?"

"I wanted you. Only you."

"We tried. But it didn't work." He refrained from adding a humorless laugh.

"I know." She shrieked and pulled Kelsey's hair. Kelsey let out a whimper. "Which is why all this ends now."

Trace took another step forward.

"Don't come any closer," Maeve seethed.

Even in college, he'd noticed red flags—her opinionated mind and self-centered attitude. Clearly that manifested all the more as an adult. It hadn't been attractive then, and it certainly didn't appeal to him in the present.

Especially with her threats to kill the woman he did want to be with. Trace nearly choked on his own saliva at the thought.

Yet the reality of the matter remained. He'd fallen for Kelsey Scott, whether he'd wanted to or not.

And now he needed God's help to find a way to save her.

He didn't like how Kelsey's frame sagged. Her resolve sank by the second.

"What do you want me to do?" Trace lifted his hands. He felt clueless with what to say to make Maeve stand down. He usually treated people's physical ailments, not their hearts.

That was Kelsey's job. One she excelled at.

"I want you to say you love me. Not her." Maeve slapped Kelsey's arm.

"Don't treat her like that." Trace bit his lip. "That's a tall order to ask."

"Then watch her die."

"Wait." Trace put out his hand. If she wanted to play this game, he'd take a stab at it. "Why do you want to be with me?" He risked taking a step closer.

"You're a hero, Trace. You save the day."

Trace longed to hear those words and know what he did mattered. He shook his head to erase the sentiment. Because those words were an enemy's kisses. "I'm honored you see me that way."

"I knew you'd understand," Maeve said. "Took you long enough to figure it out."

"You're right. I don't know why I didn't see that truth all along." He inched closer still and held his breath. No rebuttal came, so he took another step.

"You can finally have the life you've always wanted. Put aside all the past heartache."

"You're right, we could." Trace shoved his hands in his pockets as the wind picked up and blew leaves around. "But first you need to let Kelsey go."

"Oh, Trace. I can't do that. Your mind would be distracted

then. I need you to only have eyes for me."

"I will," Trace said. The words tasted sour on his tongue and made him want to gag.

"I want to know you mean it." Maeve's voice demanded an audience.

He stood close enough to them now that he could see her wide eyes.

"How?" This wasn't going the way he'd anticipated. Maeve hadn't wavered her aim with the gun, and Kelsey remained silent next to Maeve.

"Ask me to marry you."

Trace nearly coughed at the request. Instead, he cleared his throat to cover it up. She wanted him to propose in front of her burning house while she held Kelsey hostage?

Police stood at the ready. Except they wouldn't take a shot with Kelsey in the crosshairs.

"I knew it. You don't really mean it. I'm done waiting," Maeve growled.

"I'll propose right now." Trace rushed to get the words out, and they ran along his tongue like rough sandpaper.

Maeve scoffed. "Yeah, right."

"I have a ring." Trace placed his hand on his chest. The ring he'd held close ever since that fatal day. A sign of the vows he'd made to the first person he'd loved.

"Trace, don't. Please," Kelsey said in a breathy voice, like it hurt too much to gather her words.

"Shut up." Maeve shoved the gun against Kelsey's head. "You get to watch the proposal of a lifetime. The one you never deserved."

Trace couldn't believe how crass Maeve sounded.

He swallowed hard and bit down on his lip. The metallic taste of blood filled his mouth. A fitting way to go into this fake profession of love. He pulled the necklace out from under his shirt and swung it over his head.

He fingered the ring, the diamond mounted high while several small ones encircled the band. For a moment, Trace no longer stood outside on a cold September night. Instead, with his knee bent, he stared into Renee's eyes on a sandy beach, excited about the start of their future together.

"I'm waiting." Maeve drew Trace back to the present.

"This ring holds special value to me." Trace held the ring out so she could see he actually had it. "And you reminded me why I do what I do. To save and protect people."

Maeve stared at the diamond, but he wasn't focused on her.

His gaze locked with the woman next to her, who'd turned his world upside down in all the best ways possible. A woman who wanted him to live to the fullest and wasn't afraid to tell it straight to his face. Who'd made him reconsider what it might be like to open his heart and love someone again.

She'd shown him the beauty of helping people. And how to trust God in the pain.

There was no one like Kelsey Scott.

"We've gone through a lot over the years. From study sessions to late night hangouts with friends to experiencing the devastation of loss. I'm learning God can take broken things and make them whole again. That He uses it for good. For His glory."

Kelsey stared intently at him from her position in Maeve's grip.

He continued. "Now is our time to make a declaration of love and show what God can restore. You are the girl for me, and there's no one else but you."

Trace shifted his attention back to Maeve, who couldn't care less whether he stood in front of her or not.

The ring captured her attention, and he noticed her hand waver as she loosened her grip on the gun and inched toward him.

Trace closed the distance and dropped to the ground,

shielding Kelsey with his own body. He breathed hard, waiting for a gunshot to pierce the air. Pierce him.

Footsteps pounded beside him. "Stand down!"

"Police! Hands in the air!" Men yelled the commands.

Maeve let out a cry. "Let go of me."

Trace shielded Kelsey with his body and turned. Officers pinned Maeve to the ground. One of them clamped cuffs around her wrists.

Trace pulled Kelsey to her feet. "You okay?"

She stared wide-eyed at him. "Is it really over?"

Trace rubbed her arms. "Yes. We have proof too."

"What do you mean?"

"She had a room in the house I stumbled upon. Filled with pictures of every targeted attack. Notes. Articles." Trace pulled her closer. Her heart beat steadily against his chest, the sound like a strong current pulling him in. Over and over.

She was here. And alive. If she let him, he would never leave.

Kelsey put her hand on his chest. A burning sensation worked its way through his shoulder. He grunted.

Suddenly she jerked back. "Trace."

"Yes." His voice came out husky, and he cleared his throat.

"You're bleeding." She raised her hand. Her fingers dripped red.

Nausea welled up inside him. The adrenaline rush began to wear off, and pain set in.

"I just need to sit. Rest." He took her hand in his and began to walk toward the crew on the street.

With each step, his vision grew hazier. He wanted to push through the throbbing, but his body wouldn't let him. If he wasn't able to save himself, so be it. At least God had helped him rescue Kelsey.

His hand slipped from hers.

The last thing he heard was Kelsey's cry. "I need a medic!"

34

Kelsey sat in the hospital waiting room with one leg propped up on a chair. Her crutches stood against the wall to her left.

When they got to the hospital, Trace had been whisked away to surgery. He'd crumpled in front of her at Maeve's house, and Kelsey thought he wouldn't make it. His once strong body had grown limp. Everything else with the fire and Maeve's arrest had faded into the background as she'd screamed for help. Now she'd stay up all night praying, asking God to intervene. To help Trace make it through surgery.

Maeve had taken so much from her. She refused to focus on what had been though. She'd gotten treatment for her cuts and bruised shoulder. Now she waited. But she wasn't alone. Her friends were here. Jamie sat next to her, and several of the firefighters who weren't on duty stood around.

"You sure you don't want me to take you home so you can get some sleep?" Jamie yawned. "It's after midnight."

"Not a chance." Kelsey shifted to get more comfortable. The hard-backed chair dug into her spine. "I want to be here when they say we can go back to Trace's room." She was wide awake and wouldn't be sleeping anytime soon.

"Well, I'm going to get some coffee, otherwise I will fall asleep." Jamie stretched her arms and stood. "Excuse me." She brushed past Logan, who jumped back like he'd been burned.

"What was that about?" Charlie hooked a finger in their direction.

"A story for another time." Kelsey frowned. Clearly her friend had some healing of her own to work through.

"Oh, good. You're here." Natalie rushed into the room with Macon and Dean on her heels.

She dropped her purse on the floor and took Jamie's vacant seat next to Kelsey. "Are you okay?" Natalie wrapped her in a hug.

Kelsey patted Natalie's back. Was she really hugging her? She and Natalie hadn't spoken since Natalie's seizure. Although, her friend didn't appear mad.

"What happened?" Natalie leaned back.

"Maeve set fire to her house and shot Trace. He's in the recovery unit now."

"How are you?" Natalie raised her brows.

"Just a few bruises." Kelsey couldn't believe she'd walked away from all this alive. And that Jamie and Natalie were okay too. Why did Natalie act like everything was fine between them?

"Aren't you upset with me?" Kelsey squinted.

"Why should I be?" Natalie crossed her legs.

"I haven't heard from you since you got sick. I was sure you were upset with me."

"Oh, Kels." Natalie shook her head. "I'd never think that. I'm so sorry you thought I was mad. I tried calling you to make sure you were okay after Trace found out Maeve was behind things, but you didn't answer."

Oh. Kelsey grimaced. "Maeve broke my phone. But I left a

voicemail for you right after your seizure."

"You did?" Natalie pulled out her phone. "Whoops. My mailbox is full." She held up the screen. "After I got home from the hospital, I was exhausted. Didn't have much of an appetite either. I couldn't even think about talking with people. I'm sorry I didn't reach out sooner."

"It's okay. I'm just thankful you're alive and here."

"Me too." Natalie gave her another hug. "I couldn't imagine anything happening to you."

"We're all glad you're okay, Kelsey." Dean walked over and smiled.

"You're not mad either?" Kelsey stood and used her crutches for support.

"You had no control over the situation. I'm just grateful Maeve is behind bars and you can focus on your clients again."

"Wait. You're not going to switch roles and let someone else take over the grant program?" Kelsey scrunched her forehead.

Dean laughed. "You're one of the best counselors we've got. Between you and Natalie, our patients are fortunate to work with such empathetic people."

"Thank you." Kelsey blinked away tears.

"Oh, come here." Natalie waved everyone over. "You all make the best team." The crew circled each other in one big hug.

Yes. Kelsey agreed. These people weren't just friends. They'd become family. People who understood her weaknesses and championed her nonetheless.

"Excuse me," someone said. "Which one of you is here for Trace Bently?" Charlotte checked her clipboard.

"She is." Natalie pointed to Kelsey.

"Actually, we all are." Kelsey glanced around the room.

"He's awake and ready for visitors. Except only one person at a time can go back." She scrunched her nose. "Which one of you wants to go first?"

"Go ahead, Kelsey." Macon nodded.

"He'll want to see you first." Logan's eyes glistened.

Kelsey followed the nurse to Trace's room. "You're awake." She set her purse on the table and walked over to his bed.

"The doc should be in soon," Charlotte said before closing the door.

"What happened?" Trace pushed himself up and winced.

"You want the abridged version or the novel?" Kelsey chuckled.

"How much time do we have?" Trace scanned the wall.

"However long I get to stay by your side." She smiled.

"I like the sound of that." He trailed his thumb down the side of her face before he tucked a strand of hair behind her ear.

The gesture sent goosebumps across her arms.

Lines creased his brow. "Please tell me you haven't been up all night."

Kelsey leaned forward. "I've endured far worse. And a couple hours of no sleep is nothing in my book."

"Where's Maeve?" Trace's eyes widened and he gripped the edge of the bed.

"It's okay." Kelsey squeezed his arm. "She's in custody. I'm not in danger anymore." Kelsey pulled in a breath. The threats were contained. No one wanted to harm her anymore. God and her friends had helped her. Even Trace, who'd taken a bullet on her behalf.

Trace leaned his head back against the pillow. "I'm sorry." Trace took her hand in his.

"Don't be. We're both alive. And for that I'm grateful."

Trace cleared his throat.

Kelsey grabbed the Styrofoam cup of water, which sat right next to Renee's ring on the table. "Here." She handed him the drink.

Silence lengthened.

Kelsey wasn't sure if she should bring up the proposal. She could have sworn he'd spoken to her while Maeve stood captivated by the sparkling diamond. Although, Trace might have forgotten. And it could have been a ruse to distract Maeve. Regardless of what he meant by it, Kelsey learned a lot during those moments when Maeve had the upper hand.

"What's going on inside that pretty head of yours?" Trace winked.

Kelsey squeezed his hand. The monitor beeped its rhythmic sound behind her. "I'm sorry for pushing you away. It wasn't fair of me to treat you that way or get flustered like I did. I was afraid to let you in only to be ridiculed or watch you leave. But I know now you wanted to help because you care."

She searched the well of compassion that flowed from his brown eyes—a sweetness she wanted to bask in. Kelsey waited for the *I told you so*. But it never came.

"When I was alone in that house with Maeve, I realized something," she carried on.

"What's that?"

"Sometimes it's okay to ask for help. We can't do it all on our own anyway."

"You're right. I know now myself; God wants us to run to Him. With the good, bad, and ugly."

"I knew those walls would crack eventually, Mr. Bently." She waggled her finger and smiled.

"I was a basket case from the beginning, wasn't I?" Trace said, half-jokingly.

"So was I." Kelsey chuckled.

Trace sobered. "I'm just glad you're okay."

"You and me both."

"When I discovered Maeve plotted everything, I nearly lost it. The thought of you left alone in her clutches terrified me."

"How did you figure it out?" Kelsey asked.

"Remember Noah?"

"From the yearbooks, yes."

"She stole his car, and my buddy, Gage, traced the trail back to Maeve's dad's autobody shop. I pulled up his website, and he still had a picture of her as a kid helping him fix cars."

"Wow." Kelsey processed what he said. "She planned each step."

Maeve had knowingly followed through with destructive choices that had hurt multiple people and she'd hidden them for years. "I'm so sorry about Renee." Kelsey choked on her words.

"Me too." Trace rubbed his jaw. "At least now the truth is out. I'm not left wondering what happened."

It didn't make the reality any easier. "Those were some good acting skills you pulled off with that proposal though." That ring meant the world to him.

"It wasn't that hard when the words were spoken from a place of healing and truth."

"Oh." Kelsey swallowed.

"You've taught me a lot over the short time we've spent together."

"So have you. I love you, Trace." She leaned in, ready to show him how much she meant those words. But he put his finger against her lips to stop her.

"I need some time to sort things out. Then we can talk more." He smiled, but his words did nothing to assure her.

He hadn't said he loved her back.

Maybe she'd misunderstood his declaration previously. After all, they'd been in a moment of life or death when they'd professed their feelings earlier.

Someone knocked on the door, and Dr. Welch popped his head into the room. "Trace. I'm glad the surgery went well."

Kelsey stood. The chair squeaked along the waxed linoleum. "I'll be outside."

And with that, Kelsey walked out, filled with questions.

35

Trace's hands shook as he put the car in Park two days later. He stared at the brick building in front of him. Rubbing his fingers over Renee's ring, he stepped up onto the sidewalk.

All these years he'd held her close to his heart. He'd given her his love and fulfilled his vows. Now it was time to let her go. To step forward into the future God had for him. To let the pain have a purpose in a new chapter.

Because his heart belonged to someone else.

A small establishment sat on the corner of the street, tucked away from the other shops that lined the road on this side of town. The yellow paint and red door screamed for a makeover, but the eclectic nature of the shop suited the contents found inside.

No other vehicles occupied the parking lot, despite the flashing green sign inside the window that read Open.

Trace rolled his shoulders. He could do this. Time kept moving, and the due date for this had come and gone a long time ago.

He grabbed the leather pouch from his pocket and placed the ring inside.

With each step toward the entrance, the wind seemed to pick up speed as if to encourage him to keep going. A gentle shove in the right direction.

You're right, Lord. You're working things for good. It's time.

The bell rang as Trace walked inside. The space around him was filled with trinkets that someone would soon claim as their own treasure. The musty smell that enveloped the space reminded Trace that some of these goods were antiques.

A sign hung above the counter in bold, black letters. *Take a Chance Pawn Shop.*

His heart quickened as he approached the counter. His shoes thudded on the hardwood floor in time with his pulse.

A man came out of a doorway behind the counter. He was probably in his early seventies, given the head of white hair and fine lines around his cheeks and forehead. "How can I help you?"

Trace cleared his throat and set the bag on the counter. "I'd like to sell this."

"Well, you've come to the right place." The man weighed the bag in his hand before he dumped the ring into his palm.

The diamonds caught the sun's rays that streamed through the window and sprayed an array of rainbow lights off the wall. A reminder of the promise he'd made. He and Renee had been young and innocent back then.

Trace cleared his throat and rubbed the corner of his eye.

"This is a beauty for sure." The man inspected the ring with a magnifying glass. He turned it toward himself, away from himself, clockwise, and every which way. "Forgive me for prying, but it seems you're too young to be selling a thing like this." The man's features softened as he studied Trace.

"Sometimes you have to learn to let go." Trace swallowed and attempted a smile. "Start a new season."

"Wise words from a young fellow." A knowing look crossed the man's face, like he knew the path of heartache all too well. "I can give you one grand cash for this."

"That'll do." Trace nodded.

"I wish I could give you more, but no amount of money will change a circumstance." The man pulled the cash out of the register, each bill crisp as he counted up the total and tucked it into an envelope.

The guy was right that money didn't change the past. Yet it was time to move forward. If Trace wanted a chance to really show Kelsey what she meant to him, then he'd do it a thousand times over in a heartbeat.

She loved him. The way he loved her.

It was time to discover what the future held for the two of them.

"You're all set." The man handed him the money and Trace pocketed it.

"Thanks. I appreciate it." Trace shook his hand.

"Anytime. If there's ever someone special in your life again, I'd be happy to help you find something." The man saluted before he ducked into the back office once more.

Trace ran a few more errands, checking each item off his list with more courage and less weight on his shoulders. He might not be on the clock to save anyone, but he couldn't help but think he was saving himself in the meantime.

Trace dug out his phone. He leaned his head back against the headrest in his car and listened to it ring.

"Jason's Autobody Shop, where we have all the parts for your needs. How may I help you?" A woman listed off the welcome spiel like she did it a hundred times a day and the ditty had lost its luster.

"I was hoping you guys would be able to tow a car to the junkyard."

"We can certainly arrange that." The woman typed on the other end. "Where is it currently housed?"

"It's in a storage unit off Route 75." Trace rattled off the address.

"We'll just need access to the garage and we'll be happy to take it off your hands."

Once all the details were arranged to take care of the Kia, Trace wound his way up the mountainside and found a place to park at a scenic stop along the path.

Vibrant green pine trees dotted the horizon along with an array of yellow and red trees that hadn't dropped their leaves yet. A family walked the trail nearby and stopped at the overlook to take a picture before they continued on their way.

Trace grabbed the speckled urn from the passenger seat and tucked it in the crook of his arm. This moment held considerable sentiment, but it would be much easier to keep emotions out of it. He'd mourned long enough.

Trace trudged through a few muddy patches where the dirt squished under the soles of his shoes. When he got to a more secluded area that overlooked the valley below, he breathed in deeply.

His mind ran in circles, conjuring nothing. What was he supposed to say?

"I know you'd want me to get back to living life, so that's what I'm going to do." He whispered the words into the air and turned around to make sure he still stood alone.

Certain that he could do this in peace, he twisted the top off the container. With a flick of his wrist, he watched the contents sprinkle along the edge of the cliff and float down. They descended into the trees below before settling near the river that wound its way through the middle of the trail.

"I loved you, Renee."

He'd done what he'd promised her that day when they stood face-to-face in front of all their friends and family. Trace had fulfilled his vows to the woman he pledged to love until death parted them.

He'd spent too much time trying to maintain control. And somehow the act of letting go liberated him, because the control had only been a notion. Freedom hung in the air now. The chains he'd carried for so long finally gone.

The blue sky and warmth of the sunlight reinvigorated him. The Lord took what had been broken and bruised from the pain of losing Renee, and He had mended those pieces. And now because of Christ, Trace had been made whole again. And he had a Savior who understood his suffering. But Trace couldn't stay in the past. Not if he wanted to walk in hope.

He was ready now to move forward.

And show Kelsey how much she meant to him. A woman who could hold her own in every way and didn't need him to rescue her. Yet Trace wanted to protect her if she'd let him.

And he had the perfect way to show her his intentions too.

Trace headed over to Macon's house.

He'd barely finished knocking when the door swung open and Macon greeted him.

"I need your help with something." Trace cocked his head and smiled.

"Everything okay?" Macon raised a brow and ushered him inside.

"Couldn't be better."

Trace had never been in Macon's home before. The space appeared inviting and cozy. An entryway table lined the foyer, and several pictures hung on the wall. Even a blanket ladder was propped against the corner wall. "I take it this is Natalie's doing?" Trace waved his hand.

"You bet." Natalie peeped her head out from the living room. "I told him his home needed more love than his office gets." She chuckled. "Good to see you, Trace."

"You're just the people I wanted to see."

"Me too?" Natalie pointed a finger at herself.

"I have some ideas I want to run by you."

"For..." She dragged out the word.

"Kelsey."

Natalie's eyes lit up, and she gave Macon a wink. "Told you."

Trace pretended not to witness the exchange.

She grabbed Macon's arm and waved Trace into the living room, where they plopped down on the couch. "Tell me what you're thinking."

Trace relayed his thoughts to the couple, and he couldn't help but smile when they agreed to the plan.

An hour later, with a crew of people enlisted to execute his ideas, Trace called Kelsey.

She picked up on the first ring.

"How're you feeling?"

"Better by the minute."

"I'm glad."

"You doing okay?" Her voice sounded hesitant.

"I needed time to decompress and had quite a few errands to run. But I'm almost finished." He paused to gather his thoughts. "I'm tied up at the moment, but I have something I want to show you."

"Okay. When do you want to stop by?"

"Actually, Natalie said she's going to swing by to pick you up." He kept his tone even, hoping she didn't pick up on anything.

"What do you mean? You're sounding strange, Trace." She paused. "What's going on?"

"I've got a surprise for you, so don't ruin it." Trace chuckled, then hung up.

36

K elsey stared at herself in the mirror, then dabbed on some more blush. Her energy was finally back, but her body still ached after everything she'd been through at Maeve's house the other day. She'd spent the last few days resting and trying not to let her mind think about Trace.

She'd expressed her affection for him, and he'd given her a cryptic response. It was tempting to read into how he'd handle their last interaction. Especially since they hadn't talked until his random phone call an hour ago.

Her hand shook as she applied mascara. Regardless of what happened between her and Trace, she would be okay.

She groaned.

So much easier said than done. Her solace was found in God alone. She really would be okay no matter what Trace wanted.

Kelsey hoped the time apart had given Trace a chance to finally heal. Still, a small part of her wanted him to have room in his heart for her in the midst of the healing.

A knock sounded on the bathroom door and Kelsey froze.

"You almost finished, girl?" Natalie stuck her head in.

She let out a breath and leaned against the counter.

Kelsey needed to remind herself every couple of hours that Maeve now sat in a jail cell and didn't roam the streets. Yet she still caught herself peering over her shoulder to keep from being caught off guard.

She taught others how to cope with traumatic situations, and now she needed to implement those strategies on herself. The reality of that proved much harder than she wanted to admit.

"Give me two minutes." Kelsey uncapped her lip gloss. Natalie told her she wanted to show her something at the clinic, yet she'd added the caveat that Kelsey needed to look presentable. If it was something with the grant program, Kelsey wanted to be prepared. Although, Trace made it sound like he would be there too.

All of Kelsey's senses remained on high alert as she considered possible scenarios for Natalie's part in this.

The thought of seeing Trace again sent a wave of somersaults through her stomach. She cracked a smile and stepped back to study her work. She didn't want to go overboard, but at least she'd look good for whatever the situation.

Yes, the bit of makeup would suffice.

Although she was curious what Trace had been up to, she also needed to talk with him about where his heart stood as far as holding on to Renee. He still cared deeply for his wife, and in a way he probably always would. Now, with the added wrench of Maeve's role in her death, Kelsey didn't know how he was coping with it.

It wouldn't be fair to let her feelings run wild if the past still held him hostage.

Clarification was key.

Then again, he'd had time to process things while recovering too. She tucked the thread of hope inside. Soon enough she would have an answer.

"All right. I'm ready." Kelsey walked out into the hall.

"Great." Natalie clapped her hands. "This is going to be great."

"I'm glad you're excited. But I'm slightly suspicious." Kelsey narrowed her gaze.

"Whoa." Natalie held up her hands. "Why do you think I need a reason to be happy? Just the other day I nearly died from rat poison, and you were drugged and shot. And we're both still alive." She waved her finger in the air like she scolded a toddler. "I'd say that's reason enough to be grateful."

Kelsey winced and opened her mouth.

"Uh-uh." Natalie wiggled her finger again. "Don't even go there. It wasn't your fault I got sick. God had it all under control."

"You're absolutely right." Kelsey crossed her arms. "But that doesn't mean something else isn't about to go down."

"Oh, come on." Natalie grabbed Kelsey's arm and led her to the entryway.

Kelsey waited while Natalie locked up the house, then they headed for the car. "Is Macon working the weekend shift again?"

"He's working all right." Natalie skipped to the car.

"You sure you don't mind driving?"

"Not at all. I'd do anything for you, friend."

Kelsey smiled. She was incredibly blessed by the *true* friendships God had given her.

"Where are we going again?" Kelsey climbed into the passenger seat.

"The Ridgeman Center." Natalie winked.

They pulled in and Kelsey was surprised to see all the cars in the parking lot. "Is there an outpatient therapy session happening that I forgot about?" Normally Sunday evenings were quiet on the campus.

Kelsey went through the calendar in her mind, trying to place what event Dean had scheduled.

"No idea." Natalie's innocent look didn't fool Kelsey.

"What exactly does Trace have to show me?" Kelsey glanced over as they walked to the front door.

"Something I think you'll appreciate."

They stepped into the lobby, and when Kelsey opened the door, darkness encircled the area. "Why are the lights off, Nat?" Kelsey reached for the light switch.

She flicked them on and a crowd of cheers burst toward her as people stood. "Surprise!"

"What in the world?" She put her hand on her chest.

Streamers and balloons hung from the ceiling, and a table by the side wall was filled with food and desserts.

Trace stood in the center of the area along with Dean, his wife Ellie, Macon, Andi and Jude, Allen Frees and his wife Pepper along with their daughter Victory, and the rest of the counseling staff, the truck crew and rescue squad. Gerald, Alice, Thatcher, and Chrissy stood smiling. Even Jamie was there, though she gave Logan a wide berth.

Kelsey looked behind her at Natalie. "What's this for?"

Natalie just smiled and nodded in front of her.

Kelsey turned back around to see Trace make his way over. "What's the special occasion?" She looked around the room as everyone mingled with one another.

Trace braced his hands on her arms. "Why does there need to be a reason for a celebration?" He winked.

"There's always a reason." Kelsey rolled her eyes. She'd rather he stop joking around, but she loved this mischievous side of him.

"Remember how Renee threw a party in college with all our friends to celebrate you making it to your clinicals in counseling?"

"Of course. How could I ever forget that?" Kelsey searched his eyes. "So what are you saying?"

"That was just because. And so is this."

Kelsey opened her mouth to debate the statement but then closed it shut. Technically there'd been a reason that party happened—celebrating her success. Clearly Trace went through a lot of effort to corral everyone together for tonight. Probably just because they'd all been through plenty.

"Thank you." She wanted to give him a hug, but his mention of Renee held her back. She needed more information first. "What made you decide to do this?"

"I realized I'd been holding on to the past for too long." His expression softened. "I'd stopped living. In the process, I could have lost something else that was right in front of me the whole time."

"What was that?" She couldn't keep the hope from her question.

"You." Trace's voice came out in a husky whisper.

All the commotion around them faded as Kelsey hung on to that simple word. She moved closer to him, unsure if she should expose herself to the risk of what might come next. Regardless, she held her breath and waited for him to continue.

"I sold Renee's engagement ring today."

Kelsey's jaw dropped and she tried to gather her composure. Tears pricked her eyes. It must have been so hard for him to let go like that. The urge to ask him to repeat what he'd said hung in the balance, but she bit her tongue.

"I had her car towed away. And I finally spread her ashes." The edges of his lips turned down, and a crease stretched across his forehead.

"I can't imagine how difficult that must have been for you," Kelsey said.

"Oddly enough, I have peace now for the first time in years. I fulfilled my promise to her, and I know she'd want me to move on. Live my life."

"I'm glad you've come to terms with everything." Kelsey wiggled her toes. Just in case this was a dream. Except it wasn't.

"None of it would have been possible without God." Trace pulled her closer. "Without you." His breath tickled her skin.

"I just wanted to help a friend who seemed lost and hurt."

"Something you do best."

"I suppose we both like to help people through their pain."

"That we do." Trace stretched out his arms, and she welcomed his embrace.

His arms wrapped her frame, grounding her like a sturdy anchor unwavering in a choppy sea. She never wanted to let go. She nuzzled her head into the crevice of his shoulder and closed her eyes. Somehow a stubborn man with an alpha streak had broken through the walls she'd built, and her independence suddenly wanted a helpmate.

"I like this a lot." Kelsey leaned back.

"I didn't drive you away with all my antics?" Trace lifted his hands and rubbed her shoulders.

"You gave me all the more reason to stay." Kelsey tilted her head up. "I didn't drive you away with mine?"

"Not a chance." He tucked a wisp of hair behind her ear. "I'll always look after you, Kels." He leaned in until his forehead touched hers. The heat of his skin permeated her entire body.

"Even if I'm a total mess with this bum leg?" Sure, Maeve had caused havoc with her own sabotages, but Kelsey's body would always have challenges maintaining healthy glucose levels. She didn't want to sound needy, but Trace had to understand. Would he truly be willing to stick with her through anything?

"I'll walk through it with you every step of the way." He wrapped his hands around the base of her neck.

The sensation sent tingles down her arms. The man in front of her sent Kelsey's heartbeat into the most pleasantly abnormal rhythm, which might require a shock to keep it going. "Mm, I'll take his help any day."

"That means you actually need to listen to my advice occasionally." He winked.

Kelsey bit back a laugh. "Only if you'll let me in here." She pointed at his chest, right above his heart.

Trace's face sobered. "Always."

"All right, then," Kelsey said. "I guess that's settled."

"There's just one more thing." Trace leaned forward and trailed his finger along her lip.

"What's that?" Her voice came out in a squeak.

He answered by tilting his head and capturing his lips with hers. He worked his fingers through her hair, and Kelsey leaned in. All her worries ceased, and the only thing she could think about was the tenderness with which he kissed her.

Not rushed. Gentle and slow, like a promise of more to come.

The taste of peppermint sweetened the kiss and shot off sparks of heat. If they weren't careful, someone might need to grab a hose and contain the flames that burned with intensity.

"I called it!" She was pretty sure it was Andi who yelled that.

Kelsey opened her eyes. She laid her head on Trace's shoulder and looked out at the sea of spectators.

Andi smiled, and Jude let out a whistle.

Someone tapped her shoulder.

"I'd say this is cause for celebration." Natalie smiled. "Let's go cut some cake."

Kelsey turned to Trace.

She leaned on her tiptoes and kissed his forehead.

"I love you, Kelsey Scott. And I wouldn't want it any other way." Trace took her hands in his once more and pulled her in.

"And you, Trace Bently, are an easy man to love."

EPILOGUE

"**I**s she here yet?"

Allen glanced over his shoulder to see his wife walking down the hall toward him. "Natalie isn't here yet." He turned his wheelchair toward her so they wouldn't disturb the class field trip happening in the engine bay. Amelia had sprained her wrist the day before, so she had taken the duty of showing kids around off the chief's plate. "Macon is out on a call with Truck."

Pepper had the day off today, and it wasn't time to go pick up Victory from school yet according to the time on his watch. Tonight was the fire department fall party. Since the holidays were so busy, they'd decided to have a cookout tonight at the firehouse to celebrate, so they could hang out before all the craziness of Thanksgiving and Christmas.

So much had happened the past few months that he'd felt like they needed a celebration.

The women in his life—his wife and her niece, their adopted child—had settled into life, and he loved every minute of it. Even the ups and downs of his mobility were moments he could be thankful for what he had.

Definitely time for a party.

Pepper leaned down and kissed him. "Well, why isn't she here yet?"

The entire firehouse had been on edge all shift waiting for Natalie to show. The callout had been a much-needed distraction, one that got him to trust God would bring them all back safely.

Allen smiled. "Macon will probably be tearing his hair out the whole way back here. I, of course, played it much cooler."

Pepper laughed. "Of course."

"I knew you'd say yes." The happiest day of his life had been when he married her. "What have you been up to today?"

A mischievous note entered her expression. "It's a surprise."

"Christmas isn't for a couple of months." She wasn't going to make him wait, was she? Allen tugged her down to sit on his lap. "Tell me."

She'd been feeling under the weather lately. He didn't want to hope for the best if the situation turned the other direction. Allen had promised Pepper he would stick with her and weather whatever might come.

One eyebrow rose. "Tell you. Hmm. Or...?"

Pepper glanced around. Both Rescue and Truck were gone, out on a run. So was Ambulance 21. The command vehicle sat in the corner of the engine bay, where about twenty kids sat on the floor in front of Amelia, who had one wrist bandaged. A selection of fire gear was lined up on the ground in front of what appeared to be the lone firefighter at the station.

"Ignore the kids." Allen drew her attention back to him. "Tell me about my surprise."

The same way the firehouse had become a family over the past few months, he and Pepper had gotten married and adopted Victory. They'd started the life they were always meant to have. Since she'd come back into his life earlier in the year, he'd never been happier. His mom had been over the moon when he'd married, and she doted on Victory.

Allen couldn't wait to see what God wanted to do with the rest of their lives.

Pepper started to laugh. She slid her arms over his shoulders and touched her nose to his. "How do you feel about a baby brother or sister for Victory?"

Allen stared at her. *It was happening.* They were growing their family.

She smiled. "Breathe."

Allen gasped. He lifted his hands and touched her cheeks. "I love you."

Pepper smiled. "I know."

A light chuckle drifted to him from down the hall.

NATALIE PASSED HER COUSIN ALLEN IN THE HALL, HIS WIFE sitting on his lap on the wheelchair. Her cheeks heated. "Don't mind me."

Where was Macon, anyway?

Natalie found the first firefighter in the engine bay, surrounded by a class of kids.

Amelia held up a SCBA. "Does anyone know what this is?"

Hands shot up, and when Amelia spotted Natalie in the doorway, she waved her over.

"Everyone, say hi to Natalie real quick before we head out to watch how a firefighter clears a room during a fire."

Natalie smiled at Amelia, even though the time Natalie had gone into the smoke house had been a disaster. Macon had mentioned often how much the field trip students enjoyed the smoke house demonstrations. Amelia, however, wore an odd expression, but it was the way she fluttered her lashes that made Natalie tilt her head.

Wait.

Natalie stutter-stepped in front of the children. "*You're* the firefighter going into the smoke house, right?" Surely Amelia didn't mean for Natalie to demonstrate. The last time that happened, it hadn't exactly gone smoothly. Though, in the end, it had brought her and Macon closer.

Amelia winced. "Only if you can run the controls? Otherwise, these students will miss all the fun."

"Hi, Ms. Natalie!" Joey's voice paused Natalie's worries for a moment as she searched the group of students.

There in the back. He'd gotten a haircut since their last therapy session. He and his father had been needing her far less these days. "Hey, Joey! I didn't know it was your class touring today."

Joey flinched. "Well, actually—"

"So, you'll help us out, right?" Amelia had her trademark lieutenant scowl on. "Being an honorary firefighter and all." It wasn't really a question when Amelia placed a helmet into Natalie's side. "The rest of the crew got called out. I can't do two things at once."

Natalie pointed at the command truck. "Is the crew down a member? Why didn't Macon take—"

"There have been so many good questions today." Amelia turned and winked at the kids. "But the chief's not in here right now, so we'll have to ask him that later." She steered Natalie by the shoulders toward the exit. "This way, everyone."

Outside, Amelia organized the kids, then double-checked all of Natalie's gear. "Thanks for always helping out."

Natalie tightened her chin strap. She could do this. Needed to do this. "It's just a little smoke."

Amelia's gaze snapped up. "Maybe this isn't the best—"

"No, I got this. I want to do this. I can work through this fear." Fire and smoke no longer had ahold of her.

Amelia winced. "Remember, there'll be no flames."

Natalie adjusted the strap on her self-contained breathing apparatus. "No flames. Just a dummy waiting for me in the back room to rescue and show the kids."

A brief smirk flew across Amelia's face.

"Or will the dummy be in the front room?"

This time, Amelia laughed. "Oh, there's definitely a *dummy* in there somewhere. Use your TIC to find him." Amelia turned and walked backward toward the kids and the control room. "And the video feed won't pick up your audio...in case you forget how to clear a room. Or something."

Once in position by the smoke house entrance, Natalie tightened her grip on her thermal imaging camera and entered.

The entrance was barely even hazy. The visibility was much clearer than the last time she'd entered with Macon. A warm spot lit on her TIC. The dummy was going to be in its usual location.

She steadied her breathing and opened the door to the back room where she'd panicked before. And froze. There wasn't a dummy with a heating pad on it.

Macon was in its place.

Kneeling.

The TIC slipped from her grasp and hung against her side. Macon wasn't in his turnout gear like she was, but in his uniform that showed off his wide shoulders. The ones that proved to help her carry life's burdens.

He held his hand out and opened his palm.

A ring.

Her eyes watered, and she put her hand up to her mask.

Macon gave her his half smile. His eyes crinkled and sparked with joy. "Natalie Lynn Atkinson, will you—"

She yanked off her helmet and sprang forward. "Yes!"

His chuckle filled more than the room; it made her heart swell. Macon caught her and pulled her against his chest. Her hair was probably sticking up everywhere, but all she wanted to do was kiss the man she loved.

At the same moment Macon leaned down, Natalie rose onto her tiptoes. Their lips met. He secured her against him, and she sighed into his promise of forever.

All too soon, he eased away, his lips smiling as he peppered her with a series of quick kisses. "Don't you want to see the ring?"

Natalie met his gaze. "All I want is you. This. Us."

Macon slid the ring onto her finger and centered the diamond with his thumb. "I wanted you to have a good fire memory. That's why I asked you in here." His smile faded, and he swallowed.

Natalie cupped his cheeks. "I love you." She gave him another kiss, slow and full of proof that she wouldn't have wanted this moment to happen any other way. "Thank you for seeing my weaknesses and loving me anyway."

He stood, helping her to her feet. "Now we have a good reason for a party."

The door clanged open and hit the wall. "Is it time for cake?"

Natalie snuggled up against Macon's side. "Honey, *your* kids are getting restless again."

Macon kissed Natalie's forehead. "Don't blame me. They are definitely *our* kids. Remember, you signed off on this crew."

Yes, and she would never forget how God had used them to truly rescue her.

MUSIC AND LAUGHTER GREETED ANDI AS SHE CARRIED A BOWL OF baked beans from the kitchen to the firehouse yard. Bistro lights hung overhead, strung up that afternoon, and everyone stood around fire pits to ward off the fall chill.

Chief Macon and Natalie held hands and talked with Trace, his arm around Kelsey. Andi's stomach clenched at the glint of the new ring on Natalie's finger. Andi was happy for them—so happy—but also a little jealous.

"What've you got, Andi?" Bryce stepped into her path, eying the bowl.

"Beans."

With an unimpressed shrug he said, "You doing all right? I don't see you as much now that you're back on ambo."

Where the thought of leaving Truck would have once broken her, Andi's smile brightened with contentment. "I'm doing all right, big bro. Just keeping my head down and taking night classes on the side."

"For nursing?"

She nodded.

"You sure you're not missing someone in particular?" His teasing grin made her roll her eyes.

"I just video chatted with Jude last night," she said with a laugh.

"Is he moving soon?"

A twinge of sadness pierced her peace. "Hopefully."

She'd grown used to having Jude around while he recovered from his gunshot wound months ago. He'd taken vacation after to stay in Last Chance County, and they'd easily slipped back into the comradery of their teens with the added layer of their budding relationship.

They had been the best weeks to date, but real life had come back with a vengeance. His transfer to Denver was pending, but there were only so many video chats a girl could take without having her man hug her and tell her everything was going to be all right.

She'd considered hopping on a plane to San Diego, but her schedule made that impossible.

"It'll happen, Dee. I wouldn't worry about it." Bryce winked and walked off to join Ridge and Eddie.

She admired her brother's confidence. Jude hadn't sounded as sure on their call the night before, and Andi wondered if he was as committed to their relationship as she was.

With a groan, she set the beans on the table and turned back toward the kitchen.

A hand latched onto her arm and pulled her around. "Don't you know this is a party?" Logan grinned while showing off a terrible dance move.

"I'm not five, Logan. You don't need to cheer me up." She huffed a sigh. "I'm good."

"This is about that boy, isn't it?"

"Man, Logan. Jude is a man." *The perfect man for me.* She wrinkled her nose at the sappy line, thankful she'd kept it to herself.

"Give it to me straight. You guys pretty serious?" He leaned in, eyes narrowed.

She swallowed. She'd thought so, but after that call... "I think so."

"Wow, what a vote of confidence for the *man*." Logan's gaze flicked behind her but quickly returned. "If you need Bryce and me to go out to California and beat him up, we can do that. We could definitely take Mr. ATF."

"You'll do no such thing, Logan Bingley Crawford." He flinched as she used his forbidden middle name.

"I'm just saying—"

"Jude is doing everything he can to move." She willed the thread of doubt away. "He'll get here when he can."

"And then what's next?"

Heat flooded Andi's cheeks. "That's up to us. So, butt. Out." She emphasized the words with a pointed finger to his chest.

"Okay, I get the picture." Logan leaned in. "Just looking out for you, Andi Bear."

With a nod she didn't understand, he stepped around her, but Andi stayed rooted to the spot. Her coworkers turned friends made up the fabric of her life in Last Chance County, but Jude's absence left a gaping hole. She loved her job and her nursing classes, but maybe it was time to consider a move.

Resolve lasered her focus. She could find a job in San Diego. She could leave her beloved mountains for the beach if that meant more time with Jude. She could—

A hand landed on her shoulder. "I'm fine, Logan."

"You sure about that?"

The voice washed over her in a cascade of awareness. Andi froze.

"Aren't you going to say hi to me, Dee?"

A surge of excitement rushed through her as she whirled around. "Jude."

"Hey." Jude's warm brown eyes honed in on her and, with just one word, she was a puddle of emotions.

His arms wrapped around her in a hug that was as familiar as it was new. The cool, soft touch of his leather jacket and the spicy scent of aftershave enveloped her as his arms pulled her closer.

"How are you here?" She leaned back.

"Thought I'd fly in for some of Charlie's barbecue." He laughed and wiped a tear from her cheek. "I'm kidding, Dee. I'm here for you."

"I've missed you." Another tear escaped.

"I've missed you too. So much." His words were embers to dry brush, igniting a fire in the pit of her stomach.

Then his lips touched hers and the heat blazed to a five-alarm fire. Her arms snaked up around his neck as he pulled her close into a cocoon of warmth and safety. She was home in his embrace. Her fears fled and her heart was at peace.

"That's enough of *that*." Logan's voice pulled Andi back from the fog Jude's kiss had shrouded them in.

Jude chuckled. "I do have one other surprise, Dee."

"Yeah?" She bit her lip and noticed how his eyes caught the motion before refocusing on her.

"I'm here for you, but I'm also here as the head of the new ATF Last Chance County field office."

"Wait. You're transferring *here*?" She'd been ready to give up everything for him, but this was even better.

"It's why everything took so long. I could have been in Denver a month ago, but I thought it was worth the wait." He searched her eyes with hesitation. "Right?"

"Way better." She moved to kiss him again, but he stayed her with a question.

"Do you think that Airstream is still available?"

She laughed. "I think something can be arranged."

"I love you, Andi Jayne. Never doubt that." Jude's eyes roamed over her face like he was memorizing every line. Then his lips hovered over hers, ready to seal his love with a kiss. "And I'm here to stay."

TRACE CARRIED HIS CROCKPOT OF CHILI TO THE PICNIC TABLE outside and smiled. Jude had just flown in to surprise Andi, and he was thrilled for his partner. The two would finally be able to spend more time together in person. No more video calls at the station when they weren't on a call. Ones that had left her sad after they hung up. And with a little less pep in her step.

With the grant program expiring in three months, Trace had been thinking of ways to build his growing relationship with Kelsey. If Jude and Andi had made it work, he and Kelsey would find a way. He'd even go wherever Kelsey found a job if it meant staying by her side. He had connections in different towns, so he wasn't worried about finding a position himself.

Although Kelsey had said she had a surprise for him today, and he hoped it had something to do with her staying in town.

"You really think your chili is going to out win my barbecue?" Charlie sauntered over to the table wearing a *Real Men Cook* apron, wooden spoon in hand.

"It's classic comfort food with a secret ingredient." Trace grabbed a spoon and sampled the dish. "I wouldn't put your bets in yet." He cocked his head.

"It's official. We've got a soon-to-be Mrs. James in the house." Kelsey let out a squeal and took her friend's hand, holding it high in the air.

Trace headed over to Macon, Natalie, and Kelsey. "Congratulations." Trace shook Macon's hand.

"Thanks, man." He leaned in. "You and Jude are up next." He smirked.

Trace could only hope that day would come soon. He didn't want to rush things with Kelsey. But he'd already been thinking about what life would look like building a family together.

"What's this surprise you've been taunting me with?" Trace put his hand on the small of Kelsey's back and whispered in her ear.

"It's right here." She waved an envelope in the air. He took her hand and led her over to a bench.

"Open it." She smiled.

His finger slid under the flap and pulled out a thick manila paper. An emblazoned seal marked the top of the page. He scanned the document.

When he finished, he grinned. "They approved the grant program!"

"Yes." Kelsey clapped.

Trace picked her up and swung her around. He set her down, and Kelsey leaned up on her tiptoes. "I'm staying in Last Chance County. Permanently."

"I'm so proud of you, Kels. This is amazing."

"We're going to get a wing set up specifically for family counseling." Kelsey's eyes gleamed.

"You're the best person for the job." Trace rubbed his thumb along her cheek. He couldn't believe they would get to stay in Last Chance County, together.

"And I wouldn't want anyone else helping me through the process." She grinned.

Trace framed Kelsey's face with his hands. He dipped his head and kissed her with a passion that flamed hot and set his heart ablaze. Her tenderness spoke volumes as she melted in his embrace. Her arms wrapped around his neck and drew him closer. He'd vow to protect her and love her for the rest of his life.

Kelsey leaned back and put her hand on his chest. "I love you, Trace."

"I'm not going anywhere, Kelsey Scott. I love you." Trace tucked her under his shoulder and breathed in. God had taken the pain of his past and woven together a beautiful redemption story—all for His glory. Trace relished the scene in front of him as his friends—turned family—bantered around, laughing and celebrating.

Whatever the future held, a new chapter had begun, and he got to do it with Kelsey by his side.

ACKNOWLEDGMENTS

Writing a book takes an army of dedicated and encouraging people, and I'm incredibly grateful for those who walked with me through this process.

Susie, Lindsay, and the whole Sunrise Team - Thank you for believing in me and my story idea. Your willingness to take on a new author and provide expert guidance has been invaluable.

Lisa - Thank you for championing on my characters, letting me step into the world of Last Chance County, and mentoring me each step of the way. All the frantic questions I had, Discord chats, Zoom meetings, brainstorming sessions, and behind-the-scenes work has shown me what it truly means for writing to be a community of authors supporting each other.

First Responder Medical and Fire Department - Thank you to Matthew, Cara, Amanda, Matt, Donny, and Tim for taking the time to answer countless questions and even providing hands-on experience to the work you do every day. It has given me a greater appreciation for your diligence and sacrifice to protect others in our community. Thank you!

Megan, Emilie, and Kate - You all played integral roles in brainstorming, encouragement, and prayer. Thank you!

Jeff Bethke and the OG's - This is where it all started! Thank you for your mentorship, your belief in the stories God has laid on my heart. From the retreat, to Zoom sessions, and in-person meet-ups, your investment in me is what gave me the confidence to pursue writing. I can't say thank you enough. But now this book will always have a memory of OQ Farm and the people that hold a special place in my heart through the name of the coffee shop: Bridgewater Cafe.

Dani Pettrey - Thank you for your hospitality, kindness, and support on my writing journey. The time you've taken to listen, teach, and connect with me as an author and the stories God's given me as made the finished product that much stronger.

Mandy - Thank you for all your wisdom and input from personal experience on the medical side of the characters in this book. Your encouragement and direction helped make these character more relatable to those who have walked the road of illness. May it be a reminder that difficulties are a beautiful part of our story, and they are seen and supported.

Family and friends - If I took the time to list out each one of you, I'd write another novel! Thank you for your prayers and giving me the space to write this story. Even if that meant a pile of dirty dishes and laundry, rearranging plans, and bombarding you with fictional ideas.

David, Jared, Megan, Emily, Cristabelle, Scott, and my church family - Words cannot express the gratitude I have for the ways you've cared for me during this journey. I am blessed by each one of you and the ways you are seeking the Lord and championing me in my faith as well. Thank you, thank you, thank you.

My Lord and Savior - Nothing in life is possible apart from Your saving grace. You placed a dream on my heart to write and You saw fit to use that talent to point people back to Your Word so that Your name would be glorified. You have brought this sinner from death to life and I will use every day You give me to tell of Your wondrous works. Thank you for writing the most beautiful redemption story. From now and into eternity, may my life and the words I write be focused on an audience of One.

ABOUT THE AUTHORS

Lisa Phillips is a USA Today and top ten Publishers Weekly bestselling author of over 50 books that span Harlequin's Love Inspired Suspense line, independently published series romantic suspense, and thriller novels. She's discovered a penchant for high-stakes stories of mayhem and disaster where you can find made-for-each-other love that always ends in happily ever after.

Lisa is a British ex-pat who grew up an hour outside of London and attended Calvary Chapel Bible College, where she met her husband. He's from California, but nobody's perfect. It wasn't until her Bible College graduation that she figured out she was a writer (someone told her). As a worship leader for Calvary Chapel churches in her local area, Lisa has discovered a love for mentoring new ministry members and youth worship musicians.

Visit Lisa's Website to sign up for her mailing list to get FREE books and be the first to learn about new releases and other exciting updates! https://www.authorlisaphillips.com/sunrise

Laura Conaway grew up in the suburbs of Pennsylvania as an avid reader and writer while making every adventure a mystery to solve like Nancy Drew. As a former school librarian, she's always on the hunt for the next best read but now spends her time creating stories that leave readers on the edge of their seat with a healthy dose of suspense and happily ever afters. When she's not typing away or inhaling sweet potato fries to motivate writing, Laura spends her time playing violin and guitar and sharing about the Greatest Story ever written.

Connect with Laura at www.lauraconawayauthor.com

f facebook.com/lauraconawayauthor
⊙ instagram.com/conaway_laura
BB bookbub.com/authors/laura-conaway
g goodreads.com/lauraconaway
a amazon.com/stores/Laura-Conaway/author/B0BK235BZN

We hope you loved the action, adventure, and romance in this story. Keep reading for more exciting romantic suspense from Sunrise Publishing!

FIRE. FAMILY. FAITH.
LAST CHANCE FIRE AND RESCUE

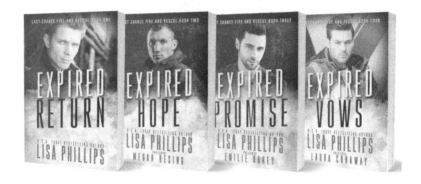

Make sure you have read all the exciting stories!

BRAINS. BEAUTY. BOLDNESS.
THE ELITE GUARDIANS WILL KEEP YOU SAFE.

Start reading the series now!

A SOLDIER, A MALINOIS, AND A STUNT WOMAN WALK ONTO A TV SET...

Experience the high-octane thrill ride that is the first book in the A Breed Apart: Legacy series.

FIND THEM ALL AT SUNRISE PUBLISHING!

CONNECT WITH SUNRISE

Thank you so much for reading *Expired Vows*. We hope you enjoyed the story. If you did, would you be willing to do us a favor and leave a review? It doesn't have to be long- just a few words to help other readers know what they're getting. (But no spoilers! We don't want to wreck the fun!) Thank you again for reading!

We'd love to hear from you- not only about this story, but about any characters or stories you'd like to read in the future. Contact us at www.sunrisepublishing.com/contact.

We also have a monthly update that contains sneak peeks, reviews, upcoming releases, and fun stuff for our reader friends. Sign up at www.sunrisepublishing.com.

OTHER LAST CHANCE COUNTY NOVELS

Last Chance Fire and Rescue Collection

Expired Return

Expired Hope

Expired Promise

Expired Vows

Last Chance County Series

Expired Refuge

Expired Secrets

Expired Cache

Expired Hero

Expired Game

Expired Plot

Expired Getaway

Expired Betrayal

Expired Flight

Expired End

Expired Vows: A Last Chance County Novel
Published by Sunrise Media Group LLC
Copyright © 2023 Sunrise Media Group LLC
Paperback ISBN: 978-1-953783-46-2
Ebook ISBN: 978-1-953783-35-6

For more information about Lisa Phillips and Laura Conaway please access
the authors' websites at the following addresses:
https://www.authorlisaphillips.com
https://www.lauraconawayauthor.com

Published in the United States of America.
Cover Design: Ryan Schwarz, thecoverdesigner.com

Printed in the USA
CPSIA information can be obtained
at www.ICGtesting.com
LVHW090441220324
775031LV00025B/138